"I've had enough! Please stop!" the inmate screamed.

They didn't listen. They beat him until they got tired. Two hours later, a white inmate committed a similar infraction against a black officer. It was Officer Harrison. He was not of the mentality of the talented seven. He was a pure nigger as Malcolm X would say.

Harrison had begun to beat the white inmate. The guy hollered and screamed. "Get off me, you bastard! Don't hit me any more! Help!"

"Hey!" a couple of white officers called to Harrison. "Take it easy on that guy!"

"Fuck you," Harrison replied. "You didn't take it easy on the black inmate an hour ago!"

He continued to whale on the white inmate's ass.

SECOND CHANCE

a novel by

JEROME DYSON WRIGHT

An Original Holloway House Edition
HOLLOWAY HOUSE PUBLISHING CO.
LOS ANGELES, CALIFORNIA

This novel is a work of fiction. Names, characters, places and incidents are either the product of the author's imagination or are used fictitiously. Any resemblance to actual events or locales or persons, living or dead, is entirely coincidental.

Published by
HOLLOWAY HOUSE PUBLISHING COMPANY
8060 Melrose Avenue, Los Angeles, CA 90046
All rights reserved. No part of this book may be reproduced or transmitted in any form or by any means, electronic or mechanical, including photocopying, recording or by any information storage and retrieval system, without permission in writing from the Publisher.
Copyright © 1983, 1986 by Jerome Dyson Wright. Any similarity to persons living or dead is purely coincidental.
International Standard Book Number 0-87067-834-5
Printed in the United States of America
Cover photograph by Jeffery
Cover design by Kim Smock

Published by arrangement with J. W. Productions and adapted from the hardback edition entitled *Shadows of Hope* ISBN 533-05151-1.
Library of Congress catalog Card Number: 81-90411.

To all the caring people involved with prisons

SECOND CHANCE

Prologue

October 15, 1963, marked one and a half years since Phil had enjoyed freedom. His being incarcerated in Maryland's penitentiary was no picnic, whether he was guilty or innocent. The pain of being maneuvered as a robot became unbearable at times. Phil was monitored twenty-four hours a day, which made him feel that he would rather be dead, especially if there was no hope of his being released in the near future.

He received mail from Vickie—the only woman he'd ever loved—which made him feel very much alive. She kept him informed of all the changes and progress which were taking place in Baltimore; she told him about being a member of the NAACP since her early teens. Most of all, she kept him informed about their son whom he had never seen in the flesh, but the pictures were beautiful.

He had just read her letter for the second time in the courtyard while gazing at the sun and biting his fingernails, as memories of her smiling and teasing him the way she used to do gave his mind a mental-therapy workout. Those few minutes cleared his mind of prison life and took him into her living room or some exclusive restaurant or nightclub. He was all wrapped up in his thoughts when a young boy of eighteen or nineteen, whom he had seen enter the prison a couple of weeks earlier, walked up to him and said, "It must be nice to read a letter and look so peaceful."

"Yeah, it is very nice. It's from my woman and I love her; it's the only thing that keeps me going."

"Well, I reckon, I'll never know anything about that because I'm in here for life."

Phil looked at the young man's sad face and said, "There is always hope, man. I'm doing life and twenty, and I have hope of hitting the bricks one day."

"What did you do?"

"Oh," he said as he sighed, "it's a long story. You won't believe it."

"Try me. I'd like to hear it."

Phil scratched his chin and said, "Let me share with you how I felt when I was sentenced." As he began to tell the story, his mind quickly flashed back to those unforgettable words and scenes.

Phil thought, feeling numb, *Goddamn, I couldn't believe the bastard judge. Sat there and tossed me life and twenty years as if he had given me a free trip to the Bahamas.*

The steel cuffs snapped on his wrist and the guard yanked him.

"C'mon, Avery, c'mon!" Phil followed the corked-face, red-necked guard, although he was oblivious of the commotion, and the shouts of injustices from the spectators. All the damned crimes that he had committed and gotten away with, he could not help but wonder, *How in the hell did I get stuck with this one of which I had no knowledge? If this is the confounded law of retribution, I wish I could understand it a little better.*

Vickie, pregnant, crying, and reaching out for him was all another part of the fog which had enveloped his mind. He stared at her beautiful face as the guard tugged at him, yet he didn't see her. He thought he saw the motion of her lips as she cried out, "Phil, I love you! I'll write you every day. We'll go to the Supreme Court!"

"Stand back, lady," the ruddy guard shouted. "You can see him in the penitentiary."

The distance from the courthouse on Calvert Street to the penitentiary on Forrest Street is about eight blocks, which is equal to approximately ten minutes in traveling time. It seemed as though it was ten years to Phillip Avery. It was as if he had taken this ride years ago during slavery. He was chained to other men, but they were faceless. The only bond of recognition was the tight-gripped chains and cuffs. He noticed that they were all young and black like himself.

"They did the whole number on you, didn't they, man?" a guy said to Phil as he looked at him with a face showing no emotion. He was chained directly to Phil, yet Phil was unaware of his presence or what he was saying. His mind kept visualizing a chain of young, black men from the past to the present being shackled and transported to plantations and prisons. Then it was in wagons with horses, now it was by trucks.

The bumpy, cobblestone street on Fallsway jarred his consciousness to the fact that this guy was talking to him. "You say something, man?" Phil asked, although he was still half out of it.

"Yeah, man," the guy replied understandingly. "I was asking if you was the guy who they gave the whole number to?"

"Yeah," Phil answered with bitterness. "Bastard gave me

life and twenty. What you get?"

"A dime, man. Two burglaries. How old are you?"

Phil didn't know why he asked, probably just making conversation. "Twenty-two, man, and you?"

"Same, man." Then he asked, "Did you drop out of school?"

Phil answered, "Yeah," as his mind flashed back remembering Miss Bell and the people who had tried to encourage him, but to whom he didn't listen. He had dropped out.

"I dropped out in the ninth grade. You?"

"Eighth, man. Wished the hell I had stayed. I couldn't even read my indictment papers."

At sixteen, Phil was shackled in a similar wagon on his way to Hagerstown to serve a ten-year sentence. That was a good ninety miles from Baltimore, but in no way did it seem as long as the eight-block trip that he was now taking. He had heard many tales about the penitentiary, but he didn't think that he would one day end up there. *This shit just isn't real*, Phil thought.

"All right, guys," a guard shouted as the truck came to a stop, "you're home. This is the Maryland State Penitentiary."

In all, there were eight of them. The guard herded them through three giant steel-grill gates, which had individual booming clamps. Phil had the devastating feeling as each door clanged, that that would be the last time that he would ever see freedom again. He was unaware that he had not breathed until he had entered the third grill. It was then that he exhaled breathlessly, realizing that subconsciously, he was attempting to preserve and carry in with him his last breath of "free air."

After entering the third grill, they were herded down two flights of stairs which seemed to have no ending. To Phil, it was as if he had died and was descending the stairs to hell. As it happened, hell turned out to be a big receiving room with several benches opposite a long counter. On the other side of the counter, there were two seasoned white inmates who waited patiently while the guards unshackled them.

"Okay," the white, gray-haired inmate shouted. "First man come get your gear." Phil walked over to the counter. "I don't want to know your name," the guy said. "Here is your gear and this is your number—6772. You get two pairs of jeans, two pairs of shorts, and two shirts. Don't sell this stuff because this is all you get for a year. And you get it cleaned once a week." Phil silently picked up his gear, which included a white book.

Phil inquired, "What is this book for?"

"That's your rule book, man. You eat and sleep with it. It tells you all about the do's and don'ts. Whether you read it or not, they're gonna tell you that ignorance is no excuse for breaking the rules. If you don't follow the book, take my advice, drink plenty of water and walk slow."

Whatever this shit means, Phil thought, *all I can do is walk slow with life and twenty.*

That same day, the prison authorities snapped pictures, took fingerprints and assigned cells. When the cell door clanged shut behind Phil, it was the sound of finality. "Damn," he said aloud, "I'm in this fucking penitentiary for life."

The cell was a four-by-nine, cold, gray and impersonal cubicle. Despite the bleached and scrubbed smell, it stunk with human suffering—suffering one could smell and sense with the mind. Besides the atmosphere of suffering, everything else in it was the pits—the dirty mattress on the little, rusty, iron cot and the stopped-up toilet.

Now that Phil was in the penitentiary, he felt alone and empty. During his entire life, he had never known such a violation of his soul. It was all like a public kidnapping as he played it back in his mind.

First, those bastard officers just stopped his car and arrested him.

Second, the judge demolished every human feeling that he possessed by telling him that he was guilty and that he must serve life and twenty years in a stinking cell.

His whole life could be summed up as one cold, gray cell, one toilet, one washbowl, one bunk, one bed, and one sad, broken-hearted, violated—Phillip Avery.

Part One
Becoming Institutionalized

Chapter 1

The Maryland Penitentiary was cold, gray and unfriendly. In his chosen career, it was considered the college of colleges, and with the stiff sentence that had been laid on him, his intentions were to get his doctorate.

Crash courses in fighting off the diversified approaches of homosexuals were the first lessons to be learned. Then came the dope, the gambling, the violence committed by both the inmates and the officials, the slavery, and the sports. These things numbed your mind, but there was a small corner of prison life where true education could be sought.

The first year, Phil's life was caught up in many of the available corruptions, but he managed to find that corner of education called a school system located on the third floor over the laundry industry. It had five classrooms staffed mostly by inmate teachers. These guys were so good that it was at least one month before he realized that they were inmates like himself. They were extremely dedicated and most effective, a combination which enticed him to become a good student for the first time in his life.

Phil thought, *Never will I forget the short math teacher, David Carter, who stood before the class lecturing about life and education.* His gray hair was trimmed closely around his brown forehead and his eyes blinked seriously in intervals as he said, "You missed your education on the street. It's here for you a second time, right here." He scanned the twenty or so students, his eyes going blinkity blink as he continued, "You can disrespect me if you want to because I'm an inmate. But, remember this—I've got mine. You got yours to get. Also, I have double life and twenty years . . ."

Damn, Phil said to himself. *He's got more time than I do.*

From the middle of the class, he could see from the expressions on their faces that some of the new inmates shared his surprise.

"Yes, they had me in the death house and I was scheduled to be executed, thirteen years ago, but I refused to recognize defeat. Dammit, I studied, wrote petitions, wrote the governor and every court that exists. Finally, because I was persistent, my sentence was reduced to double life and twenty. In two years, I hope to have my feet back on the bricks."

He was speaking to all the class as his eyes continued their blinking, gazing to see if his words were being heeded. Somehow, Phil felt that he was speaking to him personally.

"It will do you good," he said, "to remember what I am about to say. That is, the educational system here is just a small thing, but you should get all you can and remember—regardless of your number (sentence), anything that the mind can conceive and believe, it can achieve."

The statement possessed power, a power which forced him to adopt it to reinforce his fortitude. Then and there he pledged that if David Carter could do it, so could he—Phillip Avery.

The institution allowed him to attend school two hours a day and to work in the sewing shop for eight. The sewing shop was one of the multimillion-dollar complexes under the State Use Industry which included other shops such as the metal shop, tag shop, wood shop, shoe shop, print shop, and laundry, to mention a few of the slave camps.

Each of these complexes provides services and products, which are greatly used throughout the State of Maryland by other state agencies. The shops individually were grossing in excess of several million dollars annually, and all inmates clearly understood that nothing could stop the productivity of these shops, not inmate education, nor the implementation of constructive programs, nor the abolishment of slavery during the Civil War.

For working in these shops, the inmates received an average of thirty cents a day. Phil's worksite was on the fourth floor. Beneath that site was the metal shop, the shoe shop, and the knit shop. He worked in the almighty sewing shop.

After having worked in the sewing shop for about two weeks, he realized that the inmates were being treated as nothing more than slaves.

"Hey, new man," the fellow whom he recognized as Shorty Rogers shouted to him. "Bring me some material!"

His machine and table were one out of a hundred that he had to supply with materials. Shorty was stationed ten feet from the large table which Phil distributed from. It was located in the rear of the huge one hundred by seventy-five foot room. The sounds of the sewing machines, which were lined up in six rows, made a constant "zieb, zieb, zieb" noise as miles of goods rolled in and out of them.

"Yeah," Phil responded. "What you need?"

"Need some more that white man's goods, boy. That's what I need." His smile was pleasant as he waved his little stubby hands. "C'mon, c'mon, nigger. Can't keep this white man's machine idle. If you were in my hometown before this shit was processed, I'd just say bring me some cotton, nigger. Now come on with it."

By this time, he was used to Shorty Rogers' wisecracks and comical way of referring to the South, a place that he had never lived in his forty-two years.

"Coming right up, Shorty." As depressed as Phil might feel, he always smiled whenever Shorty Rogers spoke. Still smiling, he lifted the heavy bundle of pre-cut pants sections, walked the distance between the aisles and placed the bundle on Shorty's table.

"Here you go, Shorty. Hurry up before the white man sees this machine taking a breather."

"You know," Shorty said nonchalantly, as his finger flicked the cut-off switch, "I like you. You've got a lot of smarts for a young man. The best thing you did was to tell that white man you couldn't work one of these damn machines. You get good on one of these bastards and you will never get out of here. They need good niggers to run these machines forever."

The machine turned over at the flick of his finger on the switch. He lined a piece of material up and let it slip through.

"How much time you doing, youngblood?"

It pained Phil to think of it, but he answered, "Life and twenty."

His expression flipped from smile to concern. "Goddamn! Didn't figure you for that kind of time. What you do, rape and kill the president's wife?"

"Naw, man. I didn't do a damned thing."

As Phil was about to elaborate, the inmate supervisor walked towards them. He was slender, a youthful forty, wore glasses, and his dark complexion accentuated his Cheshire cat grin. The twin to that was an insecure smile.

"Okay, Avery, don't hold up production. These pants got to get out. You're holding up a good man."

Phil's feet were in motion to move when Shorty Rogers said in his own style, "Get off the kid's back, you Tomming son of a bitch, you. You drive harder than the damned white man. In the old days, they called Tomming bastards like you, 'nigger overseers.' This kid is doing life and twenty. He don't want that bullshit out of one of you five-year Tomming bastards."

It is the custom in everyday jail life that joking and panning is the agenda of the day. You either get used to it or you fight every day. True to this custom, "Nigger Boss," as we jokingly referred to him said, "Damn, I didn't know you had that kind of time. But, if I was you, I'd go give the warden a blow job just as quick as I could and try to get out of here."

With that, he moved off quickly and laughed when he reached a distance and stopped to fumble with material on another inmate's table. Phil smiled as he observed his face across the room, checking to see how he had taken his remark. His smile obviously told him that he could take ribbing. The reformatory had prepared him for that.

"Don't let him get you, youngblood." Shorty's voice was sympathetic. "He jokes with everybody. He's a Tomming bastard."

"I got to live here, man. I can take it."

"Yeah, but it hurts me to see a kid like you with all this time. Damned place is getting full with young, black kids." He reached for more material, lined it up, and let it zip through the machine. "You know, kid ... they stopped slavery in 1865. They freed all the unskilled niggers and recaptured them for trying to survive, and placed them right here in the cotton fields of the penitentiary. The soup is the same—just warmed over. Just look around you. Right here in this shop, what do you see? Wall-to-wall niggers. More whites commit crimes than we do, but we get the most time."

Phil's eyes scanned the room briefly, observing the six rows of manned machines, only to see ten white inmates out of one hundred.

"See what I mean," Shorty continued. "Your best bet is to get all you can get out of that school and get to know this old man named Cowhand. He's the jailhouse lawyer. You learn what you can from him. Write yourself some petitions and try to get the hell out of here."

Chapter 2

One Saturday, a full week after the conversation with Shorty Rogers, Phil had the occasion to meet Cowhand. The courtyard was crowded. All the shops were closed, and this was the inmates' big day of courtyard socializing. The yard was huge, bounded by four, gray, medieval-looking walls of intimidating stature, especially to an escape artist. Even if one was to manage to scale the walls, there was still the shotgun crew who were stationed strategically in towers.

The center of the yard was being used for a football field, as the Raiders and Panthers tore at each other. To the left and right were rows of bleachers occupied by groups of men doing their individual things. Some were watching the game; some were playing checkers; and some were openly or surreptitiously kissing their homosexual mates.

Phil had been told that he could always find Cowhand in the upper-righthand bleachers from the basketball court which was southeast of the football field near the guarded wall of gray. Both of Phil's hands were dug deeply in his jacket pockets, protecting them from the cold bitter air of December, as he strolled through the yard. The yard was bustling with activities. It was too much to take in at one glance. What attracted his attention was the voice of the officer who yelled, "Hey, Ironpipe, take your tongue out of that young man's mouth. Where the hell you think you at?"

The guard's head shook in amazement, but he smiled. The inmate continued to embrace and kiss the young man. It was difficult to believe that that was the extent of the incident, but a moment's observation made Phil aware that this was common in this place.

After about five minutes of walking and observing, he spotted a thin, elderly gentleman who was handling stacks of papers that could only be petitions. There were at least a half dozen clients waiting to see him as he sat on the fifth row of the bleachers to the right of the football field. His horn-rimmed glasses were wrapped snugly around his smooth, brown face. There was no suggestion of sternness in his expression, just a look of patience, sadness and alertness.

Seeing that Cowhand was quite busy, there was nothing for him to do, but stand and wait in the crowded bleachers. While doing so, he watched the game between the Raiders and the Panthers. The Raiders were in the lead by twelve points. Slim, whom he had grown up with, was quarterbacking and had just completed a fifty-yard pass. *My God,* Phil thought, *he has been here since he was a kid—ever since 1954. He's been here at least six years now.*

"Hey, Phil," a guy yelled to him. "I heard they got you big this time."

"Pete?" He was uncertain. They hadn't seen each other since the A&P days on Linden Avenue.

"Yeah, man. How you doing, Phil?"

"Bad, with life and twenty."

As Pete walked through the crowd, he observed the sea of faces throughout the yard. Many he recognized and many he had never seen before. Again, it hit him that most of the men were black. His count was that there were only two hundred whites out of the nine hundred inmates who were in the yard that day.

"Phillip Avery! How in the hell did you get caught up in this shit? Maybe I would have been better off with Gumbo, lying in my grave somewhere."

His thoughts raced back to when he was in elementary school in Miss Bell's class. *None of those students ended up here, just me. My God, what I would give to be back in those days, playing with Vickie's hair. Lord, keep Vickie strong for me. Please take care of our child. I hope he will be strong, too, and not end up here.*

"Did you want to see me, young man?" The voice that interrupted Phil's thoughts was that of Cowhand.

"If you are Mr. Cowhand, I sure do want to see you." Phil rubbed his hands together vigorously, and then he stuffed them back into his pockets.

Cowhand adjusted his glasses, slowly and deliberately, with his right hand. With his left hand, he offered him a seat.

"What do you want to see me about?"

"A court move. I want to put a petition in court."

His expression indicated that he was leery of Phil. His next question confirmed just that.

"Why come to me? I don't write petitions. Don't you know they don't allow petition-writing in here?" His gaze was intense as his eyes locked with Phil's.

"Well," said Phil, "someone told me that if anybody could help me, it would be you."

"Look, these white folks told me if they catch me writing petitions, they are going to put me on the south wing forever. You could be a plant. Now, who told you to come to me?"

For a moment, he hesitated, but then he said, "Shorty Rogers told me to come to you."

Shorty's name pushed the relax button.

"Sit down; sit here. It's cold out here, but you'll get used to it. Better than that cell. How much time you got, young man?"

"Life and twenty years."

He did a slow take, adjusted his glasses, and said, "That's a lot of time for a young man. What'd you do?"

For the next hour Phil explained the circumstances of his case, the incident that led to his arrest, his past record and the many crimes that he had committed and had gotten away with, concluding that it was still unfair to convict him for something that he did not do. After Cowhand had heard him completely, he said, "The law of compensation caught up with you, but let's see if the law of legalities can free you. I'm going to write you an appeal."

That night, Phil's first feeling of hope came over him as he sat on his bunk in his cell writing a letter to Vickie.

His cell partner, Ken Ray, was on the bottom bunk. He was doing a thirty-year sentence and he continually reminded Jesus Christ aloud in the most vile language that he was prejudiced, and called him every kind of name that he could think of. When Ken was not cussing Jesus Christ, Phil could hear the other inmates yelling from tier to tier and cell to cell, communicating and shouting about every conceivable frustration. His only way of finding a moment of peace was to write to Vickie.

Dear Vickie,

This is a hell house if I ever saw one. It is driving me insane. However, my only hope is that I now have an appeal which looks quite promising. That means there is a possibility that I may be acquitted in a few months.

Needless to say, I love you and want you to stick by me. You know I do not recognize defeat and will return to you and my child soon. Whatever, neither prison walls nor time will diminish my love for you . . .

The tier and cell that he was stationed in was located in the west wing which was directly over the receiving tier, which was where the new inmates were put. In total, there were twenty tiers, front and back, extending one full block. On the west end, the tiers were bordered by the main shower area and the east end was bordered by a section of offices and a rotunda leading to the south wing which was used exclusively for solitary confinement.

Outside of the penitentiary, the streets were Warden Street to the west and Greenmount Avenue to the east. From the side facing his cell on the second tier, the only visible objects were those seen in the yard and kitchen and the silhouettes of the people in the slave shops. On the other side, the guys were more fortunate because they could see Forrest Street and had the opportunity to look at all the lovely ladies.

Simultaneously, all types of conversations were taking place, and after months and years, one became quite skillful at communicating amid loud noises to a friend several tiers away, or even around the corner on the Forrest Street side.

"Hey, Twenty," a voice from the cell down from Phil called.

"Yeah," Twenty replied from the cell next to him.

"Got a letter from that broad tonight. You know that bitch had the nerve to tell me she's pregnant!"

"What you expect, nigger! You think that woman gonna put a closed down sign on that thing 'cause you doing ten years?"

Twenty's remarks brought some laughter from other listeners.

"Hey, Heads!" someone shouted.

"Yeah, man, what'cha want?"

"Just wanted to know if you wuz still there!"

"Where the hell you think I'm going with all this steel around me?"

"I don't want you to hang it up on me, doing that life down there!"

"Get up off my time," Heads shouted back. "I don't play that shit!"

The inmate who had called Heads wasn't discouraged in the least. He continued, "I didn't tell you to come here for life. I go home next year. Gonna fuck your woman when I get out, too!"

"Hey, man," Heads shouted. "Do me a favor . . ."

"Yeah, what is it?"

"Leave me alone and go suck your cell partner's dick!"

At that everybody roared with laughter. It especially got a laugh from Phil because the guy didn't call Heads anymore.

By now, his cell partner was standing at the door of the cell, with his hands gripped around the bars. He began yelling, "Apple! I want my carton of cigarettes in the morning or else you gonna meet my iron pipe!"

"Damn, man," Apple shouted back from the same tier about four cells down. "Why you say that to me? You know I'll have your money!"

Ray turned to Phil, slamming his fist into his palm and said, "You got to be hard on bastards like that. Loan 'em money and they fuck you around. Won't pay you back unless you threaten to bust their brains out. Man, you know I got over five hundred packs loaned out."

"That's a lot of cigarettes, man. But, what the heck you gonna do with them?"

"You better get hip," he said in a serious tone. "Cigarettes are money in here. Every six packs is equal one buck. During the middle of the month when things are tight, you can get a buck for four packs. Use your head, man, you can save enough money to buy your way out."

Ken Ray went on to tell Phil how he could lend two packs out for three back or two cartons in return for three. After he accumulated several cartons, he would sell them to certain correctional officers who would give him cash.

"That's right, man," he went on, knowing he was impressing the hell out of Phil, "there's just as much cash in here as there is on the streets. You use your head, save some money, you can get anything in here you want except a woman. And, if you be here long enough and get close to Captain Muscles, he'll sneak you out for a couple hours for two hundred bucks."

That was extremely hard to believe, but Phil couldn't detect a trace of untruth in Ray's expression. He went on, "How do you think all the dope gets in here? More dope in here than on the bricks. Man, you got inmates and guards in here who done got cold rich."

Ken Ray had really been giving Phil the insides and outs of the Pen, explaining how ten dollars could buy a single cell and how fifteen could buy you the homosexual of your choice, who would be transferred to your cell with you. He was going non-stop when everyone began to holler, "Mace Peaches! Mace Peaches! They're dragging Mace Peaches across the yard. Fight them bastards, Peaches! Kill them common motherfuckers!"

"Knock it off up there!" a guard yelled.

All inmates were now at the doors of their cells watching at least fifteen officers struggle, trying to carry Mace Peaches from the south wing to the blue room. Sticks were cracking Peaches' head and shoulders, as he landed whopping blows in the faces of panic-stricken, but brutal guards. He knocked two officers unconscious and injured three others before they cleared him from the yard over to the blue room which was isolated and next to the death house.

The shouts and cries died down as guards began to patrol each tier turning out lights for the night which meant no more loud talking.

As a kid growing up on Pennsylvania Avenue in Baltimore, Phil had known Mace Peaches. He was one of the biggest dope dealers in Baltimore. He owned a Cadillac, a couple of businesses around Laurens Street and was respected among the hustlers across the country. It had been said that Mace Peaches was the constant victim of brutal attacks from correctional officials.

Very clearly, Phil remembered in 1955 when he was sentenced to the reformatory the grapevine reported that the guards were still beating Mace Peaches. And now in 1961 he could see with his own eyes that those brutal beatings hadn't stopped. By word of mouth, it was out that Mace Peaches was the toughest inmate in the history of the penitentiary. His spirit refused to be broken. This was evident by the fact that he had been fighting the violent officers on all three shifts every day for the past seven years. The orders from the main office was that Mace Peaches was to be beaten every day until they broke him and that it would be extremely dangerous to attack him with a force of less than eight officers.

Phil had been deeply impressed and concerned by the plight of Mace Peaches. Ever since he was a child, Phil was determined to find out the truth as to why this man had become a legend within the penitentiary's history.

"Ken," he asked in a whisper, lying on his bunk. "What's the real scoop on why they are so hard on Mace Peaches?"

"I tell you," Ken replied, leaning from his bunk to see if a guard was patrolling the tier, "Mace is one tough bastard. He hates to see anyone being mistreated. About seven years ago, when I first came here, let's see . . ." he paused, stretching his neck to peer through the bars, "I was about eighteen. We were all in the yard near the hospital when this inmate got to arguing with this guard and a fight broke out between them. You know, right away those other bastard guards jumped in it and really worked the guy over.

"Once they got him down, this one particular screw ... Willison was his name, he was a bastard who got pleasure handling guys on death row. Anyway, this bastard started kicking the inmate in the face and balls. He even stomped him. The rest of us started shouting, but we didn't do anything. Peaches was standing in front of us, a big son of a bitch he was too, about two hundred and fifty pounds. The expression he had on his face I'll never forget. He said, 'I'm going to get that dirty, bastard, screw Willison. I don't like what he did to that man.'

"So the next day, Peaches walked up to the guard and said, 'Hey, that was some dirty shit you did to that inmate yesterday.' When the guard asked Peaches if he wanted the same, that was it. Phil, I've never in my life seen a man get hit so hard. Peaches' fist smashed Willison's face and I heard bones shatter and crack from ten feet away. Blood gushed from that pig's face and he fell right in front of the hospital. In one punch, Mace had broke his nose and jaw in four places. Man, there wasn't an inmate who saw that who wasn't happy.

"The goon squad came to get Peaches. They had blackjacks, tear gas, and the works. About fifteen of them jumped on him, and every time Peaches landed a blow they would fall out. He must have hospitalized seven of them before they carried him away. And man, ever since that day, each shift of guards beats him. But, you know what? He fights them bastards back. They'll never break him. He's the toughest bastard in the world."

Sleep overtook Phil two hours later as he lay thinking of Mace Peaches, lying naked, in the blue room next to the death house, waiting for the guards on each shift to awaken him for his daily therapy of brutality. His dream that night was to write a petition that would free Mace Peaches from his oppression.

Chapter 3

Phil received his answer from the court of appeals in February of 1963. In short, the reply said, "We uphold the decision of the lower court and find no constitutional violation."

Reading that court's opinion in his cell that night was like being on trial again. Depression swept over him like a plague. *To think that bastard judge coldbloodedly ruled against me! The son of a bitch could see that I was innocent. But no, the opinion says that, "This court does not concern itself with guilt or innocence, but rather with a question of legality that has been deemed flagrant enough to suffice a substantiation of constitutional violation." Dammit, if only I had the money to hire one of those super lawyers!*

More and more he realized that a son of a bitch who is poor and black, is in real trouble. His hopes were frustrated to the core. His eyes were fixed on the pictures of his son who was now one year old. He had promised Vickie that he would be home with them this year. There was no way he could serve this kind of time. Just as soon as those doors were open in the morning, he would go straight to Cowhand with his bad news.

Opportunity afforded him a half hour with Cowhand the next day in the courtyard. "Son," he said, when he finished reading the document, "we'll file straight to the Fourth Circuit Court of Appeals."

Again a surge of hope came over Phil as he observed the guys playing ball, gambling, and killing time throughout the courtyard.

"Cowhand," he asked as they sat in the bleachers, "what good is this appeal going to do? I'll be just like all the rest of these guys, in here for years and years."

"Nothing beats a failure, but a try. Look at these guys. Just look all around you. Most of them have given up."

As Phil looked up observingly, he had to admit that Cowhand was right. Defeat and depression were in most of their expressions. They had substituted ball playing, dope, gambling, and homosexuality for hope and real life. Phil thought, *I'll be damned if I am going to succumb to that shit!*

That day they immediately filed a petition to the Fourth Circuit Court of Appeals, which meant that with the case in federal court the chances of it being heard objectively stood a much greater chance.

No sooner than the petition was mailed, Phil sent Vickie a letter explaining what had happened. It was two days later that she sent him a letter stating, "Just have faith. I understand about the dragged-out court procedure and will be here awaiting your release. Love you always, Vickie."

She sent him a picture of her and their son together and mentioned that she had him in a private nursery while she pursued her profession at Crownsville State Hospital. She mentioned that she expected to be transferred to Johns Hopkins in a year which meant both a promotion and a raise.

Vickie really had her life cut out for her as a doctor, mother and civil rights organizer. After reading her letter, Phil made a comparison as to what they had achieved. She was a doctor, he was a jailbird. *Well,* he thought, *at least I have received my high school diploma, even if it was achieved in prison. Who knows where I'll go from here. This place has some positive things to offer such as the human relations course, college and other learning opportunities. Dammit, if I have to fight tooth and nail to get into these things, that is what I'll do.*

It was true that these courses were only offered on a small scale and preferably to white inmates, but Phil intended to get his at any cost. Perhaps, if he stayed out of trouble and attained an abundance of knowledge, he could possibly be released for being inmate of the year. The trick of it was to juggle his work time so that he could get more school time. It was clearly understood that production in the slave shop was far more important than inmate education. This was an unwritten law sanctioned by all main officials.

If it were true that he was reaching a turning point as to his positive way of thinking, fate threw him a crushing left hook. It happened one day as he was working in the sewing shop, giving out materials as usual, when the shop foreman asked him to get some additional material from the rack.

"Coming up, Mr. Valentee," Phil replied. He climbed the four-foot metal table and reached for a bundle of material. Now his arms were full with his back turned towards the row of men working at their machines. His feet, he remembered, crunched a piece of marking chalk. He slid backwards, and a painful flashing impact shot through his head as his back slammed against the steel rail between the machines and the tables that he had stood upon.

"Goddamn! Did you see that kid fall!"

Even in his pain and semi-consciousness, Shorty Rogers' voice could be recognized.

"Send for the stretcher," someone else shouted.

"Don't touch him! Don't touch him!"

"Get back, motherfuckers, and give the man some breathing room."

Again he knew that was Shorty.

When he knew anything again, he was in the penitentiary hospital's examining room. The doctor's voice was saying, "Trying to sue the state. Nothing's wrong with him. Get down off the table and stand up."

Pain wretched through Phil's back as he tried to move and obey. His eyes focused on the baldheaded doctor. He didn't look human as he stood over him with his six-foot frame, white jacket and sardonic smile similar to that of a Nazi torturer.

"Where are you hurting?" This question he asked Phil as he edged him gently off the table to his feet.

The pain was excruciating as he doubled over, leaning over the examining table, tears filling in his eyes.

"My back, Doctor," he cried. "I can't straighten my back!"

"Well, I tell you what," he replied, "we'll put you in m.o. until you straighten your back."

M.O. He thought, dazed. *That's the blue room. That's where Mace Peaches had been for years.* It was next to the death house in an isolated area.

Next, he felt the hands of two officers grabbing each of his arms. One officer was white and the other black. The black officer he recognized as Officer Edvans. Also, he knew him from West Baltimore when he used to attend Douglas High and hang out with the uptown gang. They weren't all right in a close sense, but certainly he could see this injustice. The blue room was a mental observation area of the most barbaric type.

"Man, I'm hurt," Phil pleaded with him. "Don't let them put me in the blue room. I can't even straighten my back."

At his plaintive cry, the white officer released his arm and showed compassion. To his shock, Officer Edvans squeezed his arm tighter and gave him a jerk.

"C'mon, goddammit—get your ass to the blue room!"

As much pain as he was suffering, the black bastard's cold-blooded treatment and icy remarks numbed him like a dentist's novocaine. Tears flooded his eyes as he cursed his black mother's womb for giving his Tomming ass birth.

As he shoved him in the elevator, he made one last remark, "Man, how can you be black and do this to me when you know I'm hurt?"

If he replied or showed any human concern, so did the death house as they passed it getting off the elevator walking towards the blue room area.

"Got one for you, sarge," he said to the officer in charge of the blue room.

The officer called "sarge" was cold and to the point.

"All right, strip and get in cell three."

In pain, Phil did as he was told and was placed in the cell. The officers locked him in and left, closing the outside grill behind them. Once the outside grill was closed, his immediate feeling was that he had been dropped in space—abandoned. There was not a flicker of light nor even a sound.

On this side of the closed grill were ten single cells known as the blue room. It was called such because you couldn't tell day from night. His cell, as were the other nine, was nothing but concrete and steel. There was no washbowl, no toilet, nor any embraceable objects. There was a brass circular drain mounted in the center of the floor which water flushed every five minutes to wash away any feces or urine that got in its five-inch diameter.

His naked body lay there trembling from the cold and pain

like a wounded, trapped animal, completely helpless with no one to hear his cry.

It seemed like hours that he lay there in total darkness when he heard a ruffle in the cell next to his. Then he realized that he was not alone.

"Hey, who's that next door?"

"Jessie Shacks, man." The voice sounded strange. He asked, "Who are you?"

"Phil, man. Phil Avery." Damn, Phil was glad to hear a voice. "What you here for, Jessie?"

"I got frustrated and climbed the windows. So they called me crazy and put me in the blue room."

Now Phil remembered the guy. He would climb the height of the building on the inside and stay for hours while everyone watched. Then he would get tired, climb down, and the hacks would beat him and lock him up.

"Man," Phil said, remembering, "you been here for a while, haven't you?"

"Yeah, 'bout four months. What they got you for?"

"I hurt my back in the sewing shop. Can't straighten it up. They took me to Dr. Hobbs, and he had me put in the blue room."

Tears came from Phil's eyes, but no one knew he was crying except him.

"He's a common motherfucker," Jessie said knowingly. "The baldheaded bastard thinks you are trying to sue the state. Don't worry, man." He tried to comfort Phil. "They may not keep you too long. You got any people outside?"

"Yeah, my girl," Phil replied, thinking of Vickie for the first time since he had been in the blue room.

"Well," he went on, "when feed up comes by in the morning, get somebody to get her a message. Don't worry. When I get out this time, I'm gonna climb the window again and piss on them for you. I want to die and come back and be a bird."

"Why, Jessie?"

"So I can fly around and shit on people I don't like . . ."

Jessie didn't say that to be humorous. He really meant it. That gave Phil his first and only laugh in the blue room.

The concrete pressed hard against Phil's side as he lay there and played hide and seek with the flushing water, trying to guess accurately when it would come up again. "There you are water. Now here you come again. Oh, I missed you by one minute." Hours passed and he became silent with the darkness and solitude. Pain kept visiting his back as tears trickled down his face. Ironically, both were welcoming company amidst the deadly silence and darkness.

In his entire life, he had never known such a cold, strange solitude. His mind searched his life desperately to find what he had done to deserve this. Was he being paid for killing Big Skip a few years ago and getting away with it? God knows he was only protecting his manhood. Could this be his payback for the crimes that he had committed and gotten away with? If so, why did he receive a long sentence for a crime he did not commit?

Lord, why did you have to take Dr. McKay's life? She would have had me out of here in minutes. If my old partner, Gumbo, was living, he would kick asses from the hospital to the blue room to get me out. I would pray to you, God, to let me out of here, but I made promises to you before where you kept your end of the bargain, and I didn't keep mine. I won't ask you this time, God. But, if you just want to help me on your own, I won't mind. Can I stand this another hour? The Pain! The Cold! The Silence!

Just when the blue room was at its quietest, there was a loud, piercing, animalistic, throaty kind of sound. It came from a throat—that much Phil was sure of, but certainly it was not a human throat. His body had jerked at the sound.

His ears listened for it to happen again. His next thought was to call Jessie in the next cell to him to see if he had heard it. *No,* he thought, *maybe I was dreaming.* Maybe Phil needed to create or imagine some noise to break the silence. He eventually lay back down. As the silence came over him, he heard it again.

"Ahawk! Ahawk-awah!"

This time it was unmistakably the sound of an animal with a horrendous lung disease.

"Jessie! Jessie!" He yelled as he banged the wall. "What was that?"

"Don't get scared, Avery," Jessie paused, "that's Mace Peaches a few cells down. He's been here for years!"

In no way was he ready for what Jessie had just mentioned. No human could cough like that, not even Mace Peaches, the two hundred and fifty pound black idol from Pennsylvania Avenue, whom he once thought the sun rose and set around.

"What's the matter with him, Jessie?" Phil's concern went deeper than he felt for himself.

"Peaches," Jessie said, "got pneumonia, TB, consumption and some more diseases. Man, he's been sleeping in one inch of water for a year. His drain been stopped up that long. He sleeps in piss, shit—you name it."

Phil's thoughts raced back to the early years of Pennsylvania Avenue when Gumbo first introduced Phil to him. Mace Peaches was the talk of the town. He represented money, clothes, Cadillacs, businesses and he was the kingpin of the dope trade. Many times he had seen him before he had gone to prison—big, black, clean and rich. Other than Smooth Eddie, he was the only other guy he wanted to be like. He had heard that the guards had been beating him daily for years, but this kind of filth and brutality was beyond description.

Suddenly, his stomach was full. He had to defecate, but

couldn't. Finally, he fell asleep and dreamed that he was on an automatic revolving toilet, twenty feet high. Beneath him were ten correction officers and each time the toilet revolved, he would defecate on them. In the dream, Officer Edvans was wearing the suit of a captain. The machine got diarrhea when it revolved over him.

Jessie was right about being reincarnated as a bird. It would be a pleasure to be able to fly and drop loads on people you didn't like!

Whether he slept or remained dazed for the next few hours, it was difficult for him to determine. Then, he heard the "Clang!" His door popped open and the ray of light had a blinding effect on his eyes. He could only surmise that it was morning.

"All right, you," the officer said, watching him lie on the floor blinking his eyes. "Get up. Shower time."

Slowly, Phil pulled himself together and stood up halfway. Pain had been with him like a comrade throughout the night and it wasn't about to leave him now. Gradually, he stumbled towards the shower. Jessie walked behind him after his cell was opened.

"No talking, you two," one of the officers shouted before they opened their mouths.

Phil observed that there were at least six officers. Also, there were two inmates with water hoses to wash out the stench of their cells while they showered. While they were doing that, four of the officers walked in the direction of Mace Peaches' cell as Jessie and Phil finished their quick waterdown. They opened his door.

"Goddamn, it stinks in here," one of them jeered.

By this time, Jessie and Phil were walking slowly back towards their cells. They could hear Peaches' body splash as he turned over in his water-clogged, foul smelling cell.

One of the officers pulled Peaches' door open farther,

opened the fly on his pants and urinated in the water-filled cell, probably on Peaches. At this, another officer roared in laughter. Next, there was a spattering sound and the officer who had pissed rushed his hands towards his face to wipe off slimy human shit, some of which was smeared across his chin.

"You black motherfucker," he shouted. "You threw shit in my face!" The officer lost control and ran into the cell after Peaches. He slipped in the slime as we all heard Peaches say, "I got you, motherfucker." Fist pounded against flesh as the other officers rushed Phil and Jessie into their cells. After the prisoners were safely locked in, the guards went to the aid of the officer in the cell with Peaches. They were really afraid to step into the slime. They made comical, fumbled attempts to enter Peaches' cell while he was beating the hell out of the hollering, screaming guard. The other guards yelled for help, blew whistles and more guards arrived. By now Peaches was out in the aisles, slinging fists and shit everywhere.

Phil got a good look, peeping out of the crack in his cell. It shocked him to see that Peaches was no longer the two-hundred-and-fifty pounder that he knew. He was closer to a hundred and fifty pounds. He was still as mean as hell.

Tear gas guns went off; blackjacks cracked, and finally Peaches was out like a light.

On Phil's fourth day in the blue room, Captain Muscle made his rounds. He was with the head nigger of the inmates, Neil. It was true that no black inmate had as much influence as Neil. His power came from Captain Muscle, the bribe king of them all. However, it was reputed that any bribes taken went through Neil first and then to Captain Muscle. That way no one could say that they paid Captain Muscle directly.

In front of Phil's cell, Captain Muscle commanded, "Open this cell."

An officer responded and Phil's cell door popped open.

"Hello, Captain Muscle. Hey, Neil." Phil greeted them as he would people of high status.

"Son, how are you feeling?" There was concern and compassion in his voice.

Before he could answer, Neil injected, "That's a goddamn shame. That boy ain't got no business in here. Look at him."

"Who put you in here, son?" Again, there was concern in Captain Muscle's voice. He even appeared angry that Phil had been placed in such a position.

"Dr. Hobbs," Phil blurted out.

"That son of a bitch has no authority to do this! Get up, son. Come on out and get cleaned up. You have a visitor. Some Dr. Adkins is in the visiting room waiting for you. She's raising hell to see you."

Vickie must have gotten the message, which Phil had given one of the feed-up men to give to Shorty Rogers.

"Thank you, sir." Slowly, Phil raised himself from the floor, adjusted his eyes to the light, and walked or hopped out of the cell.

"Can you make it, man?" Neil asked. He seemed deeply concerned, noticing that he couldn't straighten his back.

"I think so," Phil replied, feeling the pain ease as they both helped him to the shower.

Captain Muscle was a big, proud-looking man with blond hair. He puffed his cigar hurriedly as he walked slowly with him, blowing the smoke across his face to Neil's who was on the other side of him.

"Captain Muscle, Mr. Neil . . ." Phil turned from one to the other. "I really appreciate you getting me out of here."

It was Neil who spoke, "Man, call me Neil. I'm an inmate like you. But, if that fucking doctor fucks with you again, let one of us know. Right, Boss?"

Captain Muscle nodded his head affirmatively.

Silently Phil said to himself about Neil, *You may be an inmate, but you are one tough nigger in this jail.*

The blue room area was off limits to inmates except for punishment. For Neil to make rounds with the captain in that area, he had to really wield some power.

Entering the visiting room, he climbed each step slowly and deliberately. Once at the top, he took his seat on the inmate's side of the counter. He saw many attractive women visiting their husbands, brothers or whomever. Then, he saw his lovely Vickie. She rushed to the opposite side of the counter, kissed him and screamed, "Who did this to you?"

Everyone looked in his direction, including the guard.

No time was wasted. Phil immediately began telling Vickie about his getting hurt, the blue room, the pain and no medical attention.

She would hear no more. She immediately stood up, walked over to the officer and said, "May I use that phone?"

"Lady," the officer replied, "visitors aren't allowed to use the phones."

Vickie barked a command. "Then you call the warden for me right now! I want this man in the hospital."

People looked up. The guard became fidgety. He made a call and told her that someone would see her at the front office when she left.

They had a nice visit. She told him that Shorty Rogers sent an officer by her house to inform her about this situation. Phil told her about the penitentiary and that he was going to attend college while serving his time and that he was hopeful that he would be out soon.

When Vickie left, they had a wheelchair waiting to rush him over to the hospital for admittance and a specialist from the university hospital was there to examine him.

Once in the hospital, they put him in traction, gave him pain-killing medicine, and the best of attention. He could not help but think that if he didn't have someone on the outside who cared he might have died in that isolated, cold, lonely dungeon. Thank God for someone who cared.

Chapter 4

A month later, Phil was released from the hospital and placed in the west wing's unemployed section, still under the doctor's care. They gave him a cane and told him to report to the hospital for hot packs and whirlpool therapy, twice a week. His back had not completely straightened, but there was improvement. The French doctor from the university hospital told him that he had one of two choices—take the hot pack and whirlpool treatment or prepare for an operation. Of course, his decision was the simpler of the two.

Phil's unemployed situation afforded him a great deal of idle time, most of which he used thinking of ways to gain his freedom. He studied law, read books, and attended school. These were basic tools needed to acquire freedom. Nevertheless, there were others such as selling dope, gambling, and writing petitions. A great deal of money could be made at these occupations and he decided to try his hand at them all.

It was quite possible that he would hustle a few thousand and hire an expensive lawyer to work on getting his sentence reduced. With the knowledge that he had gathered as to the in's and out's of the penitentiary system, he was able to find out every guard who brought dope and who would not take bribes. By knowing Shorty Rogers, Ken Ray, and a homeboy from the avenue, Ben Paul, Phil knew the whole gamut.

It was Ben Paul who came down to his cell one day and said to him, "Look, Phil, you're doing a lot of goddamned time. That going to school shit may be all right, but it can't pay no lawyer."

"You're right, Ben," Phil replied knowingly, observed how immaculate he was in his pressed penitentiary pants and civilian shirt, a privilege he possessed because of his influence with the powers that be.

He rubbed his head with both hands, right at the front area where the hairline receded, as he continued, "I've been here eight years. You know how much I've made? I've made fifteen grand in this joint selling smack. I'm leaving soon. Lawyer gonna spring me for five grand. But, I'm gonna turn you on to every guard in here who's doing wrong. That way you can use them to bring some dope to sell. That's the only way you gonna get some fast money."

"Ben, I ain't never sold no dope in my life. You know as long as I've been on the avenue, I ain't never been interested in no dope. Besides, who would be my supply man?"

Ben looked surprised that he should ask.

"Your main man, Pee Wee, got all the dope in the world on that avenue, man. Pee Wee won't do too many guys favors like that, but he'll do anything you ask as tight as you two are."

"You know what, Ben," Phil replied giving the proposal his approval, "I think I'll do that. Those bastards in court ain't gonna do me no favors unless I give them that almighty dollar."

Phil and Ben walked down the tier of the west wing flats to the rotunda which separated the west wing from the south wing, which is used for solitary confinement. When they reached the rotunda, Ben asked that he wait there and he would be back with a hack that he wanted to cut him into.

One minute later he returned with a veteran officer, an official member of the goon squad. This had to be a mistake because he knew this red-faced Irish officer wasn't taking any bribes. Why he and his brother were reputed to be the fiercest, head-busting, ass-kicking officers in the whole joint.

Ben and the officer walked up to Phil. The rotunda isolated them from view of anyone else and afforded them the two minutes of privacy needed.

"Phil," Ben said, leading the conversation, "This is Officer Stenecker." He looked from the officer to him and went on, "Officer Stenecker, this is Phil, my main man."

The officer and Phil shook hands reluctantly.

"Phil and you," Paul went on, "will be doing heavy business together. I'm leaving soon and my man, Phil, will be dealing. He's got the contacts. All you have to do is bring it to him."

Officer Stenecker observed him closely, then he looked from Phil to Ben.

"Is he all right, Ben? I got a reputation to protect."

"Man, would I do that to you? Phil and I stick together. He can take more ass-whippings than a Georgia mule and still won't open his mouth. This is one thorough nigger."

That verbal resume from Paul seemed good enough for the officer. They shook hands and sealed a partnership.

Later, he contacted Pee Wee, told him what he needed and who would be scooping for him. After that, the dope came in regularly. When it did, he immediately passed it to his push man, Flattoc. He would cut it, sell it, take his share and return the rest. In turn, he would piece off Stenecker.

Flattoe had been in and out of the institution for years. He knew all the ropes. He also knew the ropes of boxing. He was an ex-pug and was damned good with his fists. Nobody, but nobody messed with his money or his dope because he had the reputation of being a one-punch knockout king. They had known each other from the avenue. He, too, was an idol of Phil's and had contributed greatly to his knowledge of the underworld.

Speaking of knowledge, Phil was getting it all. Academically, he was doing well and even taking some college courses from the University of Maryland. But, it was obvious that his underworld knowledge far exceeded his academics. In no time flat, he learned to distribute dope, became a chronic gambler and connoisseur on the odds of most gambling pools held in the penitentiary. The one thing that he learned about selling and distributing dope was that one must have a good lieutenant to front for him and keep his reputation clean. And, a clean reputation is a must when one goes up for parole consideration. It seemed like the name of the game for everyone in this corruption pit was to make all the money you could illegally, but to protect your reputation.

As careful as some might be, funny shit starts happening to people when the cover of their reputation is ripped off. For instance, one Thanksgiving, the state purchased several hundred turkeys for the inmates' Thanksgiving dinner. My God, the institution was loaded with frozen turkeys. Every inmate there couldn't wait until Thanksgiving arrived so they could help themselves to a piece of turkey, after having eaten such terrible meals for most of the year.

However, it seemed that strange and unusual activities were going on at the back end of the year. Guards had been seen driving their cars to the back delivery gate, which works electronically. Despite the fact that it was an area restricted to inmates because of security reasons, guards were extra busy telling them to stay back this particular day.

The unusual thing was that the inmates would observe parades of guards leaving for the back gate towards their cars. All had shopping bags or huge bundles in their arms. The unusual traffic back and forth incited many inmates to speculate as to what could be in those bundles.

Phil was in the bleachers gambling, trying to win back his two hundred dollars, when he overheard two inmates talking. "There they go again," one inmate said to the other.

"Yeah, Jack," the other inmate said. "Those two got a big bundle, too. What the hell you think it is?"

"Balled up like that? Bullshit!"

Another inmate joined the conversation. He said, "Maybe those bastards have some secret weapon they are setting up at the back gate. Don't want us to know it."

By this time, there was a gathering of inmates watching and talking. What really got everyone's attention was they saw Captain Muscle and Captain Stab go towards the door with bundles. Captain Stab was also known as the Judge because he was the chief judge of facts for the inmates' kangaroo court.

"What the hell has he got?" one inmate asked.

Another replied, "Whatever it is, it's too heavy for the old, gray-headed bastard to carry."

"Maybe the warden gave them all early Christmas presents," one inmate remarked.

They all laughed.

"Hey, Captain Stab," one inmate named Iron Pipe yelled. He couldn't bear the suspense. "What you got there? A present from the warden?"

Captain Stab wheeled around slowly, feeling the weight of the bundle pulling at his decrepit frame. Anger was in his haunted face as he barked, "You'd better mind your damned business before I raid that fucking gambling game!"

With that unexpected outburst, he hurried towards the back gate.

Those of them who were gambling resumed their game of Georgia skin. They used dominoes instead of cards because they were considered contraband. After about twenty minutes, most of them had forgotten about the activity of the guards until they heard another well-known officer named "Chief" walk by in a rage blurting out, "I don't want none! I don't want anything to do with it. That shit ain't right."

Chief was shouting at another officer who appeared to be trying to convince him of something. Even though Chief was one of the top brass, he had a reputation for being straight and honest in all of his dealings.

The following day was Thanksgiving. Many inmates passed up breakfast and lunch so that they could really get into the turkey. Phil felt like he could eat a whole turkey. So after a long hard day, they were all lined up in the mess hall with the white boys in front and the blacks behind as was the custom until Dick Gregory came and refused to do a show until they were integrated. The chow line was unusually long. Everyone was impatient as hell as the shit began to hit the fan. Conversations went like this, "Hey, what's taking so long?"

"Move this goddamned line!"

"Bet you many a bastard is bucking the line."

That was the term used when inmates would sneak back for seconds.

"What?" somebody screamed from the line in front, "No more turkey!"

"Man, fuck this shit!"

"Beans," another voice shouted. "Give your mother some beans, motherfucker. Let's tear this bitch down. Let's riot."

Trays sailed and slammed against walls. A table overturned; another one overturned. One cook was pulled from behind the serving counter, punched in the face, and kicked when he hit the floor. The guards became scared. A couple of them headed for the exits. An all-out riot was in the making until Captain Muscle stood on the table and told everyone that more turkeys would be ordered.

"If you eat what's before you today, we promise you a big meal tomorrow."

The fellows quieted a bit. Some listened. Some called him a bunch of horrible names. He went on talking, "There was a mixup in the count of turkeys. The others will follow. If you bear with us until tomorrow, everyone will have twice his share."

The other hard brass were on the other side of the mess hall by themselves. All of their faces carried worried looks as if they had a trial to face. The big one whom they called Chief did not share their expression. He appeared angry. His head was shaking and the only thing they could hear him say was, "It just was not right!"

They ate beans on Thanksgiving and returned to their cells angry and disappointed.

That very next day, the word was out that Chief went straight to the warden and told on all officers who stole the turkeys. The warden's runner, Little Ace, came back and told all the inmates how things went down. He said, "Man, the warden cussed them bastards out. He called the Judge a stupid motherfucker and that bastard held his head in shame. Man, he told them bastards to come out of their pockets to pay for the turkeys and if it wasn't for a scandal, he would fire all of their asses."

The gossip was out and the pan was on. Every time they saw the guards, they would yell, "Gobble! Gobble!"

All that night and for months to come, the inmates would yell from cell to cell and tier to tier, "Turkey-stealing motherfuckers. Gobble! Gobble!"

"Ain't that a bitch! Them bastards are free and on the outside, stealing from the inmates."

One night the big guard who they all called Chief walked by while they were locked in for the evening. He received a standing ovation.

"Hurray for Chief! Hurray for Chief!"

"Yeah, man," someone yelled from the third tier. "Chief, you are the Elliot Ness of the turkey stealers!"

Chief laughed and the other inmates roared, for Chief was their hero. All inmates liked the Chief. Needless to say, he was on the shit-list of his superiors, Captain Muscle and Captain (Judge) Stab.

Ironically, the next week an inmate named Beanie was caught burglarizing the commissary. He was caught red-handed coming out with twenty cartons of cigarettes. On the day of his trial, they were waiting in the hallway of the mess hall and those of them on the far end of the line got an opportunity to see more of the trials. Captain Stab, of course, was the presiding Judge.

"All right, Beanie," one of the rookie officers called from the court door. "You're next!"

There were about ten of them in line waiting in that area.

Beanie was a small, baldheaded fellow known to be outspoken in a comical fashion. He waited until more inmates were around and then shouted, "I'm not going in there and be tried by no turkey-stealing motherfucking judge! How can a turkey-stealing motherfucking bastard try me for stealing? He's a thief!"

At that everyone in the hallway doubled over in laughter. Even the rookie guard had a suppressed smile on his face. The cry of "gobble, gobble" could be heard throughout the line. The hall was in a comical uproar for three minutes until the goon squad rushed in and beat and dragged Beanie to the south wing without a trial.

Chapter 5

Phil had seen many experiences in the penitentiary in the last four years. But, that was also the year that the law of compensation revealed a balanced justice in his life. It was now his fifth year. Phil's back had healed considerably so he was able to work in the wood shop where they made desks, chairs, tables, and other goods for state agencies all over Maryland.

The double blast of good and bad came to him one evening after leaving the wood shop and having been locked in his cell for the night. The mail came and he received three letters—one from Vickie, one from the Supreme Court and one from Sam Vogelfine, the expensive lawyer hired by him and who was paid from the receipts of the corruption money. Needless to say, he hurried and opened the letter from the Supreme Court. It was the opinion, which decided that there had been some "constitutional inconsistencies surrounding the circumstances of his case not in accordance with due process of law," that the case at the bar be remanded to the state for reconsideration.

You could hear his scream of joy throughout the west wing. Damn, was Phil happy. It didn't mean that the Supreme Court had overturned the lower court's decision, but that the case would be referred back to the state for constitutional violations.

Next, he opened the letter from Mr. Vogelfine. His letter read:

Dear Mr. Avery:

Enclosed is a copy of the opinion handed down by the Supreme Court dealing with your Writ of Certiorari, which I am sure you have. In the event that you have not received it, this is my copy. What this opinion means is that there is still no determination of your guilt or innocence, but that there is sufficient grounds to believe that the state infringed upon your constitutional rights.

The risk involved here is a new trial which means you can be found guilty or innocent, which if you are found guilty again, you could receive the same sentence with no credit for the time you have served. You could receive a death penalty, or you could be set free. At any rate, it places us in a better bargaining position to do what you hired me for initially, to get your sentence reduced.

It is entirely up to you as to how you want to go, but for an additional five thousand, I think we can convince the state to reduce your sentence to something like thirty years or less. Should you decide the latter and not risk getting the same sentence or more, please sign and return the enclosed form giving me the power of attorney to negotiate a more favorable sentence for you.

>Very truly yours,
>Sam Vogelfine, Esquire

In ten minutes, he had signed the power of attorney and had it ready for mailing. *Wait until I tell Vickie,* he thought, *this could mean that I may be eligible for parole in a couple of years.*

In his glee, he had almost forgotten Vickie's letter, which he always saved for last. He anxiously tore open her letter before he fully reclined on his bed to read it comfortably.

>December 16, 1966
>
>Dear Phil,
>
>I regret to tell you that I will not be over Christmas Day as usual, but I will send your Christmas package. It is with much misgivings that I must tell you that I can no longer postpone the marriage that you asked me not to go into. Phil, I am sorry, but I will be married to Dr. Dixson by Christmas.
>
>>Love,
>>Vickie

He leaped from the bed.

"Goddammit!" he said as his fist plunged into the concrete wall. His knuckles swelled as blood oozed from his hand, but the only pain he felt was in his mind and heart.

"No, Vickie! No!"

In his single cell, he was totally unaware that he was talking aloud. One hour later the lights went out. He pranced the eight foot cell back and forth like a lion in a cage for a thousand times. About two o'clock that morning, his next-door cellmate, Brother Jones, whispered, "Hey, Phil." The whisper penetrated Phil's depression. At that very second, he had been speculating on how it would feel to hang himself.

"Yeah, brother," Phil whispered anxiously.

"Are you all right over there? I've been hearing you prancing all night, ever since mail call."

"My girl is getting married, man. I want to hang it up."

"Man, you are stronger than that. All we know is suffering and pain. But, that life-taking shit ain't never been the answer for us. Get your goddamned mind together and let me see you alive in the morning. Okay, man?"

"Yeah, brother. I'll hang in here. Thanks, man."

Sometimes just one word, just one act of concern at the right time is all one needs to keep hanging on.

Finally, he jumped in the bed, pulled the covers over his head and cried inconsolably.

For the next month or so, he didn't care about getting out of prison. The greater part of his incentive had been Vickie and his child. She mentioned that he was in Boston with her mother. Now they both seemed far away. The thought of it all made him feel irritable, depressed and outright hostile.

One day in the courtyard as he moped along, Jimmy Davis, a dude whom he did much joking with, walked over to him.

"Damn, boy," he panned, patting him on the shoulder. "Snap out of that shit. That bitch is gone. You're lucky the bitch lasted that long. That bitch . . ."

He didn't finish what he intended to say. Phil's fist had bashed his mouth. In surprise, he held his mouth, brought a hand of blood up from it and sprang for him. Some of the homeboys broke it up before it really got started. It was not Phil's intention to blow up. They had joked around for years. Nevertheless, it was a situation that he just couldn't help.

Shortly after Phil sent the lawyer the rest of the money, he began to get really negative. He gambled excessively and lost. He borrowed money and cigarettes from all the loan sharks. They would loan him as much as he requested, fifty cartons of cigarettes, fifty dollars or one hundred dollars. The word was out that he was losing heavily. Even the dope money was being lost. This resulted in Pee Wee stopping his supply.

It was nothing for him to bet a hundred or two hundred at a skin game and tell a runner, "Hey, tell Loan Shark Billy to send me a hundred until Commissary Day."

Commissary Day or State Day was the big payday of the month. This was when all the inmates got paid. At that time, money was plentiful, both cash and cigarettes. Most of Phil's loans had been borrowed until State Day. The sharks hadn't hesitated with their loans to him because they knew he was good for the money. What they didn't know was that his source of money was cut off and that he had been in the red for well over a month.

It was the day before State Day that he realized the tremendous trouble and debt that he had gotten into. His total indebtedness was slightly over one thousand dollars in cash and cigarettes. His bank roll was zero. What in the hell was he going to do? The crucial part of the matter was that he had not borrowed from chumps, but from some of the most bloodthirsty, money-hungry, ass-loving bastards in the entire penitentiary. All were known killers. Some had killed both on the outside and inside.

It was known that loan sharks couldn't stay in business unless they had some means of getting their money back. Those means were either shank or ironpipe.

With all of Phil's avenue experiences and rough exposure, he was scared shitless.

During this period, the institution was crowded and many inmates who had single cells had been given a partner. Phil's partner's name was B.J. He was a young kid from North Carolina doing his first bit. They were locked in their cell the night before State Day when his fears were manifested.

"B.J.," he said to his cell partner, "do you have any money?"

"I just got a couple cartons of cigarettes, man. That's it."

"I need them, man. I'll pay you back."

"Sure, Phil," he really wanted to help. His expression showed much concern. "I heard you're in a lot of debt."

"Yeah, I owe some of the most bloodthirsty bastards in the jail."

They were on the west wing flats, near the shower, on the Forrest Street side. It was still early and many of the inmates who worked late shifts had to walk past on their way to the shower. One guy stopped by and said, "Phil, Big Steve sent me to tell you to have his money tomorrow or else."

"Yeah, okay man," he remarked, scared as hell as he stood there holding the bars.

In less than five minutes, the west wing tier runner, Willie, walked to his cell. He hesitated before he spoke. "Avery, I hate to tell you this, but Loan Shark Billie said to have his money in the morning or he wants some asshole."

"Fuck Billie," he replied as he trembled thinking of the people he had killed. He had killed four guys in prison that he knew. His original charge was murder. He was known to cash his reputation for the price of a young boy's ass. Billie was successful in beating his murder charges in prison because the dead inmate was always found in an isolated area of the institution with a knife in him and one in his hand. It was reported that Loan Shark Billie would take two knives with him, one to kill his victim and the other to place in the victim's hand to indicate self-defense.

Before he could digest the awesomeness of Billie's reputation, Willie returned twenty minutes later with another message.

"Hey, Phil, Charles Cash said he hopes he don't have to fuck you up about his money tomorrow. He wants to know if you'll have it."

"Tell him I'll try." That was all he could reply.

"Man," B.J. said to him, "I really feel sorry for you. Why don't you get yourself locked up on south wing?"

"Naw, I'm not going to do that. I'm already locked up and I'll be damned if I'm going to south wing to lock up for months."

B.J.'s suggestion triggered a thought, *Why don't I armor myself?*

Phil reached under his mattress, pulled out a twelve-inch steel shank made in the metal shop. It was sharp, strong and fierce-looking.

B.J.'s eyes bucked at the sight of it.

"Damn, man. That's a sword!"

Without uttering a word, he reached under his mattress and pulled out two flat pieces of board. Next, he put on his blue penitentiary jacket and stuffed the boards down his shirt to protect his chest and stomach. The other board he placed to protect his back. Once these were secured, he began stuffing magazines in his clothes to fill void spaces. While he buttoned his coat, he observed the incredible look on B.J.'s face.

B.J. clearly thought that he was crazy.

"B.J.," Phil said to him assuringly. "Take this shank and hit me in the back, hard."

He took the shank and fumbled with it.

"Man, I can't."

"Go ahead, Goddammit. You may be saving my life 'cause if this big shank of mine don't go through, ain't nothing else will. Now go ahead and hit me with it!"

B.J. came down with the shank hard. The impact made Phil tremble. The blade didn't penetrate. What he didn't know was that just as they were doing their demonstration, one of the jail expert agitators had come to his cell to deliver a message. He observed the whole scene. When he realized what was happening, he fell all over the west wing flats laughing and shouting, "Phil Avery done armored up like a fifteenth-century soldier!"

The short, bald-headed bastard laughed so hard, it appeared

that his jet-black face became three shades lighter. He had guys laughing and calling Phil all night. He was sure enough on the pan, but was serious as hell about protecting himself.

When word got around that Phil had armored up in such comical fashion, some of his debtors sent messages similar to this, "Phil, that shit is really funny. Pay me when you get it."

All the messages weren't sent in that vernacular. A few came to him this way: "I don't care what you are armed with. I'm going to kill you, motherfucker."

So that next morning, "scared" was the only description of him. As he walked towards the wood shop, his hands were dug inside his jacket, gripped tightly around his shank. Intentionally, he stayed ten feet away from everyone. Nerves were on edge.

He passed the laundry window. His eyes were scanning the several doors carefully when he heard the alarming yell, "Phil! Phil! Look out!"

Phil's reflexes sprang into action as his shank began swinging wildly in mid-air.

Donald Walden was laughing his head off at Phil responding to his "Pan Act."

Looking up at him stretching from the laundry window, he said, "Donald, you common bastard!"

He was angry and laughing at the same time. There were at least fifteen other guys around who just folded over in laughter. The news of that incident spread quicker than teletype. As comical as it was, it served a purpose. Phil was out to protect himself and was not jiving.

Two of the guys, who he most feared, had come to him man to man. The conversation went like this, "Hey, Phil. You got heart. I like you ..."

Phil stood his distance and observed Charles Cash as he talked to him. He knew he could hit a brick wall and do damage to it with his fists and he wasn't standing too close. Continuing, he said, ". . . as you get some money, just pay me a little at a time. You don't have to worry about my hurting you. I just don't like nobody deliberately taking anything from me."

"Thanks," was all Phil could say. He gave the same "thanks" to the other fellow.

There was still a threat on his life. He went to the guys and told them frankly that he would be paying them soon. He let them know that it was not his intention to beat them out of anything. With that, all he could do was hope that they listened and he continued to watch his back.

Even that fear-inspiring episode didn't stop him from gambling. One month later, he was down on the floor of the wood shop rolling dice with two dudes who were partners out to beat him. The dice were doing pretty good for him. He had a winning streak going one mile long. He was twenty-five dollars in one guy's hundred dollar bill and fifty into the other's. His point was six. At the next roll of the dice, six it was.

"Okay, Elwood, that makes seventy-five of your hundred and fifty of yours, Herb."

The two of them had him feeling quite leery. They were holding on to those bills too long.

"Look," Phil suggested, "I can change that hundred of yours, Elwood. I've got twenty-five."

"No, just shoot the twenty-five out," he sneered.

"Bet," Phil said, turning to Herb. "You betting twenty-five, too?"

The dice rolled from his hand. They stopped on eleven. That meant Elwood owed him the whole hundred and Herb owed him seventy-five.

"Okay," he said. "Elwood, that's you for your hundred. Hand it over."

Phil reached in good faith for the bill, but he didn't extend it.

"Wait and see how you make out with Herb," he said with a sneer.

"Man, Herb's money ain't got nothing to do with our bet. Give me my hundred."

Feeling that the situation didn't have far to go, he looked at Herb. "Here's twenty-five dollars. Give me your hundred and we're even."

The reply he received wasn't funny.

"Thanks, sucker," Herb said.

Phil's body came up off the floor and stood its full six feet.

"Man, you've got to be joking, as much money as I have lost in this penitentiary. Give me my money."

Elwood answered this time, "You're a sucker. We're winners. Man, you've blowed."

Tears started to flow from Phil's eyes. They were not tears of weakness but were tears of anger.

"Don't cry. We don't like weakness," said Herb—the tall dark one.

Again, Phil attempted to reason with them, explaining all the debt he was into, ending with, "Please give me my money."

The short one, Elwood, gave this reply, "If you don't get away from here and back to your work table, you are going to get more than your money."

Phil walked towards his worktable, angry as hell. His eyes took in the seventy-five other inmates in the shop who were hammering away at their chores. Once at his table, his homeboy, George, could see he was somewhat in a daze.

"George," Phil said to him nonchalantly, "keep these dice for me until I come out of lockup."

He took the dice. His face was confused as he tried to understand what he was talking about. It dawned on him when he lifted his hammer.

"Phil, Phil, don't . . . don't . . . get . . . get yourself in no . . . no troub . . . trouble." He stuttered when he talked. He knew that at that point it was useless to try stopping Phil.

He began walking. The shop sounds were very loud. The inmates were busy at their craft. Elwood and Herb were standing at the table talking and laughing about how easy they took Phil. They were doing that as he walked up.

As he stood before them with the hammer behind his back, he said two words before he started swinging, "Why me?"

The hammer whammed on Elwood's head first. Blood spurted. In that same instant, it banged against Herb's head. With repeated blows, he banged one head and then the other. One hollered and the other screamed. They ran in circles crashing into each other. Blood was everywhere. Realizing they had been beaten senselessly and that he might kill them, he threw the hammer down. Still filled with anger, he beat them with his fists. By this time, the crowd had gathered. It looked as if he had beaten them only with his fists. The scene appeared more awesome than it was, to the onlooking inmates.

"Kill them bastards, Phil!"

"Man, you see him beat them motherfuckers with his bare fists! Look at that blood!"

"They are going to die," someone else shouted as Elwood and Herb staggered senselessly from table to table.

When they were completely out of it, he walked back to his table. The goon squad was on their way.

Twelve of them rushed in. They immediately grabbed Elwood and Herb, thinking they had fought each other.

As they dragged Elwood and Herb out, he was busy working at his table. Inmates laughed at the mistake. The laughter was short-lived. Ten minutes later, they returned to take Phil to the hole. After that, it was six months of solitary confinement.

Chapter 6

The hole, as it was called because it was underground, was better than the prison's blue room. That was because it had one luxury, a toilet. They gave Phil bread and water three times a day and a comfortable mattress.

Phil slept well on that mattress the first night until about ten p.m. Clang! went the sound of his cell lock. The door popped open. Two guards stepped in.

"All right, you black son of a bitch, give me that mattress."

His sleepy eyes focused upon the two officers. The name-caller was blacker than he. His name was Whitaker. It was obvious that if he did not roll off that mattress, he would beat him to a pulp to impress the white officer with him that he was a real nigger-hater.

His body curled over, and his feet touched the cold floor. Instantly, they snatched the mattress.

"Have a good sleep," Whitaker sneered.

"Clang!" The door shut and they were gone.

It was difficult to sleep again after that bit of cruelty. Most of Phil's time that night was spent analyzing the mentality of the black officer.

There were at least ten black officers working in the penitentiary at that time. Seven of them had the mentality of Officer Edvans and Officer Whitaker. If you were black, they would beat you to death in the presence of the white officer. All too often, the white officer had to pull the black one away before he killed his inmate slave brother.

On the other hand, the black officers were afraid to put their hands on a white inmate. It didn't matter if that white inmate had broken every rule in the institution and topped it with calling the black officer all types of foul names. The master-slave mentality was prevalent in these seven black officers. They had silently accepted the role of being black overseers of the master's plantation—to beat them and let the master know that they were doing a good job.

Phil's mind reflected a year ago, when several white officers beat a black inmate unmercifully.

"I've had enough! Please stop!" the inmate screamed.

They didn't listen. They beat him until they got tired. Two hours later, a white inmate committed a similar infraction against a black officer. It was Officer Harrison. He was not of the mentality of the talented seven. He was a pure nigger as Malcolm X would say.

Harrison had begun to beat the white inmate. The guy hollered and screamed. "Get off me, you bastard! Don't hit me any more! Help!"

"Hey!" a couple of white officers called to Harrison. "Take it easy on that guy!"

"Fuck you," Harrison replied. "You didn't take it easy on the black inmate an hour ago!"

He continued to whale on the white inmate's ass.

That bit of news spread throughout the inmate population. Every black inmate in the institution had deep respect for Officer Harrison, not because he beat up a white inmate, but because he had balls. Needless to say, he didn't keep his job long. Phil was remembering that it was soon after he got into a hassle with the big power, Captain Muscle. It was rumored that Captain Muscle wanted to shake Officer Harrison down for possibly bringing in some contraband.

Harrison, being a proud person, refused by saying, "Why you dope-dealing, bribe-taking, Georgia cracker, red motherfucker, where did you get the nerve to search me?"

Inevitably, an argument ensued. Harrison's big fist struck Captain Muscle. He hit the floor and Harrison barked, "You don't have to fire me. I quit!"

That was the last black officer whom Phil had known that had that type of gumption.

Finally, the cold concrete numbed his mind and body. Sleep overtook him.

Six months in lockup, solitary confinement, if you will, was a trying experience for him. It was a suffering, torturing experience. There is absolutely nothing to do but think, think, suffer, pace the floor, and masturbate.

Masturbation came last because it was the highlight of his activities. If it is treated with dignity, one must know that there is an art to masturbation. In your frustration and confinement, you summon to your mind any female who has once given you pleasure. The scene is recreated as your mind places her right in the cell with you. At the same time, your hand becomes her warm body, you stroke insanely, making her scream, call your name, begging you to, "Please stop!" As you are wrapped in the emotion of it all, your arm is in continuous motion per minute. After a certain amount of rhythmic motions, you experience this tremendous orgasm. A feeling of relaxation overcomes you, but you find that two minutes later you are angry at yourself for wasting precious seed that could be had by a woman.

Once out of the mental fantasy you say to yourself aloud, "Damn, I must be sick. I'm not doing this crazy shit anymore." But, it isn't that easy. Phil had known two addictions in his life: gambling and masturbation. He masturbated incessantly. Many times three times a day. There were times when he was afraid that he had ruined himself. There was a time when nothing would come out of him but blood. It scared him to death, but he could no more stop than a junkie living in a shooting gallery (dope house).

If it was any one thing that his mind lingered on in prison, it was the lack of female companionship. The separation of men from women in prison makes a sheer mockery of the constitutional words, ". . . cruel and unusual punishment . . ." Mentally, he made bargains with both God and the devil—or anyone else in power—that they could take his right arm, if he could just spend one hour with a woman.

Not only was he hurting for a female from the sexual sense, but there was a pronounced emotional void, which tortured him painfully in the absence of female companionship. He observed that many inmates substituted for this void by falling in love with homosexuals and living with them as if husband and wife. While this may have been the ultimate substitute for human need, the situation still was not real for him. It was a damned shame too, because of the absence of female companionship that many otherwise normal males had turned to homosexuality unintentionally.

Many guys shacked up with homosexuals, rubbing them, kissing them and constantly making love. In the course of these affairs as emotions intensified, the passive homosexuals began to caress and kiss in return. As a result, in all too many cases, the passive homosexual caressed the buttocks of his man, invoking passion ignored by him while under the heat of emotion. This feeling is taken advantage of by the passive homosexual who flips over and inserts into the aggressive male until both have lost their roles. In the penitentiary the term for this is "rub partners."

There were so many ways that inmates got stripped of their manhood and became homosexuals. The strong-arm method is usually applied towards the young and scared. That is simply done by an ass bandit who catches a guy alone, places his arm around his throat, and squeezes him out. To the guy who is scared to death, the bandit does not have to use the strong arm method. All he has to do is threaten him with the violence of using a shank or ironpipe.

The homosexual classic in the institution happens when a young boy of seventeen or eighteen is in awe and fear of a known muscular asshole bandit and suddenly finds himself mysteriously transferred into the bandit's cell permanently. In the young boy's mind, pure torture is a mild description as he thinks of what the situation will be when the lights go out.

In a few surprising cases the situation goes thusly: "Take off your clothes," the muscular brute demands of the young, innocent boy.

The boy, knowing that he could be torn apart with one blow, reluctantly complies by stripping. Then he watches the bandit strip. With fear for his life and manhood, he stands there and trembles, only to be told by the bandit, "Now fuck me. If you tell, I'll kill you." This homosexual goes on for years with the mean reputation of molesting young boys when, in truth, he is the nail seeker.

The smooth-off method is one of the most widely used and sophisticated forms of homosexuality throughout the penitentiary. It involves a tremendous use of psychology and employs various methods. For instance, loan sharks and other smooth guys would get guys into debt, constantly urging them to borrow more than they could pay back, building great feelings of obligation. Once the obligation is established, they would drop lines of rap such as, "Look, you can square that debt off sexually between you and me," adding, "Your line of credit will always be good." Sixty percent of the time the person obligated would agree because of two reasons: the promise of secrecy and the need for material necessities such as cigarettes, special goods and pressed clothes. Another popular style of homosexuality is "rub buddies."

In many situations, dope and homosexuality go hand in hand. That is because the penitentiary is a known frustration den. Dope is the easiest attainable answer, and the inmates who become hooked readily submit to homosexual acts to get their fix.

Never would Phil forget the seventeen-year-old kid who was raped in the shower by fifteen hardcore convicts. Phil was locked in his cell when he heard the screams.

"Please, I can't take it!"

"Lay down, bitch," someone shouted as the sound of the hard slap on his face echoed.

"Help, help!" the boy kept calling. Each time a different man mounted him, his screams intensified.

"Why don't you go down and help that kid?" Phil asked a guard who was standing near his cell.

"I didn't ask that kid to come here. They might fuck me, too!" With that, he walked away and left the kid to be slaughtered.

Later, the kid lost his mind, and within a few months he was released without having therapy only to return to prison with a life sentence for raping a ten-year-old girl and jamming a Coke bottle into her womb.

Phil thought that these damned correctional officials don't give a damn what happens to the men in this hell pit.

If they had any feelings at all, they could help lessen the

brutal encounters which the inmates faced day to day.

The hours dragged into days and the days into weeks. Two months later, his mind was still stretched beyond solitary confinement trying to figure out how in the hell Phillip Avery's life ended here. The realization of it all as he reflected was— there were hundreds, even thousands of black Phillip Averys. *How did they get here? Why, dammit,* Phil questioned, *were there so many blacks in prison and so few whites?* All statistics clearly state that whites commit more crimes than blacks. *Are we born criminals?* His mind seriously began to reflect the possibility as to whether they were totally guilty of having the criminal mentality that led them to crime. *Was the system our psychological co-conspirator?*

The answer to these questions bothered him. It was impossible to escape feeling that a deck had been systematically stacked against imprisoned blacks. His hand was just another deal in the game. Phil remembered the conversations of Pop Corn and other dudes whom he had grown up with and how they had told him, "Man, I was just twelve when I first got locked up ... been in and out of jail ever since ..."

"Who," he questioned, "are these thousands of blacks— myself included—who constantly make up the prison population? What relation do they have with the present and past society in the systematic scheme of things?" The answer was simple. The present relation was prison. The past relation was slavery. Like a thunderbolt, it hit him. There was no difference between slavery and incarceration. In his studies, he read that slavery was supposed to have ended in 1865. At that time, millions of slaves were released from bondage with no skills, no money and no structure. If a root trace could be placed on these releasees, in terms of survival, they could be classified as those with positive Master's influences; those with negative Master's influence and those with a hit of both. This, Phil guessed, wouldn't include those blacks who were always free and hip to the game of survival.

At any rate, he concluded that those with the Master's positive influence, today would be the blacks with middle class jobs and who possessed the type of family structure that would be manifested in their offspring in a degree of unity and education. Those with a bit of the Master's negative-positive influence would, today, be those skillful at the manipulation game, playing both ends against the middle, slipping frequently from side to side when it was convenient.

Finally, he reasoned that the root trace would reveal that the blacks influenced by the Master's negative force would remain in slavery today as in the past.

This would be, he continued, because the majority of them have never had any positive influence to pass on to posterity, despite the fact that sociological, educational, and economic knowledge was in abundance around them. It is these people, in the millions, who comprise the welfare population, the dope population, the crime population, and inevitably, the prison population.

Recalling a conversation from the past, Phil remembered an elderly man once saying to him, "Look, I came out of that same background. I never stole anything, worked all my life, and never been to jail."

Eight years ago, when he mentioned that to him, he had no answer for him. Today, he would tell him, "For everyone who made it, there are one hundred who don't get the exposure of what influenced you."

More and more, as he thought, his conclusion spelled, slavery is prison and prison is slavery. That system would never cease to exist for the people with the least root trace.

Passages from history and law books flashed before his mind. Phil recalled reading that the first prison was built in 1795. That prison was not built for blacks—a reasonable fact being that most blacks were property and you didn't lock up your property. However, there were a few free blacks who were incarcerated, but the whites far outnumbered them until 1865. It was that year when millions of slaves were freed that the prison population surged with blacks. A transition took place. A transition from slavery without walls to slavery with walls.

As Shorty Rogers said, "We are dealing with processed cotton rather than raw cotton."

He once read that during slavery, the many plantations would use slave labor to provide the state with its needs. A profit was made from slave labor. The same thing was happening in the plantations of the State Use Industry, and he didn't need to read it from a book.

In thinking about it all, it was extremely frightening to realize that each one of those slave shops run by the State Use Industry was making in excess of a million dollars and needed at least seven hundred or eight hundred slaves to run them at all times. This clearly meant that if the state were to create a successful rehabilitation program on a large scale, there wouldn't be any slaves to run this multi-million dollar plantation. It would be outright indefensible for the state to successfully rehabilitate inmates who brought in millions of dollars from goods sold to other state agencies.

To him, it appeared that the state was getting over like a fat rat. The prison received millions in tax money to incarcerate inmates. Adding these in his mind, all he could see was flesh-making money under the auspices of the state. His conclusion was that crime is big business—not for the perpetrator, not for the victim, but for the biggest pimp of them all, the state.

Taking in the scope of this total picture, Phil decided that if he were ever to get out of prison, he had better reconstruct his own program.

Going into his fourth month in solitary confinement and

after much mental reflection, he decided to write a book. He worked on that book day and night. Many times he would not eat or allow any interruptions.

The one interruption that he allowed to take up some of his time was the letter from Mr. Vogelfine informing him that his sentence had been reduced to thirty years.

Chapter 7

After six months of confinement, Phil was released from lockup. Once back into the prison population, he was given a job at the school as an aide. Working at the school enabled him to study more and to take advantage of two outside courses that truly changed his life and style of thinking. The Dale Carnegie course was the first impressive course and the Napoleon Hill course was the second. Some referred to it as the science of personal achievement.

In memory, vivid impressions of the Dale Carnegie instructor, Ed Vaney, remained with him as he visualized him standing before them spouting positive words such as, "initiative means originality, doing something on your own without waiting to be told . . ."

Each word was like a positive rebuilding of his mind. With consistency, he practiced the principle of these teachings in his everyday encounters with inmates, guards, and even with the warden.

It was the Napoleon Hill course that reinforced what he learned in the Dale Carnegie course. This course consisted of a study of five hundred of the world's most successful men and how they used certain principles to accomplish their goals. The most impressive thing that he remembered was a phrase that he heard an inmate teacher say when he had first arrived some years ago, "Anything that the mind can conceive and believe, it can achieve." They were words that he personally adopted into his thinking. The course taught him about the laws of nature, such as the law of attraction, the law of compensation, and the law of cosmic habit force.

One day as their dynamic instructor, Ben Terrace, was explaining the various laws and their relation to a positive mind, he raised his hand and asked this question: "Mr. Terrace, I am here for a crime I did not commit. However, I did associate with people of criminal background and committed other crimes. My question is, do you think this law of compensation was fair to me?"

Ben Terrace's steel blue eyes stared at him intensely as his mind formulated a reply that he will never forget.

"Yes, it was fair to you according to how you practiced the law." He folded his arms across his chest and continued, "You see, you practiced several laws of nature, negatively. You received the end result. You associated, as you mentioned, with people who had criminal backgrounds and those people will attract police, courts and convictions, all under the law of attraction. Your habits were negative and when practiced under cosmic habit force, they became established habits attracting you to more negative elements. As a result, you are introduced to the law of compensation which pays for your habits in the manner that you live them, negatively!"

He stopped there. There was no need for him to explain further because Phil knew what he said was true. Also, he knew that he could reverse his habits in a positive manner and live them positively. This knowledge was filet mignon to his hungry mind. He ate of it constantly only because he wanted to become what he ate.

Unfortunately, only nineteen inmates received the opportunity to take this course. The institution did not allow the return of this positive course after they graduated. It was, indeed, the most impressive, positive, and dynamic course ever to be offered within the gates of the penitentiary.

At the completion of the course, Mr. Terrace had the entire class write down and read aloud what was known as their goals and major purposes in life. Phil's goals were to be free and to publish his book. He wanted to see it accepted in all schools and libraries with the hope that youngsters would read it and not follow his footsteps. And, finally, he wanted the book to be a movie.

In stating their goals, they also had to write what they were willing to give in life to others. It was then that Phil stated that he would dedicate his life to helping inmates in slavery.

It was the latter part of 1967 that the penitentiary swelled in population. The tension was thick; the conditions bad. Many new faces were showing up—inmates and correction officers, as changes were taking place. Some changes were good; others were bad. Many of the black correctional officers received promotions to sergeants and lieutenants—even Edvans received a promotion.

Many of these promotions were brought about because of the pressure of desegregation, compiled with the overwhelming number of black inmates. Nevertheless, a change was in the air. Of course, the corruption and head-busting was still quite the order of the day. The warden was promoted to be the commissioner of corrections, and the deputy warden became the warden. And Captain Muscle became deputy warden. The change in rank continued on down the line.

By this time, Phil had become a full-fledged teacher and was attending college classes brought inside by the University of Maryland. Through various contacts, he was able to bring certain social and educational functions into the institution, which were of direct benefit to the inmates. Unofficially, he had created for himself a position in public relations.

It was accepted by all officials only because he presented himself in such a positive manner. No longer was he into a negative bag. Gambling, selling dope, and fighting had no place in his positive frame of mind. For him it was all school, making positive contacts and attempts at publishing his manuscript.

It was because of his manuscript that he contacted and developed relationships with Professor Turpins of Morgan; Dr. Perdale, his ex-principal; Mr. Swisser, the furrier; and Sussie Katz, the psychologist. All of them had read his manuscript and were quite impressed. They all sent him literature. They corresponded regularly which was direct support to his positive mental attitude.

Sussie Katz became involved with the institution through a course from the University of Maryland. Later, she became a regular volunteer teacher at the school where Phil worked. She taught psychology. Phil was one of her students.

To say that Sussie Katz was an attractive middle-aged woman would be to underrate her drastically. Actually she was a beautiful, black-haired Jewish woman, who could out-audition Elizabeth Taylor for the role of Cleopatra. All of her beauty was matched evenly with intelligence. The word was out that she was quite influential. Her integrity, particularly around the inmates, was impeccable. However, this did not prevent the inmates from having sexual fantasies about her. They all carried her image to their cells at night and stroked her relentlessly.

Between teaching sessions, when no guards were around,

Sussie would ask, "Hey, you guys, what's really happening around here? Is this place really helping you?"

They would tell her about the corruption, the brutality, the gambling and Mace Peaches and his blue room ordeal, which was still taking place. They told her the whole thing, not excluding those turkey-stealing bastards who were now high in rank.

"You mean," she responded to an inmate named Hubert, "that a guard actually saw fifteen inmates rape another inmate and did nothing?"

"That's right," Hubert said assuringly. "That young guy screamed and yelled for fifteen minutes or more, while each guy took his turn. The guard was about twenty feet away. He just called back, 'I didn't tell you to come here'."

There were about twelve of them sitting in the classroom circle. They all confirmed that and many similar incidents that happened. As time passed, Sussie became more and more involved with the teaching and plight of the inmates. The guards and other officials made many passes at her, all of which she ignored. The truth of the matter was that she was a committed married woman who didn't have time for bullshit, from inmates or guards.

She and Phil developed a close educational relationship, not different from her relationship with any other inmates. Her helping him with points concerning his manuscript made the relationship seem different. This eventually created an atmosphere of jealousy that increased daily, especially with the school officials and the guards. Mr. Richard Blaze, a black schoolteacher, was the only one who understood the situation and he supported the relationship.

Inevitably, the false rumor was spread on the grapevine that Sussie Katz was suspected of screwing inmates. Phil Avery was a prime suspect. Following that, mysteriously an order was sent to the school that she wasn't to be allowed in the penitentiary. At the same time, Phil was mysteriously transferred from the school to another job site.

Knowing this woman as he did, he knew that she loved her teaching and hated injustice. She was armed with enough inner resources to explode the adage, "Hell hath no fury like a woman scorned," right in the penitentiary's face.

Shortly after these transfers, things began to happen in rapid succession, all of which proved to be Sussie Katz-related. The thing that triggered Phil off was that one night a childhood friend of his, George Renser, died because of pure neglect.

"Guard! Guard! I'm sick!" He rang his cup across the bars of his cell several desperate times.

"Lie down, bastard!" The guard's reply was harsh. They all heard it throughout the west wing.

One hour later, George was found dead in his cell from a sugar condition that could have been treated had the guard allowed him to visit the hospital for a shot. That next day they rioted. They burned every shop and slave camp in the joint. Firemen, state troopers, policemen and dogs were all over the penitentiary. After that, everyone was locked up. The guards came around to feed them in their cells. They kept Sussie Katz informed as to every move that took place.

The warden gave his account of the situation to the news media, stating, "It's just a case of restless inmates who are dissatisfied with the food again."

There was no mention that they were upset over a dead brother who called out for help and was refused. In the public's eyes, they were just some more barbarians destroying property that their tax money paid for.

Every inmate who had anyone on the outside smuggled letters, telling them the truth as to what happened. They directed that all information was to be shared with Sussie Katz who already had accumulated a wealth of information.

Within one week, the impossible happened because of the

"scorn of a woman." First, the commissioner of corrections lost his job, the warden was replaced and the deputy warden, Muscle, was fired. Major Stab, the judge and king of the turkey-stealers, resigned. The two Irish brothers and the brutality chief were removed. The guard, who refused to give George assistance, was fired. Mysteriously, Phil was transferred from lockup to the Eastern Shore, which was one of the minimum security camp centers.

On the day of Phil's transfer, a sad event occurred. Mace Peaches died. He died of every known type of disease imaginable. He took with him a piece of every inmate there. He also left them with a memory of an unbroken spirit which would always be respected and long remembered. Should the occasion arise for a testimony of brutality in the correctional system, Mace Peaches would have to be cited as the classic example of man's dehumanization of man in the Maryland penal system.

Part Two
Hidden Slavery

Chapter 8

Phil was given the status of work release after being transferred to Eastern Shore. This meant that by law, he would be allowed to work for private business and be paid minimum wages for labor. Finally, he was getting a break!

The camp center, where he had been sent, had about one hundred and twenty men. Twenty of them had just been transferred. They were anxious for that outside air and a chance to make good, hard-earned cash. They couldn't wait until morning to see what type of jobs they would be assigned. They were housed in Kent County Dormitory. In it were rows of beds and lockers on both sides of the long room. Willie, who had been transferred with Phil, was on one bunk beside Phil, and Charlie was on the other. They talked about what the morning would be like on their first day of fresh air in years.

"Man" Willie said gleefully, rubbing his hands together,

"I can't wait. Hope they put me on a good job."

"Yeah," Phil added, "I like that canning factory in Chestertown. Tell me they got women working there!"

"Stop worrying, you guys," Charlie joined in. "You'll get a chance to get your pricks wet. We're over the hump now. I don't want no stray cunt. I'm sending to Jersey for my woman first chance I get."

Charlie and Willie were from upstate. They were big-timers on the outside. Both of them were on a charge together, and the three of them had formed a kind of trio because of mutual respect and because they all had long sentences. They were doing twenty apiece and Phil was down to thirty.

They found many things to talk about that they had in common. They talked about gambling, hustling, and what they used to do on the outside.

"Man," Willie said, "I remember the time when I wouldn't work in a pie factory. Somebody mention work to me, I'd tell them to keep the disease away from me. But, I tell you now, I'd work ten hours a day shoveling shit if they asked me to, just to be in the open air."

"You're right, Willie," Charlie submissively agreed. "I'd do the same thing."

"Just think, you guys," Phil added, "we'll be making one dollar and sixty-five cents an hour tomorrow."

They went on talking and passing the time away until finally the lights went out and sleep overtook them. The night didn't seem particularly long. Phil had a dream or two. One dream had to do with his completing his sentence, being released and having saved several thousand dollars. In the dream, he invested the money towards the publication of his manuscript. Some indescribable expert told him, "Son, that is very foolish. You should never attempt to publish your own manuscript . . ." Before he could answer him, his positive thinking instructor, Ben Terrace, interceded and replied,

"Anything that this young man can conceive and believe, he can achieve, Mr. Negative."

After that second dream, it seemed that six a.m. arrived in no time. It was time to get up, eat and be assigned to work details.

Captain Red was the officer-in-charge of the camp. He came into the Kent County dormitory and barked the following order, "All right, men, you will eat and report to the front yard when you finish!"

They gulped the food, oatmeal and toast, and in fifteen minutes, they were headed for the front yard, all twenty of them. Once in the front yard, he saw a bunch of farmers, yakking, laughing and eyeing them as if they had just stepped from the slave boat. Some were leaning on their pickup trucks. Others were just standing and talking crop talk.

"Hey, Captain Red," one ruddy-faced, dirty farmer shouted. "Can I get three of 'em todee? Bye Gawd, I got a heap of work awaiting me on that land of mine!"

Pages from a book Phil once read flashed before his mind, as he observed the scene before him. *What was the name of that book? That's right,* he remembered, *it was* Slave Trading in the Old South.

"You got three, Sam," Captain Red said. He peered at the list in his hands and called off names, "Willie Staples, Charlie Redshirt and Phillip Avery, come forward."

As Phil looked at the sturdily-built, red-faced captain, he wanted to shout, "No, captain bossman. Please don't send us off to this one!" Instead, he walked forward along with Charlie and Willie.

"You three men will be working for Sam Andre today. It's a tryout for a while. If you do good, you'll be assigned to a regular job later. Got that?"

All we could say was, "Yes, sir."

"All right then, boys, get in the back of that pickup." Sam

Andre picked up the rest of the conversation. "That there green one is mine."

Charlie was the first to head for the pickup. Willie and Phil moved slowly and reluctantly. Their slow motions enabled them to hear what was said by one poor looking farmer who eased up to Captain Red and said, "Captain Red, can I get four of them niggers and just pay you sixty-five dollars?"

"Jim Albert, you know these niggers is twenty dollars a head."

"When my crops pay off, I will make it all up—you know that, captain," the man pleaded.

"C'mon, boys," Farmer Andre shouted to Willie and Phil. "We got work to do!"

They hastened their walk, climbed over the back of the pickup as they heard Captain Red say, "All right! I want four men to go on the Jim Albert farm. Ed Davis, John Taylor . . ."

Farmer Andre's motor drowned the other sounds as they pulled off towards Centersville, Maryland.

It was hot that morning when they arrived at the Andre Plantation. Once on his property, it seemed like they rode for an hour before they reached the section designated for them to work in.

"What the hell is this shit?" Charlie asked. They were still riding.

"You're on your master's plantation, nigger," Willie replied.

"You mean," Phil put in, "we ain't gonna get paid for this?"

"You heard what the captain said," Charlie interjected, "this is a tryout."

"Yeah, man, but these bastards are selling us to these farmers. Tell him, Willie," Phil urged, "what we heard that farmer say to Captain Red."

"I swear, Charlie," Willie said, "the state gets twenty dollars a head for us."

"What the hell," Charlie replied, defeatedly. "We're in jail, aren't we? It's better than the penitentiary."

The truck halted. Farmer Andre climbed out. Immediately, he barked some commands through the juices of his tobacco.

"You two," he said, looking from Phil to Willie, "get them pick-axes and start digging me a four-foot hole 'bout twelve feet round. Wanta build me a silo."

He probably picked them because they were both tall and strong-looking.

Turning to Charlie, he asked, "Can you run a tractor, boy?"

No sooner had Charlie nodded affirmatively when Andre had him plowing on the endless land.

In Phil's opinion, Andre was a pig. On a zero to ten rating, he would have given him a zero-minus every time. Compared to how Willie felt about him, Phil's feelings were kindergarten. For three hours, he stood over Willie and Phil in the hot, blazing sun, pointing and shouting where to strike the pick-axe.

This digging crap was as foreign to him as it was to Willie. Sweat popped from both of them as they rested a second to compare blisters.

"Go'on! Go'on! Goddamn-it! Niggers ain't good for shit!"

Willie dropped his axe and stared with hatred at the farmer. "What did you say, man?"

Thinking of how much they had been through in the penitentiary, Phil said, "Cool it, Willie. It ain't worth it."

He listened. Reluctantly, he restrained himself, swinging the axe vigorously into the earth.

The farmer jabbered on. "Worked since I was eight. Great Grandaddy owned this land. Built it up with blood and sweat. We ain't never worried 'bout no damn blister . . ."

After a while, they were not only tired, hot and had blisters, but they were outright thirsty. Willie had too much pride and anger to ask for water. So Phil did.

"Can we have a jar of water, Mr. Andre?" The question

was asked as mildly and politely as possible.

"Hell no! You get water on lunch break. I pay for your time. Don't pay for you to drink no water. Bad enough I got to pay for lunch. No water 'til lunchtime!"

At this point Willie couldn't take anymore. The level of Phil's anger was a notch below Willie's.

The farmer walked over to the pickup truck to light his pipe. Willie's hand gripped the pick-axe firmly.

"Avery," he said calmly, "let's take these axes, kill this cracker motherfucker and take the truck and his money, too."

Without giving it a second thought, Phil's reply was simply, "C'mon!"

The farmer's back was still turned toward them. They both gripped their axes. As they started towards him, Phil's positiveness regained itself. In a flash, a hundred Napoleon Hill lessons rushed to reinforce his thoughts. Immediately, Phil remembered the people who were in his corner and who had begged him not to get into trouble—Dr. Perdale, Sussie Katz, Professor Turpins, and Mr. Swisser, the furrier. Phil's axe dropped on the ground as he grabbed Willie and begged him, "No, Willie. Don't do it. The bastard ain't worth it. Listen to me. I got some people outside with influence. They'll get us out of this. Don't do it, Willie. Don't do it!"

He respected Phil. He listened to him. Finally, he loosened the grip on the axe. The farmer's back was still turned. He did not know that he had just escaped brutal death. *God, could he have used some Napoleon Hill and Dale Carnegie,* Phil thought.

Chapter 9

Lunchtime they were on their own. They didn't accept Farmer Andre's water or peanut butter sandwiches. Instead, they walked to a nearby farm and convinced an old black sister to allow them to use her phone after telling her their story.

Mr. Swisser couldn't be reached, so Phil called Mrs. Swisser.

"What?" she questioned. "They are selling you to private farmers?"

"Yes, Mrs. Swisser." He assured her that she heard correctly. "Please ask your husband to help us. I really don't want to get into deeper trouble. This is pure slavery."

"Don't worry. I will let my husband know right away. Please, just don't get into any more trouble."

The next day, the captain received a phone call from the commissioner of corrections. As a result of that phone call, Charlie Redshirt, Willie Staples and Phillip Avery were assigned to a work release detail, working for decent human beings who paid more than minimum wages. Also, they treated them, as they worked on their horse farm, like family.

Working on the horse farm was like being on a vacation, except it was hard and dangerous work. There were five hundred thoroughbred horses on the one thousand acres of land. Some had been born there; others were kept and attended by Dr. Todd, a real horse doctor, and Mr. Skipper. These two men owned the land along with several houses on the land, which they rented for additional income.

The rented houses were separated from the two mansions lived in by Dr. Todd and his family and Mr. Skipper and his family. Both Dr. Todd and Mr. Skipper seemed to understand inmates and showed no overt signs of Southern prejudice, probably because they were from up North. It was Mr. Skipper who laid on us the rap about rules and expectations on our first day of work.

"Look, men, these horses are very valuable and must be taken care of properly."

Mr. Skipper was a thin, comical-looking, gray-haired fellow whose voice never really gave off a serious sound. Yet, one could discern his seriousness by his facial expression and hand movements.

"These horses," he continued, "are to be out of the barns and into the pastures every morning. Once in the fields, their stalls are to be cleaned and fresh hay put in them. Feed and water them properly, and we'll have no problems." Throwing up his hands in finality, he added, "Once you take care of my horses and do all of your work, your time is your own until it's time to take you back to camp. If you got a girlfriend, there are over a thousand acres to do what you want. Just leave my female horses alone."

He laughed, and so did they.

With that working understanding, they needed no further orientation. But, damn, was Phil afraid of those horses.

As the months went by, Charlie, Willie and Phil became quite familiar with everything and everyone who lived on the farm. A very close relationship had developed between Phil and a couple who leased one of Mr. Skipper's horses. They were Burt and Stella Kellson. He was a famous writer and she was a housewife. Phil's relationship to him was particularly close because he was an aspiring writer.

One evening as the three of them sat at their dining room table, sipping Jack Daniels, he said, "Phillip, I finished your manuscript. It's damned good. One day, I want you to autograph my copy of the published edition."

"Burt, coming from you, that is the greatest compliment I can receive."

"He doesn't toss compliments around lightly, Phillip," Stella interjected, fumbling with her half-filled glass. She appeared nervous at Phil's presence and quite ill at ease with his being black and a convict. It showed in the expression of her attractive, suntanned face as her dark green eyes flickered nervously as he talked. For a woman of thirty-three, she was damned good-looking. There was not a trace of gray in her bluish-black hair.

"I read your manuscript, too. I just couldn't put it down until I completed it. I think it will sell a million. Don't you think so, Burt?"

"Yeah! Yeah! Very good."

Burt's reply was not meant to be curt in mockery. He always seemed to be preoccupied in thought. He had just completed a book on one of the country's most influential families and was working on another. His blue eyes always reflected deep thoughts. He reminded Phil of a genius for he was a true intellectual, a brilliant person. Being of Irish and Jewish descent gave him a broad knowledge of people, an exposure that made him warm and trusting towards those he liked.

"Speaking of books," Burt said, "I'm going to be in Boston for a few days to promote my latest book. Phil, I'd like you to keep Stella company and look out for her while I'm gone. Would you do that for me?"

A glance at Stella's facial expression revealed that she was thinking, *Is my husband crazy? I guess he knows people better than I.*

"Burt, I'd be glad to do that."

The clock on the dining room wall reminded him that he had fifteen minutes before he was due back at camp.

"Hey, it's time for me to leave. Give me some mints or chewing gum to kill the alcoholic smell."

Stella handed him both, and he bade them farewell until the next day. When he stepped outside, Charlie, Mr. Skipper, and Willie were just getting into the pickup for the trip back to camp.

That night at the camp as Phil lay in bed, he thought of Geraldine who had put a stop to his masturbation. They met in Chestertown one day while he was at the feed store with Dr. Todd. He told her his story and she couldn't believe that a nice guy like him was serving time.

"Could I visit you?" she asked.

Phil's "yes" reply overlapped her last word, "you," and they both laughed at his anxiousness. So she visited him on Friday at the horse farm. They made love in the back seat of her Plymouth. Phil remembered being so excited and out of practice that he couldn't find her crevice.

"Here," she whispered patiently, "let me take it for you." And she did.

Phil had no pride about needing the assistance. When she inserted him, the realization hit him that he had forgotten completely how good the private interior of a woman could be. Two minutes later when he flooded her with a gush of warm wetness, which kept pouring out, she said, "My gawd, it has been years for you!"

"I love you," he remembered whispering for lack of anything else to say. "Goddamn, that was good!"

Geraldine neither was very attractive, nor was she ugly. She had an inner beauty. It didn't matter that she was ten years his senior. What really mattered was that she was a warm, tender female, who at last had come to his physical rescue, bodily communicating that she was the natural outlet for all that had been sexually incarcerated in his physical being.

That night, Phil went to sleep thinking that just once he'd like to have his say with the department of corrections concerning the cruel and unusual punishment of male-female separation. Later, he dreamed that he had fulfilled his second goal of becoming involved at the top level of the department of corrections. In the dream, a group of inmates signed petitions stating that there should be inmate representation in policy-making positions on all things dealing with offenders. "Further," the petition went on to state, "we feel that Phillip Avery should be elected for said position."

"Yes," Phil was saying in an acceptance speech, "I do, hereby, agree to accept this position and swear that I will do all in my power to safeguard the rights of prisoners, to bring an end to the slave status, and to influence the Criminal Justice Department that it is just as illegal in 1968 as it was in the case in 1854 to allow Lady Justice to lift her skirt promiscuously if you are white while chaining her helms in chastity belts if you are black."

That next day was the beginning of an extremely close platonic relationship between Stella and Phil. Burt was in Boston for a few days. Phil was his wife's keeper for the hours that he could spare. They talked about his experience, her Southern background, interesting books that they read, and life in general.

"You know," she said after her third Jack Daniels, "you

are the first Negro person that I have really gotten to know."

"We're not so bad, once you get to know us."

"You're so intelligent," she exclaimed as if there should be some special reason for this attribute. "It is not often that you meet a Negro who has been to prison and who has written a book as well. You really should be proud."

"I am a bit proud. It wasn't easy, studying and all. But, I still have a long way to go before it's published."

The Jack Daniels was good and soothing to swallow, as his hand lowered the glass from his lips to the dining table where they sat.

"My husband, Burt, is a good judge of character. He trusts you and thinks you have good qualities. How did you ever get in prison?"

That was his cue to run the beginning of his crime life down to her. He did. His life's dissertation included the burglaries, gambling, numbers-running, the stick-ups, and finally the long sentence for the crimes he did not commit.

"But, how could they convict you like that?"

"The law can do anything it wants to a poor, black person. There is no defense. But, I'm not bitter about it anymore. I look at it like this. I was convicted by the law of compensation. My past crimes caught up with me because I was still into a negative bag. So something negative had to happen to me."

"But, when you are released, what would be your goals with a record such as yours?"

"I'll get my book published. Never will I forget this prison experience. So, I'll set up some sort of organization to assist prisoners and bring about a halt to the inhumane treatment of both prisoners and ex-offenders."

The concerned expression on her face told him that she was quite serious about what she said next.

"Phil, it's very hard to get a book published and probably

even harder to establish, with your record, an organization like the one you're talking about. How on earth do you propose that with those strikes against you, not to mention," she hesitated, "that you are Negro."

"Let me drop this on you, Stella," he replied just as seriously. He was posed in philosophical position as his chin slipped into the cup of his hand, "whether you are black, green, white or red—I know now that with a positive mind—anything that the mind can conceive and believe, it can achieve."

At that statement, he thought of his first inmate teacher, Donald, who had double life and some change who was now on the street successfully operating an accounting firm.

Still a bit confused, Stella asked, "With all that has been done to you, how can you have that kind of attitude? Frankly I would be angry with the world, just waiting for a chance to get back at it."

"I've been through that. I guess I still have some bitterness, but my head is on straight. I think positively now. But, more than that, it was people like yourself, Burt, Dr. Perdale, Professor Turpins and Mr. Swisser who turned my thinking around. Now, granted if it were not for concerned people like yourselves, I'd probably be full with hatred. Stella, it's so beautiful to know that another human being cares. It makes a world of difference."

A knock sounded upon the door. Time had moved. It was Willie and Charlie who came to tell him that it was time to return to camp. Before they left, he introduced them both to Stella, kissed her on the cheek and leaped on the waiting truck.

On the way back, Willie said, "That white man got a lot of heart trusting you around his woman. How is that thing, Phil? I know she gave you some."

Charlie smiled knowingly as they rode on the back of the

pickup.

"Don't even start that, man," Phil replied. "I dig the man and his wife. He placed a lot of trust in me and I don't intend to abuse it."

Chapter 10

Living at the camp wasn't too bad. The inmates tried to get along cordially with one another, knowing that this would help their records as far as parole was concerned. They worked on the farm six days a week. They tried to involve themselves in activities which helped their only free day to be very pleasant. The men played cards of all kinds, played ball, and told many jokes while watching various sports programs on television.

Some would gather on the outside and sing in groups. A little talent show was started on Sunday evenings. Groups gathered and sang gospel songs, rock and roll, jazz, and rhythm and blues. There were even dancing sessions which were free shows. Someone would turn on the radio, and those who thought that they could dance got in the center of the group and performed. All were good for a good laugh. Then one man would dance like a woman, switching and wiggling all over the place, while the men tagged each other to dance with this make-believe hot chick. This gave the men a lot of laughter.

One Sunday, there were three different groups singing on the talent show; of course, there were a few solos. This particular evening, Phil took his soda bottle as if were a microphone and started introducing each group's act as if he were the master of ceremonies. Then he stepped forward as the listeners were sprawled on the ground in comfortable positions. Nevertheless, he started the show by saying, "We are here to give you your money's worth. This is going to be the best show of shows. Now just sit back and enjoy some of the world's greatest a—r—t—i—s—t—s." Everyone laughed, for they knew the kind of artists that he was talking about.

As Phil clowned around between each group's performance, two guards came out to join the group. After the show was over, the guard told Phil that he liked a couple of the groups, and he could probably get some of the churches to put on a special program to hear them perform on Sunday evenings. Phil was much interested in this because it would give them a chance to leave the premises on Sundays, too.

During the week, Phil had contacted the groups and had gotten a favorable response from them. The following Sunday, the men were rehearsing in their various groups. Phil listened to all three of them practice. Then he said, "How do you all feel about becoming one big group and calling it the Maryland Wings of Heaven?" They all laughed at the idea, but they agreed to join the group and to accept their new name.

As they got in their proper voice sections—bass, baritone, and tenor—they began to sing. Their voices caused strong vibrations throughout the building. Those who were inside lying around came out to listen to them practice. This encouraged them. Their audience made them sing louder and more forcefully, and even the visitors gathered around to listen. When they had finished practicing, everyone gave them a big applause and words of encouragement.

They had just finished practicing when someone called to Phil, "Hey, man, you have a visitor." It was the guard. Phil looked in the direction which the guard was nodding his head towards. He knew it was Geraldine trying to surprise him. Phil walked to the entrance and saw Geraldine standing there in her beautiful red skirt. "Hi, how are you doing?" she said, greeting Phil with a big smile.

Phil kissed her lightly and said, "Fine, how are you?"

"Okay." She pointed to the car. "I've got two of my friends here with me. I thought that Charlie and Willie might want to have a little company," she said as she pinched and poked him in the side.

"Gerry, you're too much, lady. They sure in the hell want some company."

"Well, go get 'em."

Phil ran around the camp's buildings looking for Charlie and Willie. He had seen them earlier when they were practicing. He found Charlie and told him he had a lady who wanted to meet him.

"What? I'm ready to meet her, too. Man, Gerry is something else," said Charlie with his chest standing out, for he thought he could rap and make any woman want for days. They found Willie and told him. He jumped up and clicked his heels in mid-air.

"Well, I'll be a son-of-a-gun. I'm ready to meet any lady who looks my way."

Gerry introduced each one of the ladies to the men, and they walked to a table, which was sitting out front of the building where the visitor's section was located.

"Phil, I brought us something to eat."

"Good, I'm hungry, too." Phil and Gerry walked to the car

to get the food. She had the trunk of the car loaded with good-smelling foods; Phil felt his mouth watering like a hungry beast. She had one box which contained four potato pies and two cakes, a bucket of fried chicken, a big roasting pan with a huge roast in it, a large container of potato salad, and a cooler with sodas in it. Phil said, "I'm afraid that I'm going to be sick this day."

Geraldine replied, "I just want you to eat all you want and to enjoy yourself."

They spread the food on the table and ate until they couldn't eat anymore. Phil got the boys in the singing group, and they finished the remains. They toured the campgrounds and made plans for the ladies to come to the farm on Wednesday of that week. Phil told Geraldine about the group. She was so excited.

"That means I can see you on Sundays when the group sings because I'll be at every one of 'em; just let me know when."

Phil and the group were performing at the First Baptist Church in Church Hill; there was standing room only. Phil introduced the group as the "Maryland Wings of Heaven." The men were dressed in their jeans and shirts. People were staring at them first as if they were from another planet, but after they sang their first notes it sounded so good with all the sections blending together, that the audience took on another expression towards them. Their voices were so forceful even the windowpanes vibrated.

They were singing midway through the third song when one old lady jumped up and began to shout. The group felt good then. They sang even louder with the hands and facial expressions of hard-working Christian singers. The men would look at one another as they swayed from right to left, wanting to laugh at the way some of them were acting as if they were feeling the spirit. The first lady who shouted started a number of ladies shouting all over the church.

There were people parked as far as a mile who had come just to hear them sing. A lot of the men stayed on the outside and listened through the windows and the doors. Some sat on top of the cars, which were parked close to the windows. Things were looking better for them.

After they finished singing, they were given dinner. There were all kinds of food—spareribs, fried chicken, and potatoes cooked in every way one could think of, and cakes and pies of every flavor. It was a feast to behold. The group showed its appreciation, too, for they ate as if eating was going out of style. All that they didn't eat, the ladies packed in boxes for them to take home.

The group had gotten so popular throughout the town and the counties that they traveled practically every other Sunday. The members of First Baptist made robes for them and brought Phil a suit since he was the master of ceremonies or the spokesman of the group.

Geraldine was at every church were they performed, and she didn't mind anyone knowing that she knew Phil personally. They would always sit together and eat together after each performance.

The men couldn't wait to get back to camp and tell the others how the sisters would throw those big legs and shake those boobs and big hips while shouting. The clowns of the group would demonstrate and this would make the men roar with laughter. Besides adding inspiration to the group, it added more members to the group. Perhaps, the talk of the food and the ride to and from camp was the important reason for others wanting to join the group.

The winter months were approaching and the men didn't get as many invitations to sing. They were doing well to get an invitation once a month. Nevertheless, the inmates, who were their audience, didn't let them stop practicing. Every

Saturday night, the group would get together and practice their gospel songs; then they would sing rhythm and blues, jazz, and rock 'n roll songs. The entertainment session was a favorite of the non-card players.

Phil became the spokesman for the group and a friend of two of the guards since he had become trustworthy. He occasionally went with Geraldine home some Sundays, although no one knew about this but Charlie, Willie and the guards.

One Sunday, Geraldine said to him when she came to pick him up, "I've just got two brand new tires with that money you gave me. Let's go to Baltimore."

Phil couldn't believe it. "Are you serious?"

"Yeah, I'm serious. Tell the guard that you want to see your folks."

"I don't know whether they will approve of that."

"Go ask them."

The guard was not in favor of Phil's going to Baltimore. As long as he was going over to Geraldine's house, or for a ride in the country, it didn't matter, but his going to Baltimore was asking a little too much. Phil said that he just wanted to see his family for an hour or two; then he would come straight back to the camp. The guard, not wanting to go along with this, told Phil to be back before he got off from work. Phil grinned and thanked him with a handshake.

Geraldine and Phil drove down the avenue. He pointed out various places where he used to hang around. They drove to Phil's aunt's house on Fulton Avenue. They knocked on the door, for he knew that she slept late on Sundays from her late Saturday night hours.

"Who'n the hell is down there?" she called out of a window above their heads.

"Aunt Ellen, it's me, Phil."

"Who?"

"Phil, Aunt Ellen. Your nephew."

She scrambled down the stairs and opened the door. "Boy, what are you doing here? How long have you been out?"

"Aunt Ellen, I'm not out yet."

She threw her hands to her mouth. "Oh Lawd, no, you haven't broke—"

Phil interrupted her, "No, I haven't escaped. I got permission to come to see my family."

"Thank goodness, boy. You had my nerves racing there for a minute."

She then looked at Geraldine for the first time.

"Oh, by the way, this is my friend who brought me. This is Geraldine Williams."

She looked at Geraldine, giving her the once-over and judging her with a motherly expression of disapproval.

"How you do, ma'am?" She said that to let Geraldine know that she knew that she was older than Phil.

Geraldine caught the hint very quickly, and threw one at her. "Very well, madam, how are you?" They both gave each other cold stares.

Phil interrupted, "Tell me, how's everybody doing around here?"

They talked about all the changes that were taking place on the avenue and the city. Phil finally asked about Donald. "Have you heard any more about Donald's whereabouts?"

"Naw, I haven't heard from that boy in four years. I don't know whether he is dead or alive. The last I heard from him, he was headed toward San Francisco."

"I hope he's all right."

"I reckon he's all right. Let's go and get something to eat. I know of this new place which opened up several years ago called Sampson. Boy, they cook some mighty good soul food. Let me freshen up myself and change my clothes."

The food was very delicious. Geraldine ate practically in silence because she knew that the aunt didn't approve of her, and she didn't care for her, either. They said their goodbyes and left for Church Hill. The trip had been very rewarding to Phil. He told Geraldine that he would never be able to repay her for all her kindness.

Chapter 11

The three men, Phil, Charlie and Willie, had been working on the horse farm for eight months and now Christmas was approaching. They pretty much knew all there was to know about horses and how to care for them. Everyone on the farm had become close and quite friendly, but they never forgot that business was the order of the day.

Charlie and Willie visited Burt and Stella almost as regularly as Phil did. Many days they would complete their work so quickly that it appeared that socializing was their main occupation.

It appeared that he had become the favorite of Stella and Burt while Charlie had become the favorite of Mr. Skipper and his wife, Currie. Willie seemed to hang out alone or just wait for his wife to visit from upstate. From all outward appearances, their social and sexual lives seemed to be intact. Inasmuch as circumstances would allow, Geraldine visited Phil regularly and she brought the most delicious home-cooked meals.

When Mr. Skipper found out that Phil was a skillful typist, he immediately extracted him from the fields and placed him in a comfortable office within the confines of his seventeenth-century mansion. "Avery," he said, "I hear you can type."

Phil threw his head up like one of his thoroughbred stallions. "Oh, yes, sir, I can type pretty well, not too much speed, though."

He then said, "That's okay about the speed as long as the accuracy is up to par. I have plenty of work you can do for me. As a matter of fact, you can do more for me on the inside than you can on the outside. Come inside tomorrow, and I'll show you what I'm talking about."

This pleased Phil greatly, especially since the cold weather had set in, making the work with the horses quite dangerous. Phil browsed around the library. It looked like a small public library. He became aware of many books and authors that he had never seen nor heard of before. After he finished his typing for the day, he could read the books of his choice, if he so desired.

When Phil had completed typing the last page of his workload for the day, he stretched and looked at the clock. It was only ten thirty a.m.—that meant that he was free to do whatever he wanted to do for the balance of the day.

He thought quickly, *The boys said that they were going to town today. I hope they haven't left.* He sprang from his chair and ran out of the house and down the road to the barn. The pickup truck was parked near the gate with a trailer hooked up to it. He hopped the fence, hoping that he was in time to send a message to Geraldine, or better still, he would see her himself. As he entered the barn, Charlie and Willie were cleaning the stables where the horses were sheltered during the night.

"Hey, you cats going to town today?"

"Yeah, just as soon as we get the stables cleaned, and Mr. Skipper returns. Why?"

"You want to go, Mr. Executive?"

"Yep," Phil threw the slur right back. "Your second boss has the rest of the day off, and he thinks he wants to play in the hay."

They all laughed, knowing that he was talking about Geraldine. Phil took a brush broom and started helping them clean the stables. They had completed the last two stalls when Mr. Skipper blew the horn.

They climbed up on the back of the truck. This was like riding the MTA to them, for they enjoyed riding into town. They were teasing Phil about the good time that he was going to have that afternoon. Phil said, "I don't know whether or not I can contact her since I didn't notify her earlier."

Charlie hit Phil on the back. "You'll find a way to contact her, even if you have to catch a falcon and train him within a couple of hours."

They all had a big laugh. The ride into town was always refreshing to them. It was like putting the cream on the pie. Just to be around people and feel the freedom of not being guarded every step was worth every muscle of strength used in laboring on the farm.

Mr. Skipper drove the truck to the supply store. They jumped off the truck, knowing that if they loaded the truck hurriedly, they would have time to browse around in town. "I'll be back to help you guys," said Phil. "I've got to make a telephone call."

Phil took long strides down the street while looking for a telephone booth. He saw one, but a man was standing in a pose that reflected that he was going to be there for a while. Phil walked on a few blocks more, for Church Hill was a small town, and he'd better stay in the area where he saw blacks hanging around. Church Hill was just like any other hick town when it came to blacks integrating.

All at once, he remembered the little cafe that Geraldine had told him about. He saw a delivery boy. He asked him to tell him where it was located. "Do you know where Calhound's Cafe is?"

"It's down on the south end. You are on the north end," said the boy. "You'd better go around that building and then walk six blocks and you'll see it."

Phil thanked him and started walking in that direction; he saw the little shabby building. Several elderly men were sitting on a bench outside. They were passing a bottle among themselves. Phil spoke politely. They looked up and greeted him with a puzzled stare, for they knew everyone who hung around this end of town.

Phil walked into the cafe and looked around for a telephone booth. He saw one in a corner at the end of the area where the dancing section seemed to be. The lady behind the counter looked at him as if he were going to rob her. He pointed to the telephone and said, "I'd like to use your telephone, please."

"It only cost a dime," she said, nodding towards the telephone. Phil looked at her and called her a nice, nasty name under his breath.

He took out the folded envelope from his pocket and took a slip of paper out with Geraldine's employer's number on it. She worked for one of the store owners there in Church Hill. He dialed the number. Geraldine answered, "Hello, Mr. Gloss's residence."

Phil was elated that he didn't have to speak to Mrs. Gloss. "Hi, Miss Lady."

"Hey, my little man, where you at?"

"I'm down here on south end at the cafe."

"What? Why didn't you tell me last week that you were coming to town?"

"I didn't know then. Can you get off today?"

"I—I reckon I could, but I gotta do a pretty piece of lying. How long are you gonna be in town?"

"I'll be down at the supply store for about an hour or so, but I've got the rest of the day off."

"Whoopee! Boy, I'll get off if I have to faint or something. I tell you what, come out to the farm and stop near the bridge on the south side where the grazing section is. All right? Then I'll meet you within the next two hours, okay?"

Phil responded, "I'll see you then. 'Bye."

Phil walked rapidly to the supply store. Charlie and Willie were nearly half finished loading the sacks of feed on the truck and trailer. Phil gave them a big broad smile and said, "Gonna play in the hay today."

The men said in unison, "M.F." and they laughed heartily. Phil swung a bag on the trailer. He seemed to have energy that he had been suppressing, and he joked with the guys.

They completed the loading of the truck and were ready for action. Phil told them about the cafe and that some girls might be coming there for lunch. They were about to leave when Mr. Skipper called out, "You guys have only thirty minutes. We've got to be getting back early today."

Charlie called him a red-withered S.O.B. under his breath. They all laughed. He must have felt the vibrations because he looked at them as they continued to laugh and walk down the street. Phil felt sorry for them because if they had longer, they might have drummed up a little business as he had done with Geraldine.

They let Phil off at the bridge where he had told Geraldine to meet him. They slapped him on the rear as he jumped off the truck. Charlie yelled, "Throw a mean curve for me."

Willie called out as the truck began to move, "Eat your

heart out." Phil gave him the finger sign and smiled.

Phil walked lazily over to a patch of tall grass and kicked around it to drive out any snakes or rats that might be hibernating undernearth. He lay on the grass, looking up at the sky. He felt so good to have this kind of freedom. It was worth thousands of dollars even though it was only for eight hours. To top all of that, he felt like a king having a queen come and be with him in his little kingdom. He rolled over in the grass so that it would lay flat, for this would be their little cocoon.

He had grown a little jittery. Perhaps, Geraldine couldn't get off from work. He walked down to the bridge and began to throw rocks into the water. At last, his mind was relieved when he saw Geraldine's car coming around the curve. That red Plymouth was a welcome sight to his eyes. He felt a surge of tension racing from his head to his toes. He ran up to the road and flagged. She then parked on the side of the road and jumped out of the car, with a big bag in one arm.

Phil ran up to her, picked her and the bag up, and swung her around in the air. "Put me down! Put me down before you let me fall down this hill." Phil put her down, half out of breath, then he kissed her face. Leading her by the hand as he carried the bag, he led her to the little cocoon he had made for them. Geraldine looked up at him as she spotted the little patch of grass and spoke, "Are you hungry? I brought something to eat because when I get through with you, you will need this and more."

"Show me, baby. Show me what you are talking about." They dropped down on the grass and began to tumble in the grass, while tickling each other and hollering and laughing.

After they completely satisfied each other, they ran over to the pond where the horses were grazing nearby. They played in the water. Phil started splashing water in Geraldine's face when she yelled, "Stop! Stop! I just got my hair fixed

Saturday."

"I'm sorry," said Phil, as he walked out farther into the pond to where the water came halfway up his body. "Come on in," he said.

"No, this is all the water I need, right here."

Phil looked at her and said, "You, Jane. Me, Tarzan." They both laughed, for they were enjoying life as if they were in their own private jungle.

Geraldine drove Phil to the farm around four thirty p.m. He kissed her very affectionately and said, "This has been one of the happiest times that I've had in my life, and I thank you very much."

"You have made me happy too, young man, more than words can express." They were interrupted by Charlie and Willie as they came out of the barn.

"Honeymooners," called Charlie.

Willie started to make sounds. "Coo—Coo—Coo, cuddle-doves—Coo—Coo."

They laughed and then Charlie said, "Stop that. You've had all day to do whatever you had to do or say. Come on over here because it's lockup time."

They were getting ready to go back to the camp. Geraldine said, "I'd better be going because it looks as if you all are ready to go."

"All right, baby," said Phil, "I'll see you soon, okay?" He kissed her and she got into the car and sped down the road.

Chapter 12

While reading the history of the Civil War, Phil said aloud, "Damn, a house nigger. I'll be damned if I ain't a house nigger." He sat there for a few minutes in total concentration on a recent book he had read by Malcolm X speaking of the house niggers and the situation from which they were chosen, and how they responded as grateful puppets. The reality brought itself clear remembering how Charlie would execute all of his communications with Mr. Skipper and Dr. Todd with such phrases as "Yes, sir, boss," or "Right, boss," and on and on.

Willie was very resentful and expressed it by his silence. He thought of Phil as "pet miracle slave," probably an offspring of the master's seed attributing to the fact that Phil was smart and could do chores other than manual labor. Adding to the atmosphere, the mansion still looked as it did in the nineteenth century with its horrible slave quarters.

It really didn't matter that both Mr. Skipper and Dr. Todd treated them kindly and humanely. What mattered was that Phil deeply resented his circumstances and he smelled the blood of his ancestors in the soil of the land—all over those one thousand acres. It was getting so that he couldn't turn anywhere without feeling the presence of his ancestors. There was a oneness in the atmosphere that was so strong, that many times he became oblivious to the twentieth century and looked for Harriet Tubman to walk over him and slap his face for not expressing the knowledge that he felt to the other slaves.

Clearly, he heard Malcolm X say to him again, "You're living in the master's house, but you're still a Tom if you don't express what you feel, knowing that the stench of your ancestors' blood is rooted in this mansion and all over this land."

Phil had become very restless. The more he read and thought about things, the more his mind became like a puma shut up inside of a big cage. Although he was waiting for Geraldine on the north end of the farm, he wasn't in a receptive mood for her today. He thought, *Damn, what in the hell is the matter with me? I don't care too much whether I see Gerry or not.* This wasn't like Phil at all, for Geraldine had meant the whole world to him, since she was the only woman he had had sexual encounters with since he was locked up seven years ago. Deep down inside, he knew what was wrong. He wanted to be free, not just free to roam around on that damn plantation and then get locked up at night like a big buck slave. *Yes,* he thought, *that's exactly what I am.*

His thoughts were interrupted by the sound of a horn. Geraldine was coming to a stop. She hopped out of the car with a big bounce and ran down the trail to where Phil was standing. Normally, he would run to meet her and tickle and hug her because he would be so delighted that she was there. She sensed the difference and walked up to where Phil was standing. "How're you doing?" She looked at him, trying to figure him out. He wasn't acting like himself at all.

"I'm okay, I guess."

She grabbed his head in her hands and held it so that his eyes were gazing in hers. "Baby, what is it? Tell me. I know you by now. Are you in trouble or something?"

Phil took her hands from that headlock that she was holding, and he kissed her palms. "Naw, baby, I'm just so damned depressed that I can hardly think straight."

She pulled him down to the ground. "Let's talk, big boy. You say there is nothing wrong, yet you say that you are depressed. You don't get depressed over nothing. Now tell me what in the hell is wrong with you."

Phil snapped a long piece of grass and put it in his mouth, not knowing how to start. "Geraldine, I feel like a damned buck slave on this big plantation. Besides feeling like a slave, I'm tired of being the house nigger."

"Phil," she interrupted, "I thought you said that this place was the best thing that happened to you in years. You told me that these white folks were damned good to all of you. And you said . . ."

"I know what I said," Phil snapped at her. "I'm ready to do more than work all day and get locked up at night like the prize slave of the stock."

"Boy, you need a drink or something to settle your mind because you're really talking foolish talk. Where did you get that slave shit from?" She jumped up and ran up to the car and opened the trunk. She took out two bags—one had food in it, and the other had Johnny Walker Red.

She walked back to their spot and spread the food on a blanket that she had taken from the trunk. Phil poured himself a big glass of Johnny Walker and gazed in it as he felt the hot sensations running all over his body. Geraldine was making sandwiches as she watched him from the corner of her eyes. She'd hoped the Scotch would calm him down because he had a wild look in his eyes and strange attitude concerning the farm and the freedom that he was allowed to have. Geraldine was at a loss for consoling words.

Finally, she spoke. "Hey, you'd better eat before you have a big headache, or you get sick in the stomach."

"I don't want any food just yet," he said.

She thought that she'd better not push him because he was a Leo and he really was acting like a wild-ass lion. She sat there eating her sandwich slowly, not saying a word. Phil got up and walked a short distance, stood, and looked across the fields as if he were looking for a ship to dock in a minute.

Geraldine was very pensive, for she had never seen Phil look and act this way. He turned down food and liquor, but above all, he turned her down. All of this had made her lose her appetite.

Phil walked back to where she was sitting. He looked as if he had solved his problem. "Geraldine, I just thought of something!"

"What?"

"I'm going to run for it."

"Oh, gawd, naw." She threw her hands up to her mouth.

"Yeah, that's what I'm going to do. I can make it through the back woods and get a ride to Pennsylvania and then to New York."

She grabbed him around his neck. "Naw, Phil, please don't do that. You're gonna ruin your chances of ever being free." Her voice was trembling and she began to cry. "Ain't I what you want, baby? Ain't I been good to you? What do you want me to do for you, baby? I'll do it, just don't run away." She was sobbing and crying like someone was about to take her life. It was so pitiful that Phil almost forgot what he'd planned only a few minutes ago.

He took her in his arms. "Geraldine, don't cry. I'll be all right, baby. I know that I can make it. I'll send for you when

I get settled."

She held him around the waist as if she was a drowning person. "Please don't. Please don't, Phil. I beg you. Just think about the other guys—they won't be allowed to have freedom anymore, all because of you." Those last words hit him like a bolt of lightning. Geraldine was making a hell of a lot of sense. He would screw up all the good times for Charlie and Willie and whomever else they might hire from the camp.

Phil hugged Geraldine and cried with his head buried in her shoulders. He was sobbing now. "I'm tired of this way of life, I just want to be free, free—that's all, free."

Geraldine was rocking him backwards and forwards like a helpless child. "It's okay, baby. Let it all out. I know what you're feeling. Let it all out."

Phil and Geraldine drove to the farmhouse, and she soothed his face with her hand and said, "Everything is going to be all right; you'll see. Now, promise me that you ain't gonna think about running away." Phil nodded his head.

"I said promise me."

Phil said, "I promise."

That wasn't good enough for Geraldine. "Swear on your Mama's grave that you won't run away."

"Damn, Gerry," he said. "I promise."

"Say it."

"Damn, I promise on my Mama's grave. Satisfied?"

She smiled and squeezed his hand and winked at him. "I'll be back on the weekend because we've got some unfinished business to take care of. Now, think about how you are gonna take care of it, and your mind won't have room for nothing else."

Phil liked it when she spoke in a devilish manner to him. He kissed her and pinched her on the rear. "I'll do just that!"

He stood there looking at the car until it was completely out of sight. He was still depressed, but grateful that she had talked him out of trying to escape that afternoon. He didn't know how to put all that had transpired into its proper perspective. However, as the old saying goes, "Everything works out for the best."

One day while he was thinking about the present state of affairs, he said to Charlie and Willie as he stood in one of the horse barns, "You know, we ain't nothing but Toms. We think more of this damn plantation than Skipper and Todd. We are a bunch of goddamned slaves."

"What do you mean?" Charlie asked angrily. "This white man is good to us. He gives us money, buys us food, and lets us have our women. What more can you ask?"

"It's just getting to me, Charlie. You are always saying boss this and boss that. Damn that shit! Me working in that goddamn big house, knowing that slaves used to live and work there doing some of the same shit. Can't you all feel nothing in the atmosphere?"

"Man, I know what you mean," Willie interjected. "I feel this shit every day. Sure they are nice and all, but they also work the shit out of us with that niceness. I feel like I'm back in 1805 or something. Charlie, you've changed. Upstate, you had white men working for you; and man, you're my partner, but you are a real Tomming bastard. That just ain't you."

"Man, I know what I'm doing," Charlie said, appearing to have a knowledge they didn't know about. "Y'all hang in here with me. It's going to be all right."

Some minutes later, Dr. Todd made his presence known. He had been at the other end of the barn, listening to the entire conversation. He didn't say anything. He just looked at Phil as if he didn't think he was capable of feeling what he expressed.

Needless to say, soon after that Mr. Skipper informed him that he was of no more use in the office. "Business is getting slow," he said. Then, not looking Phil in the face, he added,

"Phillip, I may have to let you go in a few days."

"I understand, Mr. Skipper."

"What will you do now that you won't be working here?"

"Probably be hired out to other farmers until I get a paying job."

"That shouldn't be too long for you. I understand that Burt sent letters of recommendation to the parole board for all three of you."

As Mr. Skipper talked, his expression communicated an understanding as to what he was feeling. Yet, it told him that business was first, and that was the way it had to be. They exchanged a few more expressions and concerns, shook hands as men with mutual respect, before they parted for the day's work.

Two days later, the law of compensation struck like a rigged jackpot. "Avery," called the captain. "Boy, you must know some high-up folks, 'cause you've been transferred to Jessup Correction Camp and from there, you'll be working for Mr. Swisser." He then rubbed the side of his face, waiting for Phil's response. He thought he had better say something.

"Uh, uh, do you know where I'll be working?"

"Sure do, boy. You'll be working at the South Charles Hospital. You sure got a step up from the fields, boy. You better make something good of it, too."

Phil looked at him and he turned and walked away. He thought, *To hell with you, I'll be working for my friend, Mr. Swisser, who is the president of the hospital, and besides that he's a furrier—a rich man will be on my side for once in my life.*

Packing that night before leaving for Jessup, Phil kept thinking, *Freedom! Freedom! Sure will be nice to be back in B'more and have all that freedom.* Then a part of his goal came back to haunt him again. *I can't ever be free until I do something to help my incarcerated brothers.*

Part Three
Incredible Dreams

Chapter 13

Jessup's Correctional Camp Center was not nearly as bad as other places Phil had been. It was a minimum security camp used as a transition spot for inmates who would be ready for release within ninety days to one year. The few small discomforts that it presented were blocked out and overlooked by the fact that he worked in Baltimore five days a week.

Believe me, he thought, *my hometown never looked so good,* as the correctional camp bus drove through the city dropping different inmates off at their work sites. They were let off a half block from the work site at seven a.m. and picked up at five p.m. Fortunately, he was the only one who worked at South Charles Hospital and none of the employees knew that he was an inmate.

His first morning at the hospital, Mr. Swisser sent for him, and they talked in a private office that he temporarily borrowed from the head nurse.

She looked at him strangely as he entered, as she wondered who he was that she had to be asked out of her office so that he could have a private conference with the president, Mr. Swisser.

"Close the door, Phillip," he said, smiling as he stood to take his hand.

"Hi, Mr. Swisser," he pumped his hand firmly after closing the door, "I can't ever thank you enough."

Mr. Swisser was about seventy—a small, rugged man with parted gray hair. He wore a striking blue suit with a tiny gold pin over the lapel. His small frame couldn't have weighed much over one hundred and forty. Yet, there was a presence about him which gave the impression of wisdom, strength and kindness.

"Don't thank me in words," he cut Phil off, motioning him to sit down. "Just stay out of trouble and learn all you can."

Besides himself, Mr. Swisser was the slowest-talking person whom he had ever met. Yet, he wanted to frame his every word because he was a wise Jewish man.

"Now, Phillip, there is no reason to tell anyone that you're in prison. It's none of their damned business. You'll be working in the maintenance shop, around all whites. If they give you a hard time, let me know. I have a fur store downtown. Here's my number."

He handed Phil a card with the words "Swisser—Furrier" on it and a phone number.

"I visit this place," he continued, "twice a day. I'll be looking for you whenever I come. We can have lunch together."

Most of the time, Phil was silent. Needless to say, he was in awe of this tiny, powerful millionaire. He was so damn humane and polite and he spoke to him as if they had grown up together. For five years, they wrote to each other. For five years, his wife had sent Phil books to study, but never did he realize that people of this caliber could be so humane.

"Mr. Swisser, please tell your wife that I appreciate everything that she did for me as well."

"She knows, Phillip, she knows. She feels that your book is very good, but that you should continue your education."

"I am. I'm going to be attending Morgan at night. I'll be studying day and night. Then I'll get my book published and become a writer."

"What about a trade? It's always important to have a trade. That is why I want you to learn from those guys at the shop."

"I'll learn a trade on the side, too."

It took another ten minutes for Mr. Swisser to brief him on the history and character of the hospital. Of course, he didn't fail to warn Phil to be careful of all the pretty ladies who worked there. "Also, you'll find more ladies here than men. You'll have to be careful, Phillip. I know they will be a big temptation because you have been without them for some time. But be careful; they can get you in trouble. Just remember, your objective is to get out and then you can get all the 'leg' you can handle. You understand where I'm coming from?"

Phil said, "Yes, sir, I understand. I'll stay out of trouble. Boy, I've looked out the corner of my eye at every woman who has passed." He thought to himself, *If I hadn't been with Geraldine, I probably would have had to work all day with an apron on.*

As Phil walked on, a young lady looked at him, smiled, and said, "Hi, handsome."

One hour later, Phil began working in the maintenance shop for a very prejudiced supervisor. He was an old man with a drawn face, small in stature and mean as hell. "Boy, I ain't much on saying things twice, you hear? So you listen good the first time, and if your head ain't as thick as it looks, you can learn some things just by paying attention. You got me?"

"I understand," Phil said.

He looked at Phil sharply. Phil thought, *I'm not going to say "Yes, sir" to this redneck.* He knew that he was put there to learn a trade and he was determined to see that he learned just that, if it meant lifting air conditioners, sweeping the front or cleaning up the alley. Many of these chores he didn't mind because it afforded him the opportunity to travel all over the hospital and to meet all of the gorgeous ladies.

The fifth floor record department was his favorite. There were women there who didn't wear uniforms and who didn't appear so military.

One afternoon as he walked idly through the north wing of the hospital, a brown, slim chick from the record department approached him boldly.

"Hey, Phillip, I want to ask you something."

"Yeah, go ahead," he said casually as he stopped, glancing at her from head to toe. She was a slender, small package. Her face exuded sex as her eyes fixed momentarily on his fly.

"I've been watching you around here for a month. You're not like the other guys, cracking on all the women. Are you married?"

"No, I am not!"

"Well," she continued with a mischievous smile, "you know, I like you. I am not married. Why don't you come visit me some time? I'd take some of that preacher out of your system for you."

Damn, he said to himself, *if you only knew.*

Aloud, he said, "No, you see, I live out of town. I don't have a car and don't know anything about the city."

"Country boy, huh. Got a girlfriend?"

"Yeah, I got a girl. I don't mess around on her."

"I ain't never heard no man talk like you. All men mess around. I bet you are a faggot, ain't you?" She lowered her voice to a whisper. "Go ahead, you can tell me. I got a lot of fag friends."

She had made him angry by now. His inclination was to prove to her right there that he was a real man. But he remembered what Mr. Swisser had told him about not revealing that he was an inmate because some people might try to take advantage of his situation, especially some females.

"Look," he said to her a bit nervously, "I'd better get back to the shop. Talk to you later. See you."

As he walked in the opposite direction, she giggled like a turned-on schoolgirl who had gotten her thing off.

The sad thing about it all was that he wanted her sexually just like he wanted many of the others, but he couldn't chance it in the hospital or after he was off, knowing that he had to be on the camp bus at five p.m. If he missed the bus, it would be considered as an automatic escape. The driver would wait ten minutes and not a second after.

Around the hospital, he earned the reputation of being the quiet, clean-cut young man who was always doing small favors for everyone. As a matter of fact, whenever some minor or major incident needed taking care of, especially if it didn't require skill, the different departments would call maintenance and Mr. Steval, his supervisor, would oblige them by sending him. His favorite words were, "I'm not sending my skilled mechanics to take care of that bullshit. Phillip, go take care of that."

Off he would run. Phil hated the position he was in, but he loved to do favors for the ladies. Even though he hated the subservient work, he knew that he was qualified for better and would not allow that position to take anything away from his inner pride. One day he would be someone's boss, but for now, he would be content to be a follower.

His thoughts were interrupted by Mr. Steval's call, "Phillip, come over here. Do you think you can put this air conditioner in successfully?"

Phil said, "I feel that I can, and this one is no sweat."

He said, "Okay then, make sure you can, because this is for one of the head doctors, Dr. Leon Flack, and we want to give him top quality service."

Dr. Flack lived down the street from the hospital. He was a big Jewish doctor, who sometimes looked and acted black. His personality was warm and jazzy whenever he was not talking medicine.

Dr. Flack opened the door to his house after a few rings of the bell.

"My boss," Phil said, "sent me down here to move an air conditioner from your window."

"Come on in, son." He stood there six feet tall, with twenty-five pounds on the other side of three hundred. Phil's first thought was not ever to make him mad.

"You're Phillip, aren't you, young man?"

"Yes, sir."

"Everyone speaks well of you. I have watched you around the hospital. I think you are a fine young man. Look, I don't use people. What's in this house doesn't belong to the hospital. So I am going to give you ten bucks to take my old air conditioner out and put this new one in. I can't help you; I have a bad back."

"Is this your house?" Phil asked in awe, looking around at the three-storied monster.

"Sure is. Lived in it all by myself. Why, are you looking for a room?"

"I am, but I only need it for the mornings. You see, I'm from out of town—Eastern Shore. I get here every morning about two hours before it is time for me to start work. So, I just need a place to change clothes and to use a little. I won't really need a place to live until another two months when I move in town."

"Fine! Fine! Young man, I'll make a deal with you. I've

got a private basement apartment. No one is using it. If you set out my trash and do small jobs for me around the house, you can have the apartment."

If Phil thought his arms could have reached around Dr. Flack, he would have hugged him. Instead, he shook his hands and thanked him three times.

In no time flat, he exchanged the air conditioners, received ten bucks, and a set of keys to his apartment.

Chapter 14

After working in Baltimore for one month, things were going smoothly until Phil kicked a can and out came the worms. It happened one morning at seven a.m. as he was getting off the state bus at the usual location. A cab stopped in front of the bus, and out stepped Ramona.

"Phillip," she said, somewhat alarmed. "What are you doing getting off that prison bus?" Her hand covered her mouth in disbelief as the realization hit her. "All the time," she continued, "I thought you were a fag. You've been in prison. Don't worry, I'll never tell anyone. I promise. Your secret is mine."

"Ramona," Phil said as he walked towards the hospital from Twenty-Seventh Street, "I don't need anyone to know I'm in jail. Keep your mouth shut."

"How long have you been in?" she asked with deep curiosity.

"Nine years."

"What! Nine years? You ain't had none in nine years. I bet you got plenty stored up in you. All I want is a little piece of you. Our business is our business."

Her expression and tone reminded him of something Sadie had said to him years ago: "Women with freak qualities can't resist you."

Avoiding her opening, he asked, "What are you doing here so early? I thought you weren't due until nine."

"Just thought I would come in early to catch up on my work. I goofed off yesterday and got behind. I don't have to be in until nine. Why? What you got in mind for two hours?" she said teasingly.

Why not? he thought to himself. *It's been a couple of months since Geraldine, and this chick is just begging me. Besides, she probably won't tell my secret if I make love to her.*

"Come on and go with me," he said effortlessly. "I'm going to kidnap you for an hour."

She followed without the slightest protest until he reached the house.

"This is Dr. Flack's house," she protested at the front steps, showing some fear.

"Come on. Don't worry. I've got a spot in here, in the basement." He grabbed her hand gently and urged her inside. The apprehensive expression on Ramona's thin face told him that she was a bit uncomfortable in the doctor's house. Her voice confirmed this.

"Are you absolutely sure, Phil, that this is okay?"

"Would I bring you to a spot that wasn't all right? Come on, sweetheart." The smoothness of his tone and the gentle caressing of her waist with his arm seemed to relax her.

Once her clothes were off, she proved to be extremely long and lean, with smooth brown skin. She had good-looking, long legs that ran up to her buttocks. They were inviting as she lay stretched upon the bed. She removed her hands from her front, revealing a mass of black, silky hairs that looked like a small acre.

Needless to say, Phil was stimulated to the point of discharge as he came out of his last piece of clothing and eased himself between those brown thighs. She was hot, frantic and completely wild. She gripped him tightly, and he was certain that she had wrapped those long legs around him twice. In a few minutes, she had literally dried him up, using all the mechanics of her body and mouth. The *coup de grace* came when she turned him on his back and finished him with a vacuum perfection. At that point, he lost his cool. He did the screaming.

As usual, he started working on time that day. The first two hours went beautifully. As soon as he had some free time on his hands, he visited the fifth floor where his favorite girls worked. His first stop would always be Neta's desk. She was the supervisor, an attractive, middle-aged white lady who could have doubled as a fashion model.

"Hi, Neta. How are you feeling this morning? Anything I can do?"

"Oh, hi, Phillip. I'm fine. Nothing today."

He couldn't be sure, but something seemed missing from her greeting. *Maybe just a bad morning,* he reasoned to himself.

"Hello, Mabel," he greeted the redhead whose back was turned to him as she sat typing. Many times he would park her car for her in the morning when she was running late. They developed a special, warm relationship.

"Hi, Phillip. What's new?"

"You. Every time I look at you, you are new."

"Flattery will get you everywhere, hon. I've got some serious talk for you later, in your best interest."

Ruby, who was sitting across from Mabel, was a six-foot,

gorgeous woman. She was light-skinned, proud and genuinely beautiful for a woman in her forties. If there was any female except Vonnie that he really desired, it was Ruby. However, he knew he stood a snowball's chance in hell of even saying anything to her other than, "Hi, Miss Ruby. How are you today?" For some reason, she was the only one that he referred to with the handle of Miss. It was like her presence demanded a "Miss" from him.

"Fine. How are you?"

"Okay, I guess," Phil replied, trying to suppress his blushing. She was one beautiful woman.

As he walked towards Vonnie's desk, he overheard Delores tell Ruby, "That young man has the hots for you."

"That young thing?" Ruby asked. Her tone told him instantly that she felt that giving him a second thought would be a waste.

When he reached the back area of the office, his main girls, Vonnie, Ginny and Faye, were chatting as they exchanged folders back and forth. All three of these women were black and beautiful. Vonnie was his favorite because she was his age and not as settled as the others, not to mention that she was the finest young sister in the hospital.

"Hello, beautiful black sisters. How are my lovely ladies today?"

He received three cold "Hi's!" Something was wrong. What the hell was it?

As he turned to leave, Vonnie followed him with a stack of papers to the elevator. When they got on, the door closed and he attempted his usual placing of his hand beneath her skirt to squeeze her upper thigh.

"None of that shit today," she said vehemently. Her eyes flashed hotly as she brushed his hand away. "Didn't you get enough? Why did you tell that big mouth, skinny bitch your business? She has told everyone in the hospital about you."

He knew what had happened now. *That damned Ramona,* he thought.

Vonnie continued, "You know there are some women here who really care for you, and your being an inmate doesn't matter. After you have fooled around with something like Ramona, they might not want to touch you with a ten-foot pole. She even told how good you were in bed."

The elevator stopped on the second floor. Phil thanked Vonnie and apologized for making a mistake. They both got off on the second floor and walked towards the isolated steps at the end of the north wing, a place where they often talked in private and stole a quick kiss when possible.

"Vonnie," he pleaded, "please understand the position that I was in. I didn't want her, and I couldn't tell you that I was in jail. So with that kind of pressure, not having a woman in a long time, I was tempted. I hadn't approached you seriously because you are married and I am a convict. Now that you know, please show me some understanding. So help me, I want you badly. Don't hold this one against me, baby."

Her eyes gave him an intense gaze. Then they mellowed under those thick, black lashes. "I'll think about it. I've got to go."

As she turned, he reached for her waist and pulled her around slowly until they were lips to lips. The wetness of her tongue as it slid into his mouth had a chill-heat effect on his body, and it felt like steam in his mouth. She backed away briefly as if to tease him.

"Vonnie," he whispered, "you know that I know you are a freak. Don't you?"

"We'll see," she whispered, expressing a mischievous smile.

As she walked down the north wing hall, he watched her fabulous body do its natural twist as the short skirt danced at the back of her knees, accentuating one of the most perfect buttocks that he had ever seen on any woman in his life.

She was built like a carved, Egyptian goddess and was truly the kind of woman that both Dr. McKay and Sadie described who would always haunt his life with unusual emotional, intellectual, and physical expressions.

Later that day, he saw Ramona and they had it out in the hallway. She explained that she loved him and only told their business to everyone there because she wanted them to know that he belonged to her.

"Look, bitch, I don't belong to you," he said angrily. "I don't want you at all. I am sorry as hell for this morning. I don't mean to hurt your feelings, but that's how it is."

"We'll see," she replied, "we'll see. If I get hold of you one more time, I'll make you climb a ceiling."

Ramona was sick. He had to smile at her. She was excellent in bed, but had no class. A couple of minutes later they returned to their work site. He cursed himself for yielding to her. More than that, he cursed that damned state bus for stopping behind that cab. *Now everyone in the hospital will probably shun me.*

As the weeks went by, Phil's expectations of how he would be treated did not come to pass. Most people went out of their way to help, including buying his lunch. It appeared that many of the females made themselves sexually available to him, simply because he was an inmate. Now he knew that he was no sex idol and didn't possess anything different from any other man, but he had to turn down sex because he just couldn't handle it all.

For a few weeks straight, Phil slipped girls in and out of Dr. Flack's house as if they were coming off a waiting list. This he had to say, hospital girls were the most articulate freaks in the world, probably because of the constant exposure to bodies during the course of their work and being unable to express urges that constantly built up and excited them. Whatever the reason, he was the enjoyable recipient of some of the most expressive sex acts imaginable.

Psychologically, he was trying to catch up on the nine years of asexuality that he had undergone. Physically, he had to realize that he could not screw every woman in that hospital and that it would do him well to cut back. He did. He confined himself to Vonnie and to Ruby, the older gorgeous lady whom he thought he didn't stand a chance with.

Phil's sexual escapades at the hospital, as he looked at it, was not necessarily a boosting of his ego, but a regaining of sexual confidence after having masturbated for years. His holding on to those two women had no definite relation to a continued overwhelming need to massage his masculine insecurity as it did with the personal satisfaction and appreciation that he enjoyed just having them for personal friends.

A situation that enabled him to hold on to them rested in the fact that both of them were married and really couldn't create a jealous scene or make great demands on his time. With Vonnie it was easy. Her husband was strict with her. Ruby's husband was much more flexible. Therefore, she began to demand more time.

If Phil had one platonic friend, it was Carolyn, the receptionist. He trusted her completely and she knew his every move. Many times he could have been fired and returned to prison. When his supervisor paged him over the box, Carolyn would leave her post and find him, urging that he return at once, leaving whomever he was with at his apartment until he returned. Carolyn was cute and slender. She was always in constant fear that Phil would be caught and fired.

"Phillip," she joked with him one day, "can't you leave those women alone until you make parole? I'm tired of lying for you."

"Carolyn, I am going to slow down. I really am. Freedom does mean more to me than sex."

The time that Carolyn really saved him occurred when Vonnie and he were in the basement apartment making love, oblivious to time and responsibility. In the midst of their intimate embraces, they literally could not quench their thirst for each other as they kissed, exploring the depths of passion expressed animalistically in sound. "You sweet, black bitch," Phil whispered in a tone that told her this was not disrespect.

"Phil," she whispered between bites on his neck, "can you believe again? If you stop . . . you bastard, I'll bite your neck off. Not now, don't stop . . . don't stop!"

Her climax and the knocking on the window confused his state of mind. At first, he thought the knocking on the window had something to do with his inner ecstasy until he heard it again.

Immediately, he jumped up and scrambled for his clothes.

"Oh, my God," Vonnie said, "it's ten minutes after four!"

He ran up the stairs, stuffed his shirt in his pants, and fastened his buttons. He opened the door. Carolyn was standing with an expression of fear on her face.

"Phillip, is she here? Is that girl, Vonnie, in here? Her husband has been waiting ten minutes for her, and your bus is across the corner waiting for you. I told them that you were doing extra work for a doctor and would be right there."

"Damn, damn! Thanks, Carolyn. You're a real lifesaver."

"Last time," she replied. "You'd better hurry. Send her out the back."

Vonnie hurriedly left from the back of the apartment, and entered the back entrance of the hospital while Phil left out the front.

In five minutes, she had punched her time card and was leaving the lobby as her husband entered. She kissed him and apologized for having to do extra work.

After having to run a block to St. Paul and Twenty-Eighth Streets, Phil caught his bus just as it was pulling away.

"Avery," the guard said to him, "you almost had an escape charge."

All he could do was wipe the sweat from his forehead and sigh. When he got back to the camp center that day, he could have sold sniffs of his fingers at two dollars a snort. Many guys still had not had a woman.

The next day as he was walking through the hospital, he heard his name being paged.

"Phil, call the operator. Phil Avery, call the operator!"

He dialed the operator from a patient's empty room. It was Carolyn's voice on the other end.

"Phil, there is a white man here to see you. He looks nervous, like he may be a policeman."

The fear and concern in her voice generated an apprehensiveness within him. To his knowledge, he had not done anything. But, what if they had brought out an old charge against him after all these years, knowing that his parole was near?

Oh, my God, he thought. *Mr. Swisser has heard about me and that Ramona. He's probably ready to send my hind-parts back to the campsite.* He stuttered a little. "Des-Describe him to me, Carolyn."

"He's short, nervous, and has blue eyes that blink every minute. It looks as if he has something large in his inside coat pocket."

"Shit, I haven't done anything. I'll be right up."

When he reached the lobby, there were several people sitting around, including four white guys. Carolyn saw him and pointed out the guy with her eyes while she was sitting behind the desk.

Recognition of the guy released all the tension within him. *Thank the Lord it isn't Mr. Swisser,* he thought. It was his friend, Burt, from the Eastern Shore.

"Hey, Burt," he said a bit loudly. "Damn, it's good to see you."

"Yeah, yeah, Phil. You look good, too."

They shook hands warmly. But Phil could tell something was really bothering Burt.

"Burt, you don't look too well."

"Is there someplace where we can talk?"

"Yeah, let's go down the street."

As they passed Carolyn's desk, he said, "Burt, this is Carolyn. Carolyn, Burt is my friend. If you need me . . . you know where I'll be."

She nodded.

They went down the street to his apartment. Once there and seated, he could immediately see that Burt was strapped down. Burt hated guns, and if he was carrying one, something was really wrong.

"Tell me about it, man," he urged. "Something is wrong."

"Phil," he started off nervously, "you know I recommended a favorable parole for you, Willie and Charlie."

"Sure, I know, and I really appreciated that."

"Well," he continued as he wiped away a drop of sweat, "I retracted Charlie's parole. As a result of my letter, they have taken him off minimum security and placed him back in the house of corrections."

"Burt," he whispered, "that does not even sound like you. Charlie must have done something awfully wrong." In his mind, he immediately thought of Stella because with the kind of good heart that Burt had, nothing could make him do that to Charlie except some involvement with his wife.

"Burt, I just don't understand." He banged his first in his palm. "You, me, and Charlie, we all got to be very close. Man, what happened?"

He hesitated, and his eyes blinked nervously. "Charlie," he went on, "has sort of lost himself. He slapped Mrs. Skipper and threatened that he would kill her if she didn't go back upstate with him when he was released. She is afraid of him and afraid to mention it to her husband. So I did what I had to do."

"Burt, I just don't understand. That does not sound like Charlie. He's too cool for that. He must have lost his mind."

"Phil, I am carrying a gun." He pulled it out, new holster and all. He handled it as if the holster would fire. "I'm scared. I know Charlie has underworld connections. Just yesterday, I was approached by two of them from upstate. They said for me to straighten the situation out or else."

Looking at Burt and thinking about Charlie, he still could not understand why he had gotten so involved. *It was not his wife, or was it? No, Stella wouldn't; how could Charlie approach her?* Something was wrong and he had to find out what.

Changing the subject, he asked, "How is Stella?"

"Oh, fine, just fine."

They talked a few minutes more before they both realized that they had to leave.

The following Saturday, Phil got a pass to visit the house of corrections for psychological evaluation. It was a phony setup. Phil's intention was to see Charlie. All proceedings and transactions were set up by inmates in key positions who could do anything, almost, for a few dollars.

Both Charlie and Phil were scheduled for the phony psychology session at ten a.m. It was in an area where there were no guards near the school. Besides Charlie and Phil, there were two other inmates who were clerks that worked in the area. They paid them to set up the passes for them.

Standing there beside the window, Charlie looked defeated and aged by the few days he had been back under maximum security.

"Damn, man, you look good," Phil lied. They shook hands and hugged each other.

"Yeah, thanks, Phil. This shit I don't need," he said sarcastically, pointing towards the barred windows and walls of gray. "All these years I fought to get out, and now I end up back in this bitch."

He didn't have to expand on what he was feeling. Just an hour or half hour in the place had done a number on him.

"Charlie, give it to me. What the fuck happened?"

"Your friend, man, your goddamned friend with the liberal feelings had me checked in. Phil, I need your help. You've got to convince him to get me back out."

"Charlie, I can probably do that, but if you fucked that man's wife, ain't no way I can ask him no shit like that."

"Stella? I care too much for the two of them to even attempt that."

With Charlie's flinging of his hands which he used to express himself, it was difficult to determine when he was lying. Also, he was getting the impression that if Charlie was not lying, he was holding something back. What—he did not know.

His final words were: "Man, I swear I never said one word to Stella out of the way."

"Charlie," he promised, "I'll do all I can to help you."

A few days later he contacted Stella by phone. "Hello, may I speak to Stella?"

"This is she speaking."

"Stella, Phillip Avery."

"Oh, hello, Phillip, how are you? What's wrong?"

"Well, that's why I'm calling, to find out what's wrong. I know you know what I'm talking about ... Huh?"

"Uh, uh, yes, Phillip, I know very well what you are talking about."

They arranged to meet at one o'clock to have sandwiches at his apartment. He was careful to have her meet him there rather than at the hospital. The tongues would really wag at the thought of Phil Avery and a white woman.

The bell rang at one minute after one. He knew it was Stella before he opened the door. She was radiantly beautiful as she stood there smiling with those green eyes.

"Stella!"

"Phil!"

They hugged and genuinely kissed each other.

They sat at the kitchen table, ate tuna fish sandwiches, and drank iced tea. They talked about her family and his.

"No, I haven't seen my brother," he told her. "Yes, Vickie is married and I don't want to see her," he lied.

"And your book, how are you doing with it?"

"Still trying to get it published!"

Finally, he asked, "Stella, tell me point blank, what the hell is going on? That was not your husband who came to see me the other day."

"Phil, promise this is between you and me."

"You know that, Stella."

Stella began, "What really happened is this. Charlie and Mrs. Skipper had been having a secret love affair. We all thought she had a special liking for him because he acted like a big son. Of course, they were in a compromising position. Burt was furious. When he told me about it, I asked, 'Why are you so furious? I'm your wife.' He told me that it just got him to his heart that Charlie would do something like that to a decent, married woman. 'After all,' he said, 'Skipper has been damned good to him. Just to think that I went to bat for him on parole recommendation. I'll just have to retract it.'"

"Stella, it still doesn't make sense. Burt is not a prejudiced bastard who can't stand a black man-white woman situation. He even writes about that kind of thing in his books—"

"Phil," she cut him off, "this hurts, but I found out later that Burt had a long secret love affair with Mrs. Skipper as well. That's where the real anger arrived."

Phil was floored by the whole thing. Now he remembered many things when he worked there, that now connected. Now he understood why Charlie would always say that he knew what he was doing and would act submissive towards Mr. Skipper with that "Yes, sir, boss." But, it blew Phil's image of Burt to think that he would resort to the tactic of sending Charlie back to prison.

Stella left one hour later. Immediately, he called Mr. Swisser and asked him to intervene in Charlie's situation on the parole board. He assured him that he would.

Chapter 15

Phil didn't go to work this particular morning because it was his parole hearing date—February 4, 1969. It was one of the most trying mornings of his life. The parole board was a three-man set-up that visited the institution where the inmates resided. They would call these individuals into a private room and relive their life's history and institutional stay, all in ten minutes.

Already, four inmates had been heard before Phil as he waited outside, biting his fingernails. Two of them were given a two-year holdover. That scared Phil to death because those two inmates had the same status as he. So to describe his feelings as uncertain would be a great understatement. He was scared as hell.

Sitting outside the closed door, he heard his name called. His body rose slowly from the bench. He walked in the room where three men sat at a long table. Two of them were white;

one was black. The black man, he was told, was the head of the parole board, the first black to head such a position in the State of Maryland. He had recently been appointed, creating a hope that some leniency and fairness would be directed towards the black inmates.

"Avery," the slender, gray-haired fellow said, "I am Mr. Turnage. This is Mr. Levin beside me," he pointed, "and the gentleman to your right is the Chairman of the Board, Mr. Masser."

"Good afternoon, gentlemen," Phil greeted them, looking briefly at them individually.

"We are here," Mr. Turnage went on, "to review your case and to determine whether you should or should not be granted parole. How long have you been in prison now?"

"Nine years, sir."

"Yes, yes, I see." He pulled out a stack of papers that looked vaguely familiar.

"Avery, here is a letter written to the parole board by you four years ago. I'd like to read it.

"Dear Mr. Chairman,

As an inmate of the Maryland Penitentiary, I feel that your policy is quite prejudicial in the fact that you give white inmates parole more readily than blacks, even though blacks serve more time and their offenses are more minor."

He paused for a moment, looked at Phil intensely, and asked, "Do you think that is the type of letter one should be writing to the parole board?"

At this question, Phil felt Mr. Masser's eyes gazing at him as if he were hoping that Phil would answer correctly, whatever that would be.

"Yes, sir, I thought that was the right type of letter to write at that time because I felt that it was true."

"I see," said Mr. Turnage, as he began to read from another letter that he had written to the governor.

"Dear Governor,

As top official in the state, I feel that you especially need to revamp the criminal justice system in this state to preclude the dual system of justice given to whites and blacks.

"As an inmate in the Maryland Penitentiary, I have witnessed this for years in criminal court judges, your parole board, which has no blacks on its panel, and your lily-white-controlled institutions that are highly populated by black inmates and few black officials, three-fourths of which are Toms . . ."

Again, he paused from reading and asked, "Do you think that is the type of letter you should be writing to the governor? As you can see for yourself, we now have a colored chairman sitting before you. Certainly, I know you aware of the high promotions in the correctional field received by Officer Whitaker; Captain Edvans is now a major and we have Officer Lakins acting as an assistant warden. How could you have written such letters in the wake of these progressive movements?"

Before replying, Phil studied his stern, blue eyes to see if he was serious. He was.

"Sir, as you mentioned before, those letters were written some four years ago, long before any of these people received promotions. However, I would like to say that in regard to the black correctional officers who received these recent promotions—why, they are no different than the whites who held the position before them. Sir, as a matter of fact, except for Officer Lyde, all of these men are worse."

"Gentlemen," Mr. Masser interrupted, "we are not here to discuss institutional racism. We are here to discuss Mr. Avery's parole consideration. In my opinion, that is where the discussion should remain." Mr. Masser hesitated, looking at his two subordinates first, then towards Phil. "Mr. Avery," he continued, "there were strong indications that during your first two years you had no intentions of straightening out your life. However, I see here that you have completed high school, attended college and have even written a book. Also, you taught school while at the penitentiary. We also have some very impressive letters of recommendation in your behalf from people such as Dr. Salis Perdale, Dr. Gross, Mr. Swisser, and the late Professor Turpins. My question is, how did you get to know these people?"

Phil looked him squarely in the face and replied, "Dr. Perdale was my high school principal years ago. He introduced me to Professor Turpins, who edited my book . . ." Phil's mind recalled the hurt look on Dr. Perdale's face when he was arrested at the age of sixteen in his school. He was distinguished, respectful and compassionate. Phil never stopped apologizing within, and he always let him know every time he did something good.

"I see," he interrupted. "Now, Dr. Gross is a white, female psychiatrist, and Mr. Swisser is Jewish. Where did you meet them?"

"Sir, with the exception of Dr. Perdale, I met them all while I was incarcerated. These people were concerned citizens who reached out to me while I was incarcerated. They influenced my entire life to the extent that I now believe that there are people out there, both black and white, who care. Had it not been for the influence that these people had on my life, I would be a vindictive, hate-infested human being today."

Without waiting for the others to join him in a decision, Mr. Masser indicated the outcome by saying, "Son, it is my professional opinion that you should have been released five years ago."

When he said that, Phil's mind reflected on the blue room, the solitary confinement, the slave-selling on the Eastern

Shore and the nine years of anguish and pure suffering. Tears flooded from Phil's eyes and he thanked God for this, at last, an outspoken, understanding black man who was sent to represent the black inmate population with fairness and a non-Tom-ish manner. The last words Phil heard before leaving the room were, "We all agree that parole should be granted."

Tears flooded his eyes. They flowed and flowed as Phil walked from that room feeling nine weighted years loosening their grip from his life.

As Phil walked back to his cell, he could feel nothing. He felt like a block of ice. His body was numb as if he had gotten a shot of Novocaine in his spine. All he could think of was being free. He finally made it to his cell, trying not to meet anyone because he was crying. He was too emotional to tell anyone how he felt. He looked at the little cell, and nine years of life flashed before his eyes.

"Phil! Phil! Hey, Phil!" Phil jumped up. He must have been sitting in that position for an hour. It was his friend, Harold. "Man, how did it go? I can tell by the way you are looking that they turned you down. Huh?"

Phil replied, "Naw, naw, man, it's over." He raised his body slowly and hugged Harold with both arms. "Man, it's over. They let me go."

"What?" said Harold. "You lucky motherfucker. You looked as if they'd told you that you got one hundred and ten more years." They were hugging and laughing at the same time.

Harold said, "Man, let's celebrate. We can make a toast with the fizzies. Let's just say it's Scotch." They both laughed and walked outside.

As Phil got in the lunch line, he felt that he would rather starve than to eat another mouthful in that hell hole. He suddenly thought of his friends and all the others who would be eating there for years and years. The least he could do was to eat a few bites. He knew they would understand that he was too full of joy to eat it all.

His buddies gathered around him at the table. "Let loose, man," one said. "What kind of shit went down with you today?"

Two more chimed in, "Yeah, let's have it." Phil told the whole story. After he had finished, the guys held their glasses up and shouted, "Right on! Right on!" Two guards looked at them and started over to their table, but the guards saw that the group was quieting down, so they stopped and just looked at them.

Phil lay in his bed all night tossing and turning, for he couldn't sleep because of his thoughts and emotions. He found himself thinking of Vickie. He thought, *Vickie, if you could have only waited. I'm free now—free! Free! Free!*

The next morning he was up and full of energy after sleeping for approximately an hour. He couldn't wait to get to the hospital so that he could tell Vonnie and Carolyn the good news. Then he thought that he'd better wait until the parole board set him free with a written document.

Two weeks later, both Charlie Redshirt and Willie were released on parole with the stipulation that they were never to set foot in Maryland again. Phil never told Charlie that Mr. Swisser had intervened for him.

The actual date of Phil's release did not occur until three weeks later. Early one morning, the bus let him off for work at the usual spot for the last time.

"Take care, fellows," Phil said as he stepped off the bus.

"Good luck, Phil," Jerry called.

"Hey, Phil," one guy yelled from the bus as it pulled away, "I don't know how you did nine, flat years, but don't come back and don't forget us. We're still in slavery."

He saluted them in a "right on" fashion as his thoughts reminded him that he must try to do something about the correctional system.

When he reached the house, Dr. Flack was eating upstairs in the kitchen and invited Phil to join him. He did just that because he wanted to talk with him, and this was perfect timing. He was dressed in his usual uniform and was rushing in order to get to work on time.

"Never see you much, son. You seem as busy as I. You're pretty quiet down there."

All of the time, Dr. Flack never knew one way or another whether he lived there sometimes or just showed up in the mornings. Many times they greeted each other as if he thought Phil had slept there the night before. His schedule was hectic, to say the least, and when he was not lecturing or studying, he was sleeping like a bear in hibernation.

"Doc," Phil said hesitantly, "there's something I've got to tell you."

"What is it, son?"

"Well, you've got drugs, money, jewelry, and all types of valuables in this house, right?"

His expression took on a look of concern as he waited for Phil to continue.

"None of it has been missing in the several months that you have allowed me to be here, has it?"

"No, as a matter of fact, it hasn't."

"Also, you must have noticed that you never see me on weekends or at night—only in the mornings."

"Yes, but I have no problem with that as long as you take care of certain work in the house for me."

"Doc, what I'm trying to say is that all this time until today, I've been serving time in prison. Now that I'm out, I'd like to continue living here."

"Son, you are a decent human being. I have trusted you from the beginning, and there is no cause or sense of my not trusting you now. You can live here as long as you wish—

rent free! Just look out for my house for me. I'm a sound sleeper and am very busy. I need a good partner to look out for me."

"All right then," Phil said, greatly relieved, "we're partners."

They shook hands and commenced a great friendship.

Phil sat looking at his plate nervously. "Dr. Flack, may I use your telephone, sir?"

"Sure thing," replied Dr. Flack.

Phil wanted to call Mr. Swisser and tell him about his release, although he knew Mr. Swisser knew before he did that the board was going to release him. He looked up Mr. Swisser's number. He was nervous as he dialed the number, for he knew it was too early in the morning to call anyone.

The housekeeper answered the phone. "Mr. Swisser's residence. May I help you?"

Phil sounded nervous. "May I speak with Mr. Swisser?"

"He isn't up at this time. May I ask who is calling, or may I take your number and have him return your call?"

"No, ma'am. I'll call back later."

Dr. Flack looked at him and took out a bottle of vodka. "Let's have a little celebration, my good man." Phil looked startled, but it was just what he needed to steady himself for the day, even though it was early in the morning.

Phil hurried to work that morning a little fired up from the two shots of vodka. He walked around smiling all morning. Finally, he was on the floor where Carolyn worked. "Hey, good-looking."

Carolyn looked up and smiled. "You've got your babes mixed up, haven't you?"

"Carolyn," he said and reached over the desk to kiss her, "let's have lunch together today. We've got a celebration to enjoy."

Carolyn looked at Phil, puzzled. "Celebration?"

"Yes, a celebration."

"What for?"

"Oh, wait until lunch."

Carolyn grabbed his arm. "Phil Avery, you'd better tell me now, or I'll be a nervous wreck until lunchtime."

Phil teased her, "You promise it's our secret?"

"Oh, for Pete's sake, Phil, do I have to make that kind of promise?"

"Well, my fair lady, I was set free as early as this morning when I got off the bus."

Carolyn gave a squeaky cry. "Oh, thank God, Phil!" She jumped up and hugged and kissed him. The patients in the office stared. She put her hand over her mouth and said, "Oh, Phil, I'm sorry."

Phil said, "Sorry for what? We are happy and we are showing it."

"You are right." She smiled and patted him on the hand. "I'll see you at lunch. We have a lot to talk about, brother!" She meant just that, too—some brotherly advice, if he knew Carolyn.

Phil was on his way to his work situation when he decided to call Mr. Swisser again. He dialed the number, identified himself, and the housekeeper said, "Just a minute, Mr. Avery."

Mr. Swisser was on the other end. "Hello, Phillip, what can I do for you?"

"Uh—Uh, how are you, Mr. Swisser? I just wanted to let you know that I was paroled as of this morning, and I wanted to thank you personally."

Mr. Swisser said, "That sounds wonderful, Phillip. I'm happy for you. There is no need to thank me. You deserved to be paroled."

"Yes, sir, but if you hadn't spoken up for me, I wouldn't have been—"

Mr. Swisser interrupted, "The pleasure was all mine, Phillip. You just try to stay out of trouble, you hear?"

"Yes, sir, I will."

"I'll see you at the hospital one day this week, okay?"

"Yes, sir." Click.

Phil skipped down the corridor as the ladies called out "hi's" to him. He was all smiles as he passed by everyone. He wanted to celebrate with every bright-eyed and bushy-tailed chick in the hospital.

He thought, *I should have a big party with all females, and in order for them to get in they'd have to show proof of no panties.* He chuckled to himself.

As he worked with a big smile on his face, one of the workers said, "Phil, did you have a good night last night? You're smiling like you just had your first piece."

Phil smiled. "Naw, not last night, but ask me tomorrow." They both laughed as they worked on installing a floor air-conditioning unit in one of the offices on the third floor.

That evening after work, Phil made arrangements to register immediately at Morgan State College for night classes. Phil's heart beat with a new kind of thump. He walked into the registrar's office and said, "Good evening."

The lady looked up and said, "Good evening, may I help you?"

"Yes, yes," said Phil. "I would like to register for some classes."

The lady asked, "Have you attended Morgan before?"

"No, ma'am, I haven't. This is my first time here."

"All right then, you'll need to see Dr. Curtis; he directs new students. Take a seat over there, please."

Phil sat there patiently, waiting, feeling more joy than any one person could ever imagine. He was now in another institution, and his goals were quite different. He thought, *My goals—I need more education. This I intend to get. I'll be housed here for some time and even though the building doesn't look plush and all, it looks like heaven compared to the walls I just spent my last weeks inside of.*

Chapter 16

Phil's goal had now become fourfold—publish his book, pursue his education, become involved in inmate assistance, and one day change the barbaric correctional system, which so heavily exploits black people.

Working on work release had enabled Phil to save quite a bit of money. Having this money at his disposal presented a great image temptation, that of buying a car and fine clothes as opposed to paying for his college and publishing his own book.

Phil lay in his bed thinking, *Damn, it would be so easy to take all of my savings and buy some fancy clothes and stroll down the avenue, letting everyone know that Phil Avery was back out and as clean as ever. Why in the hell should I spend four thousand dollars to get a book published? Who in the hell is going to read it anyway? It will probably never sell.* He slid off his little single bed and walked to the window and looked at the cars go by. He told himself again as he began to bite his fingernails, *Think positive, Phil. Think of Malcolm and how he would have said, "Don't give up, young man, the race has just begun."*

Phil walked outside and thought even more of how the hand of fate had him like a yo-yo. He thought of Professor Turpins, who was supposed to have gotten it published for him. *Why did fate have to take his life? Things would have been so easy if only he had not been struck so suddenly by cancer.*

In the wake of the temptation that freedom offered, all of his negative thoughts seemed to bombard him. Phil, feeling very depressed, thought, *Wait a minute, Phil Avery! Wait a damned minute! You are thinking as negative as hell. Remember, anything that the mind can conceive and believe, it can achieve. Even though Professor Turpins is gone, you have to learn right now that IF IT IS TO BE, IT IS UP TO YOU. Well, damn it, stop thinking negatively and do it. You will publish your book. You will sell it. People will read it. You will sell it on Pennsylvania Avenue, in bars, in libraries and all over the country. If all you really know how to do is hustle, why not hustle constructively?*

That night after school, Phil talked it over with Ruby. She was the big, gorgeous Amazon who he once thought he wouldn't have stood a snowball's chance in hell with. But, as it happened, he asked to treat her to lunch. To his surprise, she said, "Yes, I'd be delighted." She was old enough to have been his mother and attractive enough to be any man's queen. From that day on, they developed an extremely close relationship. It tickled her with delight to bring him a wrapped dinner whenever they met.

"Phil," she said, "maybe you should concentrate on school first. Then, work on publishing your book. It's not feasible to concentrate on too many major goals at once."

They were sitting in the basement of his apartment, sipping Scotch and eating the delicious baked chicken she'd brought from home.

"Yes, but what's going to happen is that I'm going to exhaust all my savings in college and won't have publishing money."

"Why don't you let me help you with college and worry about book publishing later? That's more expensive. That will be my welcome home present for you."

In some ways, Phil resented her making him this offer. But, he accepted. He also resented taking favors from women because certainly he did not classify himself as a gigolo. Yet, he always found himself on the receiving end of a woman's handout. Because this usually happened, he rationalized that they saw a potential in his character that may one day make a significant contribution toward the scheme of society. He dearly hoped this was true because his character was beginning to develop, and using women for financial gain did nothing to stroke his ego.

College money was not the only welcome home present from Ruby. They made meaningful love in such unforgettable fashion that if there is such a thing as mental reincarnation, those memories would be potent in another lifetime.

Phil felt good about going to college and having a job that provided an opportunity for his learning a trade. He counted his blessings carefully every day.

The word spread like wildfire through the hospital that he was attending college. It spread just as fast as the news spread when Ramona told several people that he was a prisoner. When he did various jobs on different floors, all of the employees started to call him "Mr. Ivy League." His new name was spread throughout the hospital and nearly everyone called him by his new name.

Phil attended classes three nights a week. Courses in American history, psychology and U.S. government kept his mind very active the first semester. Psychology was his favorite course. He liked getting into himself, and he liked understanding others. He studied very hard because he wanted to gain as much information as possible.

Vonnie didn't appreciate his going to school three nights a week. She thought that would put a restraint on her seeing him whenever she had the opportunity of slipping away some evenings after work. "You mean to tell me that I won't get a chance to see you unless your days are free? You know that I can't get away on weekends. Besides, that would make my husband suspicious if I stayed out only Wednesdays and Fridays."

"We'll work something out, Brown Sugar. Don't get your feathers ruffled."

She snapped at him, "It's not my feathers that I am concerned about."

"We'll see each other and you know that. I'm not ready to end our thing. We'll just have to fit my schooling into our schedules." Phil hoped that she was pacified with his explanation. However, he had planned to do business before pleasure.

Phil carried his books to work with him some days, especially when he was going to have an examination. Some days, he would get finished with his tasks an hour or so before the end of the work day. He used that time to study notes or read a chapter or two.

He had a hectic schedule—job, school, Ruby and Vonnie. Ruby was very discreet around the hospital. No one knew that she and Phil were seeing each other. She never was seen with him in the cafeteria or on the lawn. She went along with his "Hello" and "How are you?" as if he were nothing to her. Phil appreciated her being discreet as she called it. Although she was discreet at the hospital, she was somewhat demanding of his time regardless of if it was his spare time or not. She was helpful, though, in doing different little things for him; for instance, she ironed his clothes and cleaned his apartment from time to time.

One evening as he returned from school, Ruby was parked in front of his place, waiting for him. Phil didn't like this kind of action. He might have had someone with him, or told someone else to meet him there after class. As he parked the car, he made up his mind that he would tell Ruby how he wanted things. She got out and walked to the entrance as he slowly got out of the car and gathered his books. "Hi, honey, I thought I would surprise you," she called out.

"Yeah, I don't like these kinds of surprises."

She noticed a slight resentment. "Okay! Okay! I've got the picture." She understood exactly what he meant, and she was wrong. At that moment, she realized that she didn't own him—although she was falling in love with him and didn't want to share him with any other woman.

They walked into the apartment and she placed the small bag that she was carrying on the table. "Are you angry, baby?" She looked at Phil in a teasing manner.

"No, I'm not really angry, just caught a little off-guard, I reckon."

She started trying to explain things. "I didn't have a chance to put the note in your car today, because Marian was with me when I came out of the building. I respect your rights and, above all, your privacy, if that's what you're sore about." Now she was a little perturbed at his insolent attitude. He could tell that because of her prancing around the apartment like a racehorse at the starting line. She cleaned the table. "Here, sit down and do your homework." Phil didn't mean to let his resentment be so noticeable. She went through the house as if she were his private maid, hanging his clothes up, cleaning and dusting. He prepared his assignment, and then he reviewed some notes. Ruby interrupted him. "Phil, me roast beef sandwiches. Would you like to stop now or later?"

"uppose this time is as good as any." As she turned he kitchen, Phil caught her by the arm. "Come here." He pulled her close to him and kissed her. She looked at him with a tender feeling inside, because she knew that he was no longer angry with her. "Are you still angry with me?"

"How could I possibly stay angry with you, you sexy devil?" he said as he pinched her buttocks.

She yelled, "Phil! That hurts with your king-size hands."

They talked about his classwork and his job. Ruby told Phil that she wanted him to do well in school even if that meant her seeing him occasionally. "No woman, young or old, is worth forfeiting your education, and don't you forget that. I know that there is a lot of temptation around you." She was speaking of Vonnie and thought she'd better make him understand. "Especially people like Miss Vonnie and others." Phil kept crunching on his sandwich. He didn't even look up while she was talking. He knew that the silent treatment would change the conversation. "Are you listening to me?"

Phil looked up at her, bowed his head and said, "I hear you."

"Well, why don't you say something, damnit?"

Phil hunched his shoulders. "Why are you getting all worked up over nothing?"

She reversed the role as she sat sipping her Scotch in silence. Phil completed his sandwich and suggested that they take a break, look at television, and relax.

She asked, "Is it working okay? You might have to put it in the shop. I put it in the basement because we could only get two channels. Your reception here might be better than ours."

"Yeah, it's working fine, come see for yourself," he said

as he led her to the bedroom.

Chapter 17

One Friday evening, Phil was a little late getting off from work. He was feeling a little mischievous that evening, not knowing who he would see that night, Ruby or Vonnie. He smiled to himself and thought, *The first one who calls is going to be the one I'll see.*

Just as he came down the steps, he thought he heard his name being called. "Phil! Phil! Phil!" He stopped in his tracks, as people rushed past him, trying to see where the voice was coming from. He felt someone tapping him on his shoulder. He turned and froze in his tracks. Staring in disbelief, he couldn't believe his eyes. It was Geraldine standing there, not smiling. For he'd promised her six weeks ago that he was coming to Church Hill.

She spoke very solemnly, "How you doing?"

"Ger—Geraldine, how'd you find this hospital?"

"I have ways to find anything I want."

Phil put his arms around her and kissed her on the forehead. She kind of pulled back in resentment. Phil sensed her attitude and said, "Come on, Gerry," in a pleading tone. "Where are you parked?"

"I ain't driving. I caught the bus up here."

"All right then, my fair lady, let's walk to my place." She looked straight ahead like one of Mr. Chipper's prized mares and took long strides which equalled his.

Phil tried to think of a million interesting things to talk about, but they all seemed to turn Geraldine off. He knew that he was going to get a good tongue-lashing, and he knew why. He had written her two letters in the past six or eight weeks. He had lied to her by promising her that he would see her soon. That was his biggest mistake, for Geraldine didn't take to being lied to very calmly.

They arrived at his apartment at last. Phil invited her in as he opened the door. "Come into my web, said the spider to the fly." Whew! Geraldine rolled her eyes at him as if he had threatened to slap her. Phil knew that this was it, for Geraldine was good and ready to let him have everything that was on her mind.

As she sat down, she took a good look at the place. Phil fixed two glasses of Scotch. "Here you go," he said, as he handed her her glass.

"Why did you lie to me, Phil?"

"Lie—lie about what?" Phil asked as he tried to look innocent.

"You wrote in your first letter that you would see me the next weekend, and that damned weekend ain't got here in seven weeks."

"Uh—uh, Geraldine, I meant to come down to see you, but—"

"Meant to like hell," she interrupted. She stood up and placed one hand on her hip and waved the Scotch in the other.

"Phil Avery, if you wanted to come, you would have been there, come hell or high water."

"Geraldine . . ." Phil rose to his feet, hoping that she wouldn't get any louder. "You know how much I care for you, and I always will care for you. I didn't lie deliberately to try to give you the run-around or nothing. I just have been working, and seeing all of my old friends."

"Yeah, I bet you've been seeing your old friends, especially that Vickie, and gawd knows who else." Tears began to trickle down Geraldine's face. "I thought you cared so much for me when you were on that damned farm. I was wrong, though, for thinking it. You . . . You . . . just wanted me for a good lay. You didn't give a damn about me . . . You might as well have studded one of those big ass mares you brushed every day. I was just too damn good to you . . . You didn't give a damn."

Phil couldn't take any more. "Geraldine, please, baby," he said as he took her in his arms and she sobbed shamelessly, like a helpless child. Phil's eyes filled with water, for she had been too damned good to him for him to neglect her as he had done. He felt guilty now about all the other women who he had been seeing in the past eight or nine weeks. Taking Geraldine by the hand, he led her to the bedroom and told her to lie down and rest herself. She lay there sobbing as Phil sat there gently rubbing her back.

She finally stopped crying and stared at the wall. Phil said, "Let's go out and have dinner tonight." She didn't answer him. He kept talking to her slowly, telling her how he'd make up for doing her wrong. As he was talking, he stretched out on the bed beside her. She moved toward the edge of the bed. She didn't want Phil to touch her. He felt the negative vibes from her.

Then she sat up and said, "Phil, I'm going home now."

Phil sprang up. "What?"

"Yes, I'm going home now. I had to see you in person and tell you how you have hurt me. I didn't come here to get laid."

Phil reached for her shoulders. She stepped back and threw up both hands. "No, Phil, I don't want to hear your sweet lies anymore. I'm going home now."

"It's seven thirty now, Geraldine. You don't know whether or not a bus is scheduled for the Eastern Shore at this time."

"I didn't come not knowing how I would go to and from here. The next bus leaves at nine, and I'll be on it."

"Geraldine, I want you to stay at least tonight."

She combed her hair and put on some lipstick. "I didn't plan to stay all night. I've done what I came to do."

Phil couldn't do anything other than stare at her, for he knew that there was nothing he could do or say that would change her mind. Feeling very guilty, he knew that this was the end of a beautiful relationship.

Phil decided to hail a cab rather than use his car. He didn't want Geraldine to see the feminine articles left in the car by Ruby. Geraldine didn't say a word in the cab as they rode to the Greyhound bus station. As the cab came to a stop, Geraldine started to open her purse to pay the driver. Phil closed her purse and gave the driver five dollars. They walked into the bus station, and he asked, "Aren't you hungry now?"

"Naw, I ain't hungry, although I think I would like to have some coffee."

They went into the coffee shop, where Phil tried like hell to turn Geraldine on, but he was completely in left field. "Geraldine, will you ever find forgiveness in your heart towards me?" he asked after she had calmed down. That coffee seemed to have done the job beautifully.

Speaking in a very low-keyed tone, Geraldine said, "Phil, I ain't mad at you. I understand everything much better now. What I thought was wasn't, and what I thought is ain't."

Phil hadn't ever heard Geraldine talk in riddles like that

before. She shocked him a little. They sat in silence for a few minutes. When they had finished their second cup of coffee, Geraldine looked at her watch and said, "I'd better get my ticket checked now."

They walked outside where the bus was parked. She looked as if nothing had happened between them. They both stood there, not saying a word. Just before she gave the driver her ticket, she reached up, kissed Phil on the cheek, and said, "Goodbye, Phil. Take care."

"Geraldine . . ." Phil grabbed her hand. She looked at him and smiled a faint smile as she stepped into the bus. "Geraldine!" Phil called out again, feeling a lump in his throat because he had lost a very dear friend. He looked at her as she took her seat by the window. The bus began to roll backwards, and Phil walked along beside it, looking up at Geraldine. She gave a very feminine wave of her fingertips as the bus turned down Howard Street onto Franklin.

He caught a bus back home. On the way, he felt so alone. He couldn't begin to count his blessings for having met Geraldine. She'd meant so many things to him. She wasn't just a person to release his sexual tension with, as she had so vividly expressed. Counselor, psychologist, friend and lover had been the roles she had played in his life. He knew the goodbye that she gave him meant just that. He promised himself, as he rode and looked out at the city, "I'll find a way to make it up to you, Geraldine. I promise."

Chapter 18

Phil completed the first semester successfully. He turned his thoughts upon his two different institutions. For it had only been seven months since he had been released from Jessup. He felt good that he had fought like hell to come up from sub-zero. He had moved toward some positive directions, comparing himself with a slide rule.

He was so proud of his grades until he took them to work to show to Carolyn. Carolyn took his grades around to various people, bragging about her big brother's success in his first semester of college. Ruby smiled as she looked at Carolyn acting silly with Phil's grades. She wanted to cheer her on and say, "Show them because he deserves all the praise in the world, for he has come a hell of a long way." She was turned off instantly when Vonnie came running up to the group where Carolyn was standing.

She announced boldly, "Let me see my man's grades."

One of the women said, "If he's your man, you would have seen them before anyone else."

Vonnie didn't act offended at all. "Maybe we were too busy to talk about some damned grades," she said as she turned and strutted away with a walk that got everyone's attention. Ruby looked at her with a scornful look, for she disliked her for saying that and acting as if Phil was her private property. She was peeved because she thought that Phil had stopped fooling around with her. She couldn't wait to question him about that statement.

Spring was in the air. Phil found that with work, study and women, the winter months had passed rapidly. The news of Phil writing a manuscript with hopes of it being published caused hostility from his peers.

One day he overheard a couple of the white men talking about him while he was in the storage room without their knowing it. "I can't stand that nigger. He thinks he's smart, talking about publishing a damn trashy book. Just give 'em an inch, and they'll take a mile. Besides, I don't know what Mr. Swisser sees in that jailbird anyway."

The other one said, "Maybe his mama worked for him or something. Who knows, maybe Mr. Swisser was going with his mama. I bet you that's it. What other reason could he have for having so much interest in a jailbird nigger?"

Phil couldn't take it any longer, for his blood had begun to boil. He stepped out of the storage room, making noise so that they would know that he wasn't just coming in. They looked as if they had witnessed the resurrection. Phil looked at them and said, "Just in case you guys want to know about Mr. Swisser, my mama and me, I'll tell him what you said and that you'd like for him to tell you about my mama and me."

They both looked at him with their mouths open. They knew that if he told him what they had said, their jobs would be in jeopardy. Mr. Swisser wouldn't stand for any slurs of that kind. Phil walked out with a smirk on his face as if he was going on an errand. "I'll be back in a little while. I have something to take care of right now, okay?" The two men were so nervous because they knew that Phil was angry and was headed straight for Mr. Swisser's office or the telephone.

As Phil walked down the corridor, he had to laugh to himself as he thought, *I bet those bastards are having diarrhea problems about now. Serves them right for opening their big mouths and putting their feet in.*

As the months passed, school was the highlight of Phil's day. The used 1968 Chevy which had been bought for him by Ruby was his source of transportation for getting back and forth to Morgan.

Psychology and sociology were his majors. Without bragging, Phil considered himself to be an astute student. Professor Steve Black was an effective enlightener of dark minds, and they all enjoyed his methods of teaching. Many times he would bring in a colleague to lecture. This was an educational treat which they all looked forward to.

This particular night as the guest speaker arrived, Phil went through one of the most traumatic experiences of his life.

"Folks," Professor Black was saying as Phil's mind struggled to absorb a passage from the book before him, *My Conflict, Regression, Anxiety and Defense.* "We have with us tonight a very learned person. She is one of my colleagues. She is an associate psychologist for Johns Hopkins, and her topic will relate to reaction sensitivity and predisposition to neurosis. At this time, I introduce to you, Dr. Victoria Dixson."

As the other classmates clapped, Phil's hands wouldn't move. They were suspended in mid-air with twelve inches of space between them, probably because his mind had done the same. It froze. Suddenly, one million feelings came over him simultaneously. Every suppressed memory and emotion which had been long forgotten stood at attention within, saluting vigorously throughout his body.

"Good God, it's Vickie!" He had no idea whether he had said this aloud or to himself. He was conscious that she was into her lecture and had given him no extra attention.

"Some persons," she was saying, "are predisposed to develop neurotic behavior under pressure by a type of inner psychological equilibrium rooted within during impressionable years."

His emotions personally transposed everything that she said. He could certainly tell her something about neurotic behavior under pressure. "Don't you know, woman, that you were an integral part of my impressionable years, that my psychological equilibrium has been out of whack since the day I first played with your ponytails in kindergarten?"

Vickie was dressed in a grayish-maroon two-piece tweed suit, with a matching scarf neatly tied around her neck. She deliberately tried to suppress her curvaceous body under that conservative suit. This would have proven to be an impossibility even if she had worn a sack. Her legs were super gorgeous and strong. She wore wine-colored high heels as she paced back and forth to the chalkboard where she made frequent illustrations.

Seeing her before him brought on a stubbornness which overcame him like Niagara Falls washing away a lily. *This is my woman!* he reasoned. *Married or not, she belongs to me and, dammit, no one will have her but me and God.*

When the lecture was over, the class applauded. This time he joined them. There were questions asked. She answered them. When it was over, Vickie gathered a set of books in her arms and was saying some last-minute words to Professor Black as Phil walked behind her, waiting patiently for her attention.

When she finished and turned towards him, his question was, "Dr. Dixson, if a person becomes neurotic because he's been isolated from his object of affection for nine years, is there hope for him?"

Without really looking at him first, she recognized him by the emotional tone of his voice. Then she looked in his eyes. Her books fell, toppling all over his feet.

"My God, Phillip!"

Professor Black helped him retrieve Vickie's books.

"It's my assumption that you two know each other."

"Yes, Steve," Vickie replied, her expression still displaying disbelief. "We do."

"Dr. Dixson," he offered, "I'll see you to your car."

"That would be nice, Phillip, thank you."

Once out in the parking lot, they both agreed that they hadn't eaten and they should at least stop and have something to eat together.

"Why don't you meet me at Sampson's?" he suggested.

"You mean that place down on Fayette Street that everybody goes to for a good home-cooked meal?"

"That's it, sweetheart. They've got the best home-cooked meal in the country. You probably could use some good soul," he joked. "Bet you been eating in classy joints with the gold-striped menus and tux-wearing waiters where they serve filet mignon and caviar, and have probably never heard of hot biscuits."

"Phil, cut it, please. I am hungry. Soul food will do me fine just now. Meet you there in ten minutes."

Once in Sampson's, they ordered stewed chicken, collard greens and candied yams. The iced tea was delicious, and the biscuits were piping hot.

They ate, talked, and observed the many different calibers of people who came from all walks of life and parts of town, risking the danger of visiting the ghetto just to eat some of that good Sampson's food.

After they had dined sufficiently, he suggested that since it was still early that they should go somewhere and have a drink.

"I know just the place, Phil—the Sphinx Club. I have a card."

"Oh, you mean the private club on Pennsylvania Avenue that the members of the higher echelon patronize?"

"Yes, Phil, if you want to be sarcastic. If you can give me some ghettoism, then I certainly can give you some upper-classism."

They both laughed as he paid the big-legged waitress, dressed in a tight black uniform.

Leaving Sampson's, he took Schroeder to Lexington and Lexington to Freemont. The city had begun boarding up quite a few houses, preparing for urban renewal. Driving up Pennsylvania Avenue, the changes broke his heart. Many buildings were closed. Wilmer Court on Dolphin Street was being torn down. Passing the Royal, Phil was reminded that great entertainers would no longer appear there. It, too, was marked for demolition.

The Frolic was still open on Lafayette and Pennsylvania. The Comedy Club was closed, but the Casino was still open. The crowd hanging in front of it was a different breed than that of the old days, but nevertheless they were there as if to support one of the last famous clubs on the avenue. The old Avenue Bar was still standing at Pitcher and Pennsylvania Streets, but it, too, was scheduled for demolition.

A thousand memories appeared as Phil recalled that as a child the avenue was the only place where blacks could shop, participate in cultural affairs, and see some of the world's greatest entertainers.

It was as dear to Phil and other blacks as the Stars and Stripes are to America's other citizens. *Goddammit*, he thought, *they have in every city a Jewtown, a Germantown, a Little Italy, and a Chinatown. Pennsylvania Avenue was our Blacktown, but they are going to tear it down. How could they do that to the Royal Theater? Every black entertainer who made it came through the Royal: Nat King Cole, Sammy Davis Jr., Redd Foxx, Slappy White, Jackie "Moms" Mabley, Duke Ellington, Count Basie and Ella Fitzgerald. Many others in Baltimore will never receive the richness of our cultures because there will be no Royal.*

When Phil reached Bloom and Pennsylvania, he parked across from Leon's Pig Pen and met Vickie, who was parked there. Together they entered the Sphinx Club. Inside, it was cozy and private, with close to a dozen people in their good clothing, talking their sophisticated language and sipping their fine drinks. A trio was in the center of the floor where the bandstand was located. They were playing familiar jazz tunes, and an organist was there. There were shouts from the audience every now and then, such as "Play your number, Squeeze! Play your number!" Squeeze was a tall, slim musician who had been on the avenue before Phil was born. He was a great musician and was well-liked by all Sphinx Clubbers.

Vickie and Phil took seats at a table to the left of the bar and the band, where they ordered rum and Coke and Johnny Walker Red.

"Here's to nine years of separation, young beauty and your success," Phil said, holding his glass and sipping the Scotch in salute to Vickie.

She lifted her glass in the same fashion, sipped, and said, "Here's to your determination, your Leo quality, and our reunion."

At this point, Phil took another look at Vickie and concluded that if she was not the most gorgeous woman in the world, then the sister holding the title needed to come out of hiding and convince him otherwise.

"Vickie," he began without preliminaries or ceremonies. "He can't have you, be he Dr. Dixson or Dr. World. Can you get to what I am saying without my going into it?"

"Yes, I can, Phil. But you must remember, nine years is an awfully long time. Five of those years I have been married. You just can't abruptly come out and start picking up the pieces."

By this time, Phil had placed his glass upon the table and was gazing into her soft, beautiful eyes with all the sincerity that his emotions possessed.

"Vickie, I never put down the pieces. As a matter of fact, they were never fragmented. I just felt one huge emotion that I had to try and submerge with a million segments of life and thoughts, hoping to obscure the total object, which had been the conscious motivating force for every moment of my survival. Vickie, I love you. Unashamedly, I have no idea how you are going to work it out, but you know and I know that you do not belong to him."

Phil's every desire was to lick the trickle of tears that flowed from her eyes down her teasing brown cheeks.

"Phil, I know that I am only his on paper. Also, I know that I do not wish to disrespect my marriage. But, just as sure as I am sitting here, I cannot deny the deep inner meaning as to what I am to you and what you are to me. Phil, this sounds crazy, but it's like he's my husband and you are my man. God knows I have not been unfaithful to this man, yet I have never stopped being yours."

"Vickie," Phil interrupted, "if I said I didn't understand what you are feeling, I'd be lying. I have been with some very good women since being home. The physical aspect has been pleasing and delightful, but my mind and emotions must be involved in order for me to be fulfilled. Right now, I am involved both mentally and emotionally. I feel that I am yours as well. And goddammit, you are the only woman in the world who can do that number on me."

It was not his conscious intention to be egotistical, domineering or disrespectful towards Vickie's marriage; neither was Phil being sexually revengeful. But just as sure as he was human, he had to have his woman that night.

They went through a half hour of "Phil, not tonight . . . Let me think about it. Maybe some other time."

Finally, she said, "I'll go just to see what your place looks like."

This time they left her car parked and went in his. By the time they reached his Charles Street apartment, they both were feeling good from the drinks and each other's company.

"Vickie," he said as they entered his apartment, "I promise you won't have to stay long. I know you have a time limit."

"No, no," she cooed casually. "My husband is in Atlanta at a doctors' convention."

They had sipped a couple more drinks and talked for an hour when she asked casually, "Phil, how long have you been home?"

"Ever since March."

The next thing he felt was a slap. It was a playful one, but hard enough to sting.

"You are a real stinker," she said. "You've been home three months and I would have never known it had I not lectured at the college tonight."

"Eventually, I would have found you."

After a while, they got comfortable, took off their clothes, sipped their drinks, and talked about everything.

"I can't believe you wrote a book, Phil," she exclaimed. "Am I in it?"

"From cover to cover."

"It's going to be a best-seller, if I know you, Phil."

"Vickie." Phil hesitated. "Not changing the subject, but

how is my son?"

"He's fine. He's still in Boston with mother. Phil, I have not told him about you. He thinks you are not with us ... That's it."

"Vickie, I understand. That's on me."

Vickie was lying across the bed, sipping her drink. Her brown silk mini-slip had slid upward, exposing her smooth thighs, which were almost the color of the slip.

"One question, Vickie."

"Yes."

"Are you still as sweet as ever?"

"Only the first man who had me would be able to tell after so many years."

Memories swelled in his mind and emotions as he remembered when he first made love to her years ago as a young virgin. Now she had become a voluptuous, full-grown woman with the same spirit that had kindled a fire in him that was madly burning. Without warning, he kissed her on the thigh. She responded with a purr, which sent chills through him. As her stomach pressed against the bed in a prone position, Phil gently kissed her protruding, unblemished cheeks.

"Oh, Phil, please," she whispered breathlessly. "Don't ..."

But he did. His lips kept pressing the sweet brown smoothness of her copper-chocolate body—up, down, front and back. Vickie was sweet through and through, and he didn't care if the world knew of his emotional license to make love unashamedly to her, his woman, to the point of no restrictions. When her lips reciprocated, exploring his body, every warm, wet touch was a nerve explosion of the most sensitive kind. He pulled strands of her hair and called out, "Vickie! Vickie! Vickie!"

Finally, their bodies straddled as they absorbed each other as deeply as possible, with his wanting desperately to fertilize her with a child.

"Phil . . . Keep me, darling. Keep me, darling . . . Please keep me!"

"Vickie!" he whispered breathlessly. "I love you, darling. Honest to God!"

As they relaxed before falling off to sleep, there was no room for feeling anything short of supreme elation.

The next morning, after a lingering embrace, Phil relinquished her body slowly. "When will I see you again? Tonight, maybe?"

Vickie looked at Phil with an understanding expression. "Not tonight. My husband will be in on the ten thirty flight. And I'm supposed to meet him at the airport." She flashed her eyes up at Phil and said in a serious tone, "Phil, don't look like that. We will see each other occasionally."

Phil interrupted, "I can't live for some damned occasionally. I want you for keeps."

Vickie gave him a sharp look. "Phil, let's not get into that. Okay?" She dashed into the bathroom and took a shower. When she came out, Phil was sitting on the side of the bed. She bent over and raised his head with her fingertips, and kissed him lightly. "Come on and cheer up, Phil. Don't spoil what we've just experienced. Look happy, because this was a total revelation of joy that we felt."

Phil looked at her and said, "You're right, my love. I'm sorry." They kissed, and she headed for the door.

"When will we see each other?" he asked.

Vickie replied, "Soon. I mean real soon, too. I promise." She held her head up and kissed him. She left without looking back, for she couldn't stand that sad look he had on his face. Phil watched her spin off down the street.

Vickie arrived at work with a different stride in her walk. She also had a very cheerful tone in her voice. Her co-worker said, "Vickie, you look like you had a very restful night. That's the way I like to see people come to work. Especially when they enjoy their work."

Vickie smiled sheepishly and said without looking up at him, "I do enjoy my work very much."

He replied, "It shows, too."

Vickie thought, *But you don't know the kind of work I'm talking about.*

When Vickie looked up from her desk, it was past her lunch hour. She was gliding through her work like an airplane getting ready to land. She thought, *Airplane—funny I would think of that because I have to go to the airport, I guess. Oh, if I only had one more night with Phil.* Her emotions sent chills through her body.

Vickie went to lunch and ate by herself. She didn't want anyone to infringe on her mellow thoughts.

"Hi, Vickie, what's new with you?" asked Alice, the lab assistant. Vickie looked up and hoped she would catch her drift and move on.

"Oh, I'm just sorting out some things in my mind."

Alice said, "Study long and you'll study wrong."

Vickie smiled and waved her on. She thought of what Alice had said and grunted, "You're probably right; that might be the best psychology to go by—study long and you'll study wrong." She stirred her tea slowly, seeing Phil's eyes and smile. She thought once again about Mother Nature as being the selfish stepmother throwing out goodies to her stepchildren every now and then. This was what life was all about to her.

Vickie went back to her office and worked on a few more reports. She also had several conferences with patients. Finally, it was time to go home.

She arrived home not wanting to go inside, for this was the little world that she was ready to let go for love. Letting herself in the house, she felt a depressed feeling enveloping her. She felt emotions of guilt and loneliness simultaneously.

She turned on the radio, tried to block out everything, but she couldn't get past Phil's face.

She began to shed tears, knowing that she couldn't go to Phil for keeps. Besides, she felt that if she continued to see Phil, it would sooner or later dissolve her marriage to Bob. And she couldn't do that to him because he had been a good husband, as well as a good provider. Vickie cried out loud, "Oh, Phil! Why? Why?" Then she finally pulled herself together and prepared a light dinner for Bob.

Vickie arrived at the airport forty-five minutes early. She went into the cocktail lounge for a drink while waiting for Bob to arrive. She smiled to herself as she thought, *I need a pint to help me face Bob and to make it through the night.* Then she thought of herself telling her patients about facing the truth and not needing a crutch such as drugs or alcohol. *Face it, Vickie,* she said to herself. Her thoughts were interrupted by a distinguished, elderly man.

"Have you been waiting long, young lady?"

She smiled. "No, not very long."

Then he smiled in his modest, flirtatious way. "You look like you don't believe he's coming."

She looked at him, wishing he wasn't coming, and said, "Yes, he'll be here. I'm just a little early."

He said, "Oh, it's the other way around. You are the anxious one."

Vickie smiled and nodded her head, for she wished he wasn't coming. She didn't say anything else so the conversation ended. She sipped her drink slowly, watching the minutes tick by.

Vickie waved to Bob while she was standing at the gate as he came down the ramp. She couldn't believe her play-acting herself. She reached up and kissed him and greeted him like she'd missed the hell out of him. He was all smiles. "How's my gorgeous queen?"

"Fine," she whispered, "now that you're here." They hurried and got his luggage. While driving home, she chatted about the lecture at Morgan and the dinner at Sampson's with some friends. She felt only half-guilty now, since she had half-told the truth.

Vickie crawled into the bed beside Bob, knowing she could not give herself completely. He reached for her. Her insides froze. She knew deep down inside that she couldn't respond as she had been responding to his touch. Bob sensed a little restraint. "Come on and really show me how much you have missed me," he said.

Vickie started play-acting again. "Oh, you know how much I missed you. So if I don't do a good job, you know it's because of a long, long day."

He kissed her lightly. "I know, darling."

As he began to make love to her, Vickie's heart wanted to run to Phil and say, "I can't help what I'm doing, for I'll always be yours."

It was almost like Phil knew what was happening. He walked the floor an hour or more. He decided to go on the avenue for a few drinks. He drove to the avenue and parked, hoping he would find some peace of mind. He walked into the first bar he got to. He saw an old friend who was twisting in the middle of the floor. She looked at him for a long time and then she came over and said, "Don't I know you from somewhere?"

Phil looked at her and smiled. "I think you do. I'm Phil."

"Well, I'll be damned. Phil Avery. I heard you were ..." She stopped in the middle of the sentence.

Phil smiled and said, "You heard right."

"Uh, I didn't mean it."

Phil said, "It's okay, it's okay. It's no secret."

She began to talk more and more to Phil. She twisted her body from right to left, trying to entice him with her suggestive body language. When she saw he wasn't interested in her, she asked, "Phil, are you married or something?"

Phil replied, "No, I'm not married, and I will probably never get married."

She threw her head back and laughed. "Oh, they all say that. Just wait until someone hooks you. You'll have a new tune to sing then." She was twisting to a sound from the vendor. "Let's dance, Phil." Phil didn't want to hurt her feelings, so he went on the floor with her. He couldn't wait until the record was over; he told her he felt a little dizzy.

He thought he should leave her quickly, so he ordered her another drink and told her he had to be on his way. She looked disappointed that he hadn't asked her to go with him. She held the drink up and said, "Cheers." He smiled and walked out slowly, for he was still fighting all the emotions he had before he came down to the avenue. He decided to drive home and take a straight shot of whiskey and try not to think of anything.

Part Four
The Beginning of Dawn

Chapter 19

A little more than a year after Phil's release, it had become quite evident that his little, drawn-faced, prejudiced supervisor had no promotion in mind for him. Regardless of what Mr. Swisser had instructed the supervisor to do, Phil thought to himself, *It doesn't matter to that bastard that I am doing swell in college; nor does it bother him that much that my qualifications exceed those of many staff persons who hold positions at the hospital.* Phil's whole faith lay in the fact that if he kept going to college, kept trying to get his book published, and kept a positive outlook, no amount of alley-cleaning, errand-boy duty, or heavy lifting would take away what he was all about.

Admittedly, the tension did swell between his supervisor, Mr. Swisser, and him. It was Mr. Swisser who interceded and had him transferred to another position, that of stockroom clerk. It wasn't bad. His errand-boy status increased, but it afforded him the opportunity to come to work much cleaner. Also, it gave him a greater opportunity to travel all over the hospital.

In the midst of it all, a major change was taking place in the hospital, which greatly displeased the officials. The union was trying to get in, and for very good reason. The non-professionals were grossly overworked and underpaid. Their fringe benefits were nil, not to mention that one could be fired without recourse.

For some reason, almost every employee involved sought Phil out for advice, maybe because he was in college or just because they knew his views as to the plight of black people.

"Phillip," the general question was asked, usually in confidence, "should I join the union?"

"Damned right," was his general reply. "If your rights are being violated and you have no real benefits or protection, by all means join!"

The union people—all black—were picketing the hospital, handing out literature and trying to hold conversations with black workers as they came to and from work. It infuriated Phil to no end as he observed the black workers dodging these freedom fighters as if they had the plague. They were afraid to speak to them for fear of being fired. It was as if free blacks couldn't mingle with those confined to the plantation. Phil thought to himself, *Well, I'll be damned if I am going to refuse to speak to my brothers and sisters.*

"Hey, brother," said one of them who was approaching, "here's a piece of literature."

"Thank you, brother," he replied warmly.

It must have encouraged the brother when he stopped and spoke warmly.

"What do you think of the union?" he questioned.

"I'm into brothers and sisters reaching out to one another. If that's what the union is into, I'm all for it."

"Solid on that, brother," the fellow said and shook his hand again.

He entered the hospital and prepared for work, knowing that a fleet of spies had reported his association with the plague carriers.

Phil had not been on his detail more than an hour before he was summoned to the administrative office.

The office was small, yet it didn't cramp the two black leather chairs that sat opposite Mr. Berger's unused desk. As Phil sat, he watched Berger's beady blue eyes observe him. Finally, Berger did a quick brush of his short brown-gray hair with the back of his hand and said, "Mr. Avery . . ." He hesitated. "We are going to ask you to resign." Phil already knew from instinct that the reason was union-related, regardless of the whitewashing.

He silently stared at Berger, watching those beady blue eyes blink. Berger continued, "Now I know that you want to talk with Mr. Swisser concerning this, so feel free."

"No, no, I won't be talking to him about this. He has helped me enough, and if you are doing this, I'm sure it's within his knowledge."

"Phillip," he said, "I really hate to see you leave. But I know you will make it. You don't need to be working in a place like this, anyway. You are in college. Also, I read your manuscript. Mr. Swisser let me read it. It is excellent. You don't belong here. You are going to make it."

"Thank you, Mr. Berger." He signed the resignation and walked out.

Phil walked out of the office. He thought as he walked to a small sandwich shop, *I'll talk with Mr. Swisser concerning my being terminated.* The waitress interrupted his thoughts. "May I help you, sir?"

"Uh—uh, yes, let me have a ham and cheese sandwich."

"Something to drink?"

"Yeah, a Sprite."

"Thank you, sir." She spun around, wagging her tail like a reckless train. Phil began to think again about his job.

He said to himself, *What am I going to do now?* He smiled to himself as he traced circles on the countertop. He was visualizing what Mr. Swisser probably said when the hospital officials told him that he was considered a threat to the labor force of the hospital staff. He could hear the slow drawl, "Well, I like Avery, but I'll be damned if I'm going to let him make us lose money. Therefore, we have no other choice but to let him go. He'll find some kind of job."

The waitress interrupted his thoughts again. "Here you are, sir." As she gazed in his eyes, she smiled at him. Phil gave her a cordial smile. She said, "You sure have something on your mind today. You haven't stopped staring at that countertop since you walked in here. Whew! Boy, it must be serious."

Phil smiled and said, "I guess you could call it that." She stood there with ears and mouth open, ready to hear it all. Phil took a bite into his sandwich and chewed his first mouthful. "Um-mm-mm good."

She realized then that he wasn't going to discuss his business with her. She said, "That'll be one dollar and thirty-five cents."

Phil stopped eating and gave her one dollar and fifty cents. "Keep the change," he said.

She smiled and said, "Thanks." She walked a few steps and looked back and said, "Now stop thinking so hard. It'll work out; you'll see." She went back into the kitchen area. Phil finished his sandwich and raised his hand at her as he went out.

That evening Phil was talking to Ruby about his being terminated. She sat very patiently and listened to Phil as he poured out what he was feeling. He paused a little and then looked at her and said, "I'm going to get a job if I have to start a business myself."

Ruby asked, "Doing what? Now let's be more reasonable about this, Phil. You'll go out and find a job. And you can do that by starting tomorrow." Phil looked at her in dismay.

"Who is going to hire a 'con' man? You think they aren't going to run a check on me? I wouldn't have had that job at the hospital if it had not been for Mr. Swisser."

Ruby said, "Well, you can see he sure wasn't in love with you."

Phil replied, "I can see his point—why keep me on and have a walkout strike, which would interrupt the routines of the hospital, when he can remove the one who might cause this interruption? Can't you see his point? If I were in his shoes, I'd probably have done the same."

Ruby said, as she led Phil to the bedroom, "I guess you're right. Well, after a good night's rest, you can get an early start in the morning looking for another job. In the meantime, let's forget everything else."

Phil was restless that night thinking about employment. He tossed and turned continuously. Ruby tried to comfort him, but he was at loose ends. He finally had a bright idea that just might work. Then he went to sleep with a smile on his face, knowing that he had a solution to his problem.

Since he was not the type to allow grass to grow under his feet, Phil used the back of Dr. Flack's garage and opened a car wash business. He typed some flyers and passed them throughout the neighborhood. In no time, business was rolling in. Of course, he received most of the hospital business and all of the neighboring business.

At this point, business was so good that he developed an idea to start a mobile car wash, which enabled him to use a truck with several barrels of water and a hose. With this method, he was able to pull up beside a car while it was parked and wash it.

It was through John Bowman of *Bowling for Dollars* on channel eleven that he was able to get all the car wash business at WBAL and a private country club in Timonium. Businessmen and women sent for him all the time. It was a real enjoyment to be able to work for himself for the first time.

Of course, none of this was without struggle, obstacles and pressures. As it happened, the atmosphere was still tense with the threat of the union coming into the hospital. Many of the hospital workers were his customers, and the word was out that he was still a major influence with the workers as to their decision to join or not to join the union.

Consequently, the grapevine news said that any hospital workers caught having their cars washed at Phil's place of business would be fired. There went fifty percent of his business. The loss was tremendous, and warm weather would soon be gone. Phil thought that he should "make hay while the sun shined." At least he was saving his money towards getting his book published, should his business fold.

One evening while he was washing cars, a guy whom he had served time with pulled up to get his car washed. His name was Lloyd.

"Phil," he said, "you give a damned good car wash, but I never thought I'd see the day that you would be cut out for this. What happened to that book you wrote?"

"It's in the publisher's hands. I'm paying to have it published. It should be out in a few months."

"Phil," he said, expressing concern, "with the smarts that you got, why the hell are you out here washing somebody else's car? You know they got a halfway house over on Lanvale Street run by ex-offenders. They need a caseworker, and you would be just the man. Why don't you check them out?"

"What is it, one of those federally-funded programs?"

"Yeah, funded by Model Cities. They pay pretty good."

"I don't know, Lloyd. I may just check it out. This car wash business is getting pretty slow."

Before he left, he gave Phil the address, phone number and contact person. Later, Phil thought about it. *This could be my avenue towards my second goal. At least I could be helping ex-offenders.*

He took time out, went over, and filled out an application. Most of the workers he knew. He was told that he would be contacted one way or another as to whether he would be hired, but that position would not be available for a while.

By the end of September, it began to get a bit too cool for washing cars, but he stuck with it. There was nothing else to do. When October arrived, it brought with it cold weather, and after a few days he found it quite uncomfortable sticking his hands in the icy water. It was even more difficult when he saw the water freeze on the car as he tried to wash it. It was at this point that he knew that he had to cease being stubborn and find himself a steady job.

He didn't like the thought of working for one of those government handout programs. To him, they stripped you of your dignity. *What the hell am I going to do?* he wondered.

Chapter 20

Phil was very depressed on this dreary Friday night. He felt as if he wanted to be with people, but he really wasn't in a mood for talking, nor was he in a mood to be with any of his female companions. He wanted to be out among a lot of people. After he showered, he put on his clothes and caught the bus to North and Charles Streets. He wanted to see the flick starring Sidney Poitier. Just as he was getting a bag of popcorn from the counter, someone slapped him on the back. "Hey, my main man, how are you doing?"

Phil grabbed Douglass around the shoulders, since he was only five feet, nine inches. "Hey, Short Stuff," replied Phil. "How in the hell are you?"

He made a face and said, "So-so, man. No job, almost in the pits." Then he pulled his girlfriend over and hugged her. "Man, this is my main squeeze. If it wasn't for her, I'd be back in the joint, I reckon. Uh, meet Clara, Phil. Clara, this is Phil."

Phil extended his hand. "How are you, my fair lady?"

She beamed all over, revealing a bright gold tooth. "Just fine and yourself?"

Phil nodded and said, "Fine, thank you."

Douglass said, "Who are you with, man? I know you're not streaking by yourself."

Phil nodded and said, "Yes, I am, man. I'm by myself."

Douglass laughed. "Man, you got to be crazy. I got out before you, and I don't plan to spend but eight hours away from my woman." He rubbed Clara on the shoulder, and she beamed all over. "That'll be the time I leave for work and return from work. Man, you haven't forgotten those hard nights of wanting, wishing and hoping you'd be in the presence of any female, just let you get out." They both laughed and did the hand slap.

Phil said, "I've been making up, man. Don't you play me any shorter than this six-foot, one-inch frame."

"Hey, man," Douglass said, "the flick is about to start. Let's go in. You wanna sit with us?"

Phil replied, "Don't mind if I do."

Douglass was sitting there making comments about the movie. "Man, that Sidney is a bad M.F., ain't he?"

Phil laughed, "Sure is."

After the movie, Douglass asked, "Man, are you going home?"

Phil answered, "I really don't feel like it."

Douglass scratched his chin. Clara looked at them, knowing they could do without her company. She said, "Look, you guys, I'm gonna take a cab home. You two go on and shoot the breeze for a while."

Phil reached for her arm. "Naw, don't let me take your man from you on this good old Friday night."

She patted his hands and said, "It's okay. He'll be there

later on." She winked at Phil to let him know that she had the calling cards in this deal.

Douglass said, "Man, I wouldn't take nothing for her." She smiled. He patted her on the rear. "Come on, let me get you a cab."

Phil said, "Man, your lady is nice."

"She knows how to treat a man, too," replied Douglass. "Like I said, she's boss. By the way, man, where are you working?"

Phil replied, "No damned where."

Douglass said, "What? Man, with your smarts, you ain't got nothing to do, either?"

"Well, man, it's a long story. I had something, but I got fired. Then I started my own business, a little car-washing gig. Now it's too damned cold for that. So, man, I'm in the pits, too."

"Man, I got an idea," said Douglass. "It's near Christmas, and we need money. Let's figure out a way to get some."

Phil said, "Man, if I could, I would blow some of these bastards straight to hell and take off."

"Man, that's no sweat. We can do it." They walked into a small bar and sat at the back. The barmaid came over and took their orders.

"What are you two Prince Charmings having tonight?"

Douglass, being fast at the lips, said, "Well, let's see," as he looked her up and down. "How about you? That is, without the rocks."

She smiled. "Okay, let's have it, please."

Phil responded this time. "Make that two Budweisers, please." She turned away. Phil laughed as Douglass turned around in his seat to watch her movements. "Man, you are after them all."

"I've got to keep the women happy, my man, even if I ain't got no money. I got my game and a strong back." They laughed.

The barmaid set the beer in front of them and said, "Pay now or later?"

"Later," said Phil.

Douglass sipped his cold beer with a big gulp. "Man, I'm serious about us getting together. We can plan it so well that the FBI won't be able to catch us."

"I don't know about that," said Phil, "but what did you have in mind?"

"I know where this little liquor store is that is just the spot. It's way out. We could stop by one of my friend's house and borrow his piece. Then we could knock the place off before closing time. It's just nine-thirty."

Phil interrupted, "Man, the cops are probably swarming around that place like flies."

"Naw, man," said Douglass. "I've scoped the place out two or three times. I just didn't have anyone that I could trust to help me pull it off."

"I don't want to go back to prison for a few dollars."

"Man, this ain't no chicken scratch that I'm talking about." Phil looked a little worried, although he could have used some quick cash to help tide him over a few weeks. Douglass rose and said, "Come on, Phil." Phil placed the tab on the bar.

They caught a cab and got out at Lafayette's Court. Douglass knocked on the door. A voice rang out, "Who is it?"

The door opened. "Hi, Carolyn. Is Sam here?"

"Naw, Doug, you know Sam. You'll probably see him before I will."

Douglass smiled and said, "Okay, Carolyn. I'll see you later."

They walked on down the block, neither one saying a word. They stopped at another apartment. Douglass knocked on the door. A lady answered through the door, "Yeah?"

"Hey, is George here?"

"Hell, naw, he ain't here, and don't knock on my damned door looking for him no more."

Douglass looked at Phil and smiled. "Man, that's his old lady. They must have had a good knock-down, drag-out fight. Come on, man, I've got one more place, but I'd better call first, because it's on the east side."

Phil said, "Man, let's make plans for tomorrow night. It's closing time now."

Douglass responded, "Give me your address or, better still, let's meet at North and Charles at Clover's Bar."

Phil, remembering his lessons from Kool Eddie, said, "All right, man, let's make some plans now." They talked about the layout and how they would maneuver things. Then they departed and went home.

Phil walked around in his little apartment in a very distressed state of mind. He looked on the floor and saw a white envelope addressed to him. He grabbed it, knowing it was from Vickie. It read: "Hi, Phil, I came by earlier. I thought we could be together for a while. I heard you were out of work. So I'm treating you to dinner tomorrow night at seven-thirty. We need to talk. You've been on my mind for some reason. Please be here—Vickie."

Phil started biting his fingernails. He knew that he couldn't pull that job off now. What would Vickie say? What would Mr. Swisser and all the rest say if he were caught? *Yes, that's what they expect me to do,* he thought, *even Vickie. Why did she say that she needed to talk and that she's heard about my losing my job? Yeah, that's what she thinks, all right—I'm going back in the joint. She's trying to use that damned psychology on me. Well, I'll fool all these damned know-it-alls.* Phil was steaming mad now. His guilt and Vickie's speculation had him steaming. He continued to think. *I won't go back. I'll be damned if I will. I'll show them.* He went over to the cabinet and took a straight shot of Johnny Walker Red and went to bed.

The next day Phil was toying with the idea of what he should do about Douglass. He felt that if he went to him and explained how he had thought it over and thought that he'd better not take part in it, Douglass would think that he was afraid. On the other hand, he thought about how Douglass had placed so much confidence in him. "Damn," he said out loud. "What am I going to do?" He knew he wasn't going anywhere now that Vickie was coming over.

Phil cleaned his apartment because he wanted it to be very neat for Vickie. He went out and got a few things to cook. He wanted to surprise Vickie with dinner. Besides, he wanted to have as much time with her as possible. It seemed funny at first when he read her note that he was very angry with her, for he thought she was thinking negatively about him. Then he thought, *They have always said that the truth hurts, and the truth was that I was headed for trouble.*

Vickie arrived on time, at seven-thirty sharp. Boy, was she precise. She rapped on the door lightly. Phil opened the door with a jerk. She walked in with a big smile and said, "Hi . . . um, it smells good in here."

He winked. "What are you trying to do, save me some money?"

He took her coat and hung it in the closet. He then reached and pulled her to him. "It sure does smell good in here, now that you're here." She smiled and they kissed.

"Oh . . . Phil Avery, your flattery will get you all the way." They both laughed as they sat on the sofa.

Phil said, "So how have you been, Vickie?"

"I've been okay, Phil. I'm just moving through life like a zombie some days. I guess you know why."

"No, tell me about it," he said as he smiled, feeling a warmth in his heart that had no comparison.

Vickie went on talking about her job, home, and a few other

things. Then she said, "Now that I've opened up to you, let me hear what's been happening to you."

Phil was not ready to talk about himself at that moment. "Let's eat first."

Vickie sighed, put her hand on her hips and said, "Phil, I said I was taking you out."

"I know what you said, Miss, but I want to hibernate with you as long as I can." She smiled as Phil placed the two trays in front of the sofa; then he went back into the kitchen nook, trying to keep busy before Vickie asked him again. *Damn,* he thought, *why am I so jumpy?* He hadn't committed a crime. Just then, he almost spilled the green peas on the counter.

Vickie got up and said, "Here, let me help you. You are new at this kind of thing, so let the old pro show you how."

Phil felt a surge of relief go over him. "Okay, pro," he said as he handed her a plate.

"I didn't know you could burn, baby," teased Vickie as she bumped him with her hip. "When did you have time to learn?"

"Oh ... some things come natural to the Wonder Boy." They giggled and caressed each other.

They were about finished eating when Vickie said, "Phil, are you all right? I've had two dreams about you recently, and one wasn't so good."

Phil looked at her with a puzzled expression. "I'm a little at rock bottom," he said as he hunched his shoulders, feeling guilty again. "I guess I'm all right."

Vickie looked him in the eyes. "You can't fool me, Phil. You haven't gotten into any trouble, have you?"

Phil spoke a little above his normal tone. "Naw! Naw! What makes you think that? I'm straight."

She reached and grabbed his hand. "Okay, baby, I just asked. Don't get so defensive. I've always been on your side." He felt that she wasn't thoroughly satisfied and that she would eventually pry it all out of him before the night was over.

Phil got up and made two drinks. After they had sipped their drinks, Phil took Vickie by the hand and unbuttoned her blouse and helped her out of it. They were gazing at each other like two barracudas getting ready to attack their prey. Phil said in a hoarse tone, "Vickie, you are my life." He really meant to say, "You've saved my life." He tried to convey the message in his caressing.

"I feel the same way," said Vickie as she snuggled closer to him. Phil made love to Vickie, trying to convey gratitude coupled with his true feelings for her, for she had kept him from getting into trouble. If body language could transmit anything at all, he definitely had sent a message.

The next day, Phil felt as if he had let Douglass down. He wondered where he could reach him, since they hadn't exchanged addresses. He thought about going to North Avenue to see if he could find him. He knew that he must be quite disappointed in him, but on the other hand, Vickie might have just saved him, too.

He hoped to run across Douglass and try to explain what had happened. He thought, *Ever since my release, my schedule has been hectic with work, school and women.* At no time did he really get a chance to assess himself and what he was all about.

Since being fired from South Charles, he realized that he had taken hold of his anger and expressed it positively in a car wash business, letting the system know that he wouldn't be outdone.

Maybe I should stick them bastards up on payday, he thought. With a mask, no one would recognize him. *No,* he reasoned. *That's twenty years if I get caught.* A feeling of loneliness overcame him and he decided to go to Pennsylvania Avenue to be with his kind of people.

His mood was very negative as he drove to Pennsylvania

Avenue. He parked the car at Pennsylvania and Mosher. The avenue was lit up. There were bright lights, colorful people, hustlers, boosters, whores, pimps, dope fiends and some decent folk.

When he reached the front of the Comedy Club, it was about seven o'clock and dark. Even with their backs turned, he could spot his two old partners, Moe and Skinny. He walked up behind them and said jokingly, "Don't move, goddammit. This is a stickup."

Skinny's hands went up in the air for real. Moe, after an initial fright, recognized his voice and broke into a smile.

"Phil!"

They hugged, shook hands and did the avenue hand slap.

"Man," Skinny said, "I thought you were for real." He now had a smile on his face.

"How long you been home, man?" Moe asked.

"Close to a year, man. Been laying in across town."

"Wish the fuck I could stay out here that long, man," Moe said half-heartedly. "My ass stays in jail. Just finished ninety days yesterday at the city jail."

Moe had a hard expression on his face. His black corduroy jacket resembled a Salvation Army special. It was obvious that he had just gotten out of jail.

Skinny was neat and clean, the way he had always been from childhood days. His suede jacket was expensive-looking; so was his matching suede cap. He was still lean and not much larger than when he was a kid.

"Skinny, what you doing now?"

"Working, man, walking slow, and now and then I gamble."

"That working shit," Moe interrupted, "ain't for me. Y'all niggers done squared up. You know what I want?" His eyes lit up in a dream fashion as he extended his hands to rake in imaginary money. "I want to take me off just one big one for a hundred grand and just lay back. Take, for instance, that crap game that's across the street in Johnny's. Them niggers got 'bout twenty grand. Phil, you and me could go over there, tear them niggers off, and get over like fat rats."

"Moe," Phil said reflectively, "the shit sounds good, as broke as I am, but as much time as them people slapped on me, I don't want to see no more pistols."

"Shit, you're out now. Might as well make somebody pay for it."

Often, Phil mentally toyed with the idea of making fast money. This getting fired and the car wash folding was for the birds. But damn, if he got caught, that would be the end of it for him and Vickie.

"It's chilly out here," Skinny said, blowing a huff through his clenched fists. "Let's go over to the crap game and try to win some of the money instead of ripping it off."

"Yeah, Moe," Phil said. "C'mon."

When they walked in, a big game was in progress. Many of the faces were familiar to them. Tension was in the smoke-filled air like gold is in Fort Knox. Dudes of all descriptions stood around the table, watching the dice roll. While scanning the faces, Phil saw numbers-backers, pimps, businessmen, regular hustlers and dope dealers. The swelling tension was magnified because everyone was almost broke except the two people that all the action and tension centered around—Georgia Boy and Pee Wee.

Pee Wee could no longer be called Little Pee Wee. Now he was known as one of the biggest dope dealers on the East Coast, not to mention the fact that he was the best gambler Baltimore had ever seen.

The pot had an unbelievable amount—fifteen thousand dollars. Georgia Boy was rolling the dice. As was fashion, the gamblers talked shit to each other. All of this was part of the psyche game glamour.

With a stack of large bills already gathered in front of him,

Georgia Boy shook the dice, threw them down, and asked, "Who else bet the dice will lose?" Then, playing with the stack of bills, he added, "You know it's enough money here to burn a hole in a wet mule's ass. Want to raise the fifteen grand, Pee Wee? Why don't you add that new Eldorado you got parked out there?"

"Bet the fifteen grand, nigger," Pee Wee retorted. "If you win that, I'll send for enough cold cash to give your ass pneumonia."

"Goddamn," Moe whispered to Phil. "Man, we can take that shit off."

"Cool it, Moe. Watch the game," Phil whispered back.

Georgia Boy picked up the dice again to shoot across the pool table. When he did, the tension mounted.

"House man," Pee Wee broke in, "stick the dice to this country pimp, will you?"

"You scared of my hand, nigger?" Georgia Boy asked with a winner's smile. "I don't give a damn if Jesus sticks the dice. I'm gonna seven or eleven on your black ass for that fifteen grand."

"I can bet all you can stand to pick up, nigger. Just shake 'em and roll 'em."

The house stuck the dice to Georgia Boy. He caught them, gave a shake, and tossed them galloping down the table. One die stopped on three, the other hit the table's edge, rolled three times, spun during a tension-filled moment that seemed like hours, and stopped on four.

"Seven it is!" called the house man. "Fifteen thousand worth. Well, that broke the game."

Georgia Boy's big smile extended three inches beneath his wide-brimmed, velvet hat as he raked in the pile of impressive greens, all large bills.

Once he had it all, he asked, "You want to bet that Cadillac parked out front, Pee Wee?"

"No," Pee Wee said nonchalantly. "I'll bet you what's in it, for all you got."

Pee Wee was cool and calculating, not too far changed from the young boy who Phil used to hang around with during his earlier escapades. He was wearing the hell out of his expensive black silk suit. Now he was much too tall to be called Little Pee Wee, and with his smooth, black, handsome face, enhanced by his perfect thin frame, the Winkley's Modeling School would give top dollar for him.

"Kato," he said to his henchman, "take these keys and bring me two shopping bags from the trunk of my hog."

Kato, called such because he was swift and dangerous, responded like a Japanese servant. During his brief absence, everyone was in awe of how much money had been bet and won by Georgia Boy. In the midst of it all, Moe disappeared.

"I don't know where he went," Skinny replied to his inquiry.

"Phil," Pee Wee called to him from across the table.

"Hey, baby, I love you. I'm not speaking too tough to you now while you're taking care of business. Do what you got to do. We'll talk later!"

Kato returned, dramatically carrying two full shopping bags. Everyone watched as he handed them to Pee Wee. Pee Wee slowly dumped the contents of the table. The effect was staggering as at least one hundred thousand dollars in hundreds, tens, twenties and fifties were scattered on the table.

"Goddamn!" one spectator exclaimed.

"Son of a bitch. Never seen that much money in my fucking life!"

The fashion that it was done in was extremely colorful and typical Pennsylvania Avenue style, as only Pee Wee could execute.

"Bet that," he said to Georgia Boy, "against all that you got—your ride and ten of them ticky-time whores that you own."

Georgia was stupefied. He, too, had never seen that kind of money. Not wanting to be chumped out or outdone, he controlled the expression on his face and said, "Bet, goddammit!"

The house man gathered the dice, stuck them to Georgia Boy, and the game was on. It lasted one second. Georgia Boy shook the dice, released them, and out came craps. Everybody yelled it, "Craps!" There was silence. Everyone stared at Georgia Boy. His face was expressionless. He broke the silence with a loud, embarrassing fart. Everyone burst out laughing. It was a short laughter, interrupted by a lone masked gunman yelling, "All right, don't move!"

The bandit, masked with a stocking cap, meant business as he brandished a huge forty-five. They all lined up with their faces to the wall while he took money and stuffed it in the shopping bags.

In a flash, a gun went off. It was Kato who fired. Pieces of brains flew all over the craps table and stained the money.

In Phil's heart, he cried because poor Moe was dead before he hit the floor.

Kato scooped up the money and placed it in the bags, as the housemen lifted Moe's body, taking it towards the direction of the back alley of the gambling house.

Such was the code of the avenue that no one told. What had happened was fair. Moe was killed doing what he knew best—holding a stickup.

Phil had heard about various people being killed and being found in the alley. Although it was a common thing, when your friend was a victim of circumstances, it didn't balance in your mind as just one of those things that happened.

A young man came in with a pail of ammonia and water and began to wipe the floor where Moe's blood had stained it. He wiped it as if he were wiping up ketchup that had spilled from french fries.

Phil was standing there in a daze. The crowd was disbursing gradually. Phil couldn't believe what he had just witnessed. He was staring in Pee Wee's direction with an accusing expression on his face. "Phil, there was no other way, man." Pee Wee was looking at him with pleading eyes, which seemed to be saying, "You saw it, don't you understand?"

"Yeah, man," Phil said as he nodded and then he turned and walked outside, for he didn't want to be fingered as the one who was last seen with Moe. Yes, they were old friends, but this was a matter of his freedom.

He drove home because he was very nervous that night. As he arrived home, he poured a small glass of Scotch and drank it. It felt like every cell in his body was on fire. He prepared for bed, hoping that he would soon fall asleep. He tossed and turned for almost an hour, then he got up and went outside on the steps and smoked nearly a pack of cigarettes while sipping from the Johnny Walker Red bottle. As he sat there drinking and smoking, he felt himself getting into a stupor. He went inside and fell fast asleep.

That night he had a terrible dream, with nightmares coming at him from every direction. He dreamed that Popcorn was walking down the avenue and laughing and kidding the rest of the old gang. "You guys thought that policeman had killed me when he shot me on the street, but I fooled all of you, didn't I? Look at me, I ain't dead and I've never been dead. You all thought I was, though. I even had a fake funeral. Ha ... ha ... ha ... ha." Then Popcorn took Gumbo's hand and walked up to Pee Wee and Phil. "Come on, man, let's show 'em that we ain't dead."

Gumbo looked at Phil and pumped his hand up and down. "Man, when are you coming to see me? I miss you. Moe came to see me last night, and he said you'd be coming to see me soon. You and Pee Wee come to see us and we'll be the same old gang again—all together. Look, here comes Moe now." As Phil looked around, Moe was holding out his hand with blood all over it.

Phil woke up screaming. He sat up in bed with perspiration as big as mothballs rolling off him. He couldn't believe that he had just dreamed about all of his dead friends. The worst of it all was that Gumbo, who had been dead for ten years, was telling him to come to see him soon. Phil felt as if he were going to vomit. Reflecting further on what Gumbo had said scared him even more. For he said that Moe told him that he would be coming soon. He rubbed his chest and face as he thought that might be an omen. *Am I doing to die soon?* he thought. He tried to go back to sleep, but the only thing he thought about was that he was going to die. He finally drifted off to sleep.

The next morning, Phil got up early; he hadn't slept very much, anyway. He walked to the corner store and purchased a newspaper. He thought that he would read about Moe's death. As he scanned the paper, he didn't see any article concerning it. He'd hoped that someone had found him before that morning.

Several days later, Phil attended Moe's funeral. It was a quiet funeral. The funeral home was jammed with people from the avenue and his family. Phil was thankful that Pee Wee had paid for the funeral. He had overheard some ladies whispering in the back of the funeral home that an unknown friend had taken care of the funeral expenses for the family.

As the short minister began to raise his voice with the same old funeral ritual jargon, Phil got lost in his thoughts of how Moe looked and acted as they had gotten into mischief on the avenue. He tuned out all the other things that were being said because he wanted to remember Moe for the good times and the happy times they had shared together.

Chapter 21

A few days after Moe's funeral, Phil received a card from the Model Cities' Halfway House, asking him to come down for a final interview.

The main office was on Gay Street in the Prisoner's Aid Office, and the work site would be on East Lanvale Street. Four people, besides Phil, were called for a final interview, and they all had to be interviewed by a board of mostly ex-offenders. Most of them knew him and his sincerity in dealing with people. One board member in particular, whom they called Cocky, came out to the waiting area, saw Phil, and said, "Damn, Phil, if you are here for the interview, you got it!"

That was it. They interviewed him and gave him the job.

Working at 310 East Lanvale Street not only became his job, it was his way of life. He ate, worked, slept and dreamed of the center, twenty-four hours a day. Never in his life had he become so involved in such meaningful work.

It was a pure delight to have on staff and as his boss positive-minded ex-offenders who were sharing their experiences with younger offenders who needed to know there was something more positive to do than go in and out of prison.

Tango, an ex-offender who served ten years and knew how to relate to all ex-offenders, was his boss. His philosophy was "Counsel all the time."

Cocky was the senior counselor, an ex-loafer who had served nine years with him. He was positive and more effective than any psychiatrist. Then there was Lawrence, a dedicated counselor and ex-offender with a manner of speaking that would make anyone stop and listen. Big Red was the oldest—about fifty and quite worldly. Then there was Little John. Collectively, they had put together one of the strongest programs for an offender or ex-offender in the city.

The program was structurally tight and sound. The residents of the program received benefits that they had never received while incarcerated. Once Phil remembered Tango trying to reach a young resident who had been in and out of prison for years. The fellow was twenty-five, a slick, hustling pimp whose greatest goal in life was to hustle girls on the street and invest the money in dope for distribution.

"Man," the young guy was telling Tango, "you can't tell me nothing. I ain't working for nobody 'cause I'm the best hustler out here."

"Yes," Tango replied, gazing at him seriously, "but you keep ending up in jail."

"All hustlers take a fall now and then."

"But what do you have to show for it?"

"So I blowed it on lawyers. What the hell? I'll make it back hustling."

Tango patiently looked at the young fellow, obviously feeling sympathy for him. "Man," he said, "I've been in the joint myself for a long while and I know that they make you work in there or lock your ass up in solitary confinement. How is it that you can work in one of those joints for two years at forty cents a day and can't work out here for twenty dollars a day?"

"Well," the resident stuttered, "I—I—"

"I my ass," Tango interrupted. "Let me tell you something. Do you know the greatest pimp that ever lived? It's the state prison system. It pimps your black flesh for three or four years, gives you forty cents a day, makes a million off your black ass in those state-used shops and private farms, and then brags about what a good whore you are. Yes, I said whore. You ain't no pimp. You are a whore. You have a whore's mentality any time you constantly place yourself in a position to keep going in and out of prison to be sold, used and abused every day, year after year. You think about that. Then maybe you'll come up with the fact that the slickest thing you can do is get a job." The young guy walked away from Tango speechless, but with much on his mind.

It was this type of counseling that they as ex-offenders had to offer the residents who came into the program. They were to stay fourteen weeks, in which time it was their job to reach them mentally and help them function crime-free in society. They dealt with them from ages eighteen to thirty-five. As time passed, they were developing a track record of being able to reconstruct effectively negative thoughts, consequently preventing people from returning to prison.

Phil was working with Johnny Wilson, a young man of twenty-three. Phil thought that he could talk to anybody, and one would listen to him as long as he used logical reasoning and not authoritative reasoning. With all of this positive thinking, Johnny somehow got next to him. He had been working with Johnny for one month. He thought that he had Johnny ready to go out on his own, and ready to think positively about working extra hard, although the pay was below the normal rate of a dollar fifty an hour.

Johnny would sit and stare at Phil and agree with him as they had various conferences. For example, just before Johnny's last week at the halfway house, Tango came over to him after he had left. "Phil, my man, I hate to discourage you, but you're fighting a losing battle. That M.F. will be back in the joint before two months are up."

Phil interrupted, "Man, don't put the bad mouth on the dude. He just has to get his head on straight."

"Get his head on straight," echoed Tango. "That M.F. is a lazy S.O.B. He ain't gonna work if somebody paid him fifty dollars an hour, let alone a dollar an hour."

Phil responded, "Man, I'm going to try harder. I believe I can reach him. Look at Westley, I reached him. Now look how well he's doing at C.C.B. He's making some damned good grades, too. I've got a feeling that if I can keep shooting positive vibes, I'll reach him."

Tango said, "The hell with positive vibes. That sucker is gonna 'positive vibes' a stickup. You'll see, man. I've been out here longer than you have, and I know those who will strive to do better. And I know those who ain't gonna do shit."

Phil looked at Tango with a little disgusted expression. "Well, I'm going to keep trying, although you may be right. I'm going to work harder with him."

Tango threw up his hands as he walked away. "Don't say I didn't warn you."

Vonnie went to see Phil later that evening. He was so worked up over what Tango had said that he wasn't very good company at first. Vonnie asked, "Phil, what's wrong? You had a run-in with your supervisor or something? You've been like a 'half-ass' wild tiger ever since I arrived. Of course, we both know that ain't you, now is it?"

Phil told her the whole story. Then he looked at her and

pulled her close to him and smiled. "You're right about my acting like a . . . what kind of tiger?" They both laughed.

Vonnie sighed and said, "Phil, if you can't reach him, just think of those who you have helped and those others who you plan to help."

That night after Vonnie left, Phil read a few chapters of *Positive Thinking*. He was determined that he was going to reach Johnny somehow. He could hardly sleep for thinking of things he was going to discuss with Johnny.

The next morning, Phil arrived at the center early. He went up to Johnny's room, but he wasn't there. Phil thought, *Oh, hell, what could have happened to him? He knew perfectly well that they must return each night for the first month of their parole.*

He walked down the stairs, not wanting to tell anybody what he had just discovered, although he knew that he must make a report if Johnny hadn't signed the roster stating his leaving time. Just as he went to sit down to try to think how he could help Johnny from getting into serious trouble, one of the counselors came in and said, "How's everything?" They talked about Johnny and how he should be put on strict duties. Then the counselor signed his time-card and went to the next building.

Phil was sitting there somewhat puzzled by Johnny's absence when his thoughts were interrupted by two white policemen. One asked, "Who's the director here?"

Phil replied, "I'm one of the assistants. May I—"

The tall one interrupted, "I said 'director.' I don't wanna talk to no aide."

Phil felt a surge of anger coming over him, but he thought quickly. *Must think positive, for these S.O.B.'s can't deal with it.* "Yes, I heard what you said, but I'm in charge here this morning. Is there anything that you wish to discuss with me? I'll do my best to assist you."

The older one looked at the other one and said, "We have got to follow rules and procedures. We might as well talk with him for the sake of completing our report."

The little one nodded and said, "Okay."

Then he looked at Phil and said, "Uh, do you have a young man who lives here by the name of Johnny Wilson?"

Phil felt as if he had been splashed in the face with a bucket of urine. "Uh—uh, yes . . . he lives here. What's wrong?"

The tall one said, "He's in the hospital at Union Memorial. He was shot in an armed robbery attempt."

Phil couldn't believe what he heard. His mouth was open wide. He finally said, "Is he all right?"

"If you mean whether he's dead or alive, he is barely alive." Then he asked for Phil's signature on the report. He looked at Phil and said, "We'll be getting in touch with the center later on."

Just as they were leaving, Tango walked in. They looked at him and walked out. Phil didn't want to tell Tango because he might say, "I told you so." Nevertheless, he told him what the policemen had said.

Tango said, throwing both hands in the air, "You can't say that it is a surprise, now can ya?" Phil didn't say anything. They sat there in silence while Tango took long drags on a cigarette.

Phil finally said, "I'm going to the hospital."

Tango said, "Pull his file first and see who is the closest relative and try to contact him while you are out there."

Phil walked inside the hospital feeling as if a heavy burden was weighing on his shoulders. He kept hearing what Tango had said about Johnny. It was almost as if Tango had walked every step of the way with him. "I told you so" kept ringing in his head—"I told you so, Phil."

Phil walked inside and over to the receptionist's desk. "May I help you, sir?" she asked.

"Yes, what room is Johnny Wilson in?"

"Sir, I'm sorry, but he is not permitted to have any visitors unless they are his immediate family—for instance, his mother, father, brother, sister. Are you his brother?"

Phil was tempted to lie. He started to say that he was his brother, then he thought, *I'd better tell the truth.* "No, I'm the assistant director from the halfway house, and Mr. Wilson has been assigned to me for rehabilitation counseling. I need to see him in order to make an official report to the parole board." Phil couldn't believe himself—how his lie sounded so professional.

The receptionist looked half-puzzled, not really knowing what to do. She said, "I think I'd better ask someone else to give you permission, sir. I'm afraid that I'm not authorized to permit you." She walked into another office.

In two or three minutes, a nurse came out. "Sir, we have orders not to let anyone in to see Mr. Wilson."

"Yes, this lady told me that. As I told her, I'm his counselor from the halfway house. When he was released, he was placed in my custody. Therefore, I need to see him in order to make an official report to his relatives and the parole board."

The nurse looked at Phil, and then she looked at the manila envelope in his hand. She said, "I guess you can go up then, if that is the case. First you must sign this form and show us some identification." Phil completed the form and gave it to her. "You may go up to room two hundred and one and present this pass."

"Thank you, ma'am."

Phil walked up the stairs to the second floor. He felt that there was some good in Johnny regardless, and he hoped that he would be able to tell him why he had committed the crime.

As Phil walked up to room two hundred and one, the policeman at the door said, "I'm sorry, we have orders not to let anyone go in." Phil showed him the written pass. The policeman then questioned him. Phil told him who he was and then he said, "Okay, I guess it's all right for you to go in. You can only stay five minutes. That's the limit for his mother and any other member of his family, so I was told."

Phil nodded his head as if to say, "I understand."

When Phil walked into the room, Johnny was lying very still, with tubes running from every direction. A nurse entered the room and said, "I'm afraid that he can't have any visitors at the moment. Besides, he will still be under sedation for another two or three hours."

Phil asked, "What is his condition?"

"Sir, I'm afraid to say at this moment. As of now, he's still on the critical list."

Phil asked again, "You say that it'll be about two or three hours before I can see him?"

"It may be longer than that. It's hard to say just how long it's going to be. It might take the entire day before he'll be able to speak to you."

"In that case," Phil said, "I'll be back this afternoon."

"That would be a better time, sir."

Phil walked several blocks and caught the bus to Biddle Street on the east side. He got off the bus and walked six blocks to Milton Avenue. He knocked on the door, but there was no answer. He knocked again. Finally, he heard a window being raised above his head. "Who's that down there?" a voice asked.

"Ma'am, I'm looking for Mrs. Georgia Fields, because I have some news for her concerning Johnny Wil—"

She interrupted him, "Boy, what you mean, some news about my Johnny? I just saw him yesterday. I'm his grandmother. Go around to the back door and let yourself in and come on upstairs. I can't walk."

Phil walked up the stairs. He couldn't believe the condition which this lady's leg was in. It was swollen, with sores covering it. She had it propped up in a chair. "Sit here, son. What kind of news do you have about my Johnny?" Phil didn't know how to start. He looked at her hesitantly. "Come on, boy," she raised her voice. "I ain't got all day."

Phil felt relieved, for this was one strong old lady. She would not fall to pieces. He told her the news about Johnny. She shook her head and grunted. "He did it all for me ..."

Phil said, "Ma'am?"

"I said he did it all for me. He told me yesterday morning that he was going to help me get the money for the operation that I need on this here leg. Lawd, I didn't know my boy was gonna get himself into trouble just for me. 'Cause I ain't got long here, and I'll be gone on to glory."

Phil could feel a big relief within his mind. Johnny had done a wrong thing, but he did it for a cause. He asked, "Mrs. Fields, can you get some help from the city so you can get that operation on your leg?"

She said, "I reckon I could, but I ain't gonna turn over my property to them. This is all I got to give my Johnny when I die. So those folks told me that they can't give me no help as far as paying my hospital bill. I told Johnny what they had said. That's when he told me that he'll help get the money. But I thought that he was talking about a job and all. I didn't think that he was going to rob again, after being in prison for three whole years. I sure didn't want him to do that for me." Finally, she broke down and began to cry.

Phil could feel only sympathy for her, because he would have done the same for his grandmother if he had been in Johnny's shoes. "Mrs. Fields, is there anything that I can do for you?"

"Go downstairs, son, and make me a pot of black coffee 'cause I need something to calm my nerves."

Phil ran downstairs and made a pot of coffee. He yelled

up, "Mrs. Fields, do you want any sugar and cream?"

"Naw, son, just black coffee." She had calmed down when Phil reached the top of the stairs. "God bless you, son," she said as she reached for the coffee. "Are you going to see my Johnny this evening?"

"Yes, ma'am, I'm going to see him later on."

"You tell him that I'm praying for him, and I didn't know that he was going to get in trouble just for me. And tell him I'm gonna sell this here house and get him a good lawyer to help get him out. I made up my mind a few minutes ago that I must help my Johnny."

"I don't think Johnny would want you—'

She interrupted, "Boy, don't tell me what Johnny would want. This is what I want, you hear?"

"Yes, ma'am." Phil was ready to go after that. "Mrs. Fields, is there anything else I can do for you before I leave?"

"On your way out, take out the garbage, please."

"Yes, ma'am. I'll be back to see you, Mrs. Fields, and let you know how Johnny is getting along."

"Wait, son, I got so worked up when you told me that you had some news about Johnny, I forgot to find out what your name is and how you came to know my Johnny."

"Oh, didn't I introduce myself? I'm Phil Avery. I am Johnny's counselor down at the halfway house where he was living. I have been in prison also, but now I'm working with parolees, trying to keep them from going back to prison."

"So that's how you know my Johnny? Son, you don't look like you've been to prison. How long did you say?"

"Nine years too long."

"Ump, I guess you can tell them young fellows how it is, then, can't you?"

Phil smiled and said, "Yes, ma'am. Mrs. Fields, you take care of yourself, and I'll tell Johnny that I talked with you."

"God bless you, my son. Now, you tell Johnny what I told

you to tell him, you hear?"

"Yes, ma'am." He then walked down the steps and carried the garbage out with him.

That afternoon, Phil walked into Johnny's room. He was lying there half-awake. "Johnny, Johnny, can you hear me?" Johnny opened his eyes and looked at Phil with a long stare. It was almost like he could read Phil's mind.

"I—I ... am sorry, man ... I ... did ... it for ... Grandma."

Phil looked at him and said, "She told me all about it. How do you feel?"

"I—I'm ... floating, man ... I'm ... floating."

"Johnny, I'll be back tomorrow to see you. Get some rest and save your strength."

"O—kay, Phil ..."

One month later, Phil and Johnny were sitting in court. His grandmother had lived up to her word. She had gotten him one of the best criminal lawyers in Baltimore City, or in that sense, the state of Maryland.

Johnny looked at Phil and said, "I'm sorry that I let you and the program down. Like I said, it had to be. I had to do what I did. It seemed like the only way then."

Phil put his arms around him and said, "I understand, man. Every man deserves a second chance."

"Do me a favor, man?"

"Sure, what is it?"

"Go by those projects on Caroline and Orlean, and tell Grandma the sentence that they gave me and that I'm sorry that she sold her house just for me."

"Okay," said Phil. The guards came and motioned Johnny to end his conversation. He and Phil embraced without saying a word, for they had experienced that feeling before.

Needless to say, Phil loved his job with a passion. It was what he was totally about—most definitely one of his main goals. Without question, he decided to dedicate his life to the concepts of the center, come rain or shine.

Two years can bring about a lot of changes. It can take the sun away and bring on the rain. It did nothing to dampen Phil's love for Vickie. They remained lovers and friends, using as much discretion as possible. Because they had retained their close relationship, they always shared their problems and personal struggles.

Such was the time when they had breakfast at Sess on Wilson and Division Streets. The problem this time was the situation with Model Cities cutting the program's funds.

The waitress, Miss Rose, just served them waffles and eggs, tea and toast. Vickie sipped her tea, and with concern and some apprehension, asked, "Phil, what are you going to do?"

"All I know, Vickie, is that I am not a quitter. I love this job. I feel that the bastards are deliberately cutting this program because it is really helping young black men to stay out of prison."

"Phil, I'm not in love with the Nixon Administration, either, but I can't see them cutting federal funds deliberately to hurt programs such as yours."

"Vickie, let me tell you something, darling. All of these programs were appeasement programs to begin with, you know that. You demonstrated and fought for anti-poverty and self-help programs. They never wanted to give the money in the first place. But because of the pressure and mass demonstrations, the enlightenment of leaders such as my man, Malcolm X and Martin Luther King, they reluctantly gave appeasement money to black programs all over the nation. But the money was given for a small period of time, only to appease and not to achieve. Our program has shown great achievements, as many others have, and in the midst of our progress, they cut us back. It is designed to fail, and any program that looks as if it will survive will be financially wiped out."

"Phil, that may be a concise analysis of the program, but what do you personally intend to do? Does this mean that you'll become frustrated and return to crime? If you return to prison, I'm a walking dead woman."

"It could mean that for an awful lot of people, but not me. I'm going to be positive. I'm going to make it. I want to save this program. Vickie, I don't give up on anything; you know that by now. I just wish your husband would give you up."

They both laughed.

Continuing, Phil said his little ten-word, two-letter riddle, "If it is to be, it is up to me."

"I like that," Vickie said cheerfully. "Phil, for God's sake, stay strong. Don't end up again like your friend, Little Pee Wee."

"Yeah, I heard that he received eight years for drug distribution."

"Do you really believe that he had a hundred thousand dollars to pay F. Lee Bailey?"

Remembering the change he dumped on the gambling table, Phil said, "Yes, I believe it."

Phil thought about Little Pee Wee and the life of crime he had dedicated himself to. Sometimes he wondered if the system was trying to give an invisible license to commit crimes by forcing unbearable economic conditions. Certainly, the individuals without a positive mental frame of mind didn't have a chance to survive unless they lived under humiliating circumstances or committed crimes.

"Vickie," he said reflectively, "a lot of people are going to commit crimes before all of this budget-cutting is over. I am not sure if I'll be one of them or not."

They finished breakfast, kissed politely, and went to their respective jobs.

Chapter 22

Ruby was lying in her hospital bed, not wanting Phil to see her condition. She thought she'd better get in touch with him, since she hadn't heard from him in three weeks. She asked the nurse to dial the number and tell him that she was in the hospital.

Phil was writing a new proposal at his desk when the telephone rang and interrupted his thoughts. He answered, "Yes, this is he. What? What is the matter with her? Is it serious?"

The nurse said, "I'm afraid I can't give out any more information, Mr. Avery. Perhaps you'll have to come to see for yourself."

Phil replaced the receiver down and stared into space for a moment or two. He couldn't believe that Ruby was in the hospital very ill, for she had always been so full of life. She never looked as if she had anything wrong with her. He told one of the staff members to take charge while he went to the hospital to see a very sick friend.

Ruby asked the nurse to comb her hair and put some lipstick on her lips because her friend would be there soon. Even though Ruby knew that she looked frail, she couldn't bear to let Phil see her without her makeup. The nurse held the mirror up to her face, and she gave a faint smile, nodded, and said, "Thank you very much."

Phil arrived at the hospital, and he couldn't wait to get to her room. After getting on the elevator and pushing the fourth floor's button, he thought about flowers. He pressed the first floor's button and went to the gift shop. He purchased a beautiful bouquet of flowers. He knew that these flowers would help cheer up Ruby. He felt as if he just couldn't face her as she lay in that bed sick, for she had always been very youthful acting with him.

He walked into the room, and Ruby's eyes met his. He smiled and went over and kissed her on the forehead. She smiled back and said, "Hi." Her voice sounded very weak, which frightened him.

"Ruby, how are you feeling?"

"Tough, Phil," she said. "I don't know whether or not I'm going to make it."

"Sho-o-o-d," said Phil. "Don't talk like that. Of course you are going to be all right."

She threw her head to one side and looked down. Phil knew that something terrible must be wrong with her, but he wanted her to tell him on her own terms. He said, "You are looking lovely, as always." She smiled and squeezed his hand lightly.

As he opened his mouth to say something, Ruby's sister walked in. She began to joke and say silly things to make Ruby laugh. Phil could see that Ruby was in much pain. Then the nurse came in and said, "I'm afraid Mrs. Mason has to have some rest now." She gave Ruby two pills. Phil and her sister both kissed Ruby and told her they would see her later.

Walking down the corridor, Phil asked the sister, "What's wrong with Ruby?"

She looked at Phil and began to dab her tearful eyes. "My sister is dying, Phil. She's dying of cancer." Phil stopped in the middle of the corridor as if he'd been struck by lightning. He couldn't move or believe what he had just heard. He was just staring at her with his mouth open. He wanted to hit her and say, "You take that back; it isn't true." She looked at him as she wiped her eyes with tissues.

He said, "You can't mean that."

"Yes, yes, it's true. It's only a matter of time, a week or two or a month or more."

Phil said, "Oh, Lord, no."

As he and the sister embraced, trying to console each other's hurt, people were passing and looking at them with sympathetic eyes. They walked and talked for fifteen minutes before they were ready to depart. Phil gave her his telephone number and told her to call any time there was a change in Ruby's condition. She promised she would. They departed, both looking very sad.

He went back to the center, knowing that he could not do any more work. He just couldn't think straight. He thought about one thing and then another.

He knew that he and Ruby would never be together again, at least on this earth.

The secretary walked in as he sat staring into space. "Everything all right, Mr. Avery?"

"Well, I don't know, really. I have a friend who is in the hospital, very ill, and I'm kind of worried."

She looked at him very sympathetically and said, "I understand." Then she dashed out of the office.

He went home early. For the life of him, he just couldn't believe what was happening. He looked at pictures that he and Ruby had taken in New York, Atlantic City and the Poçonos. He just sat there staring at them, because the pictures he saw that day were so full of life.

The next day he had to see Ruby again. He headed for the hospital, thinking of a million things he was going to say to her. When he got there, he was all surprised to see her daughter and husband sitting by her bed. His feathers were ruffled because he wanted to talk with Ruby in private. He hadn't thought of her family, especially her husband. He walked in slowly, because he didn't want to make them nervous. Ruby, looking even weaker, looked up at Phil and smiled a little. Then the husband and daughter greeted him cordially. Her sister was feeding her slowly.

Ruby was so ladylike. She motioned for her sister to wipe some food particles from the corner of her lips. Even then, she wanted to look her best. He smiled at her and thought, *She knows what I'm thinking*. He reached over and squeezed her hand to try to convey a message of love to her. He knew that he could never tell her how glad he was that they were friends, and how much he appreciated her helping him.

She must have known what he was thinking, for she looked at him and blinked her eyes in a manner in which to say, *I know what you're thinking*.

He said softly, "I'll see you soon, Ruby. Get well."

Ruby said to him, "Bye, Phil. Take care." It was in such a whisper that it scared the living hell out of him. He turned and walked out, giving a glance towards her as he reached the door. He had a funny feeling that he would not see her anymore.

He was in a staff meeting that afternoon with three assistants when the secretary interrupted, "Phil, you have an urgent telephone call." Phil stopped what he was doing and walked slowly into the next office. He knew it was over for Ruby.

"Hel—Hello," he stammered out.

It was Ruby's sister, crying hysterically. "Sh—She is gone . . . Phil. Sh—She's gone."

"When?"

"This afternoon at one twenty."

Phil couldn't move. "Don't cry . . . You know she wouldn't want you to make yourself sick." He found himself babbling. "I'll see you later tonight, okay?"

She said, "Okay," and hung up.

The funeral was two days later. Phil arrived at the funeral home early and sat looking at Ruby. He thought, *She looks as if she is sleeping*. He felt very numb. His heart felt as if it were trying to wedge through his throat.

Finally, the director touched Phil on the shoulder. "Sir, you'll have to move now. The family is getting ready to come in."

Phil wanted to lash out and say, "I'm family, too." He slowly moved to the rear of the funeral home and sat listening to the eulogy. He couldn't take it any longer. He eased out of the side door and drove to Druid Hill Park.

He sat there looking at the lake for hours, thinking of so many things. First, his mother, then Dr. McKay, Gumbo, Popcorn, Moe, and now, Ruby. All of his loved ones were slipping away from him. He couldn't stand all of this. He had to talk to someone. *Vickie,* he thought. She'd understand what he was feeling, although he couldn't tell her everything. She would still understand his feelings. He finally drove to his apartment and called Vickie.

Chapter 23

The center received a notice stating that as of March 9, 1972, it would be closed. The entire staff were sitting around discussing the situation and venting their frustrations.

"Ain't that a bitch," Cocky was saying as they all sat in the office, stunned by the news. "We are doing one of the most effective jobs in the country in fighting crimes, and they are closing us down right in the middle of our prime."

"Programs," Big Red said angrily, "are designed to fail. The bastards didn't want us to succeed. This program did more for me than it did for many of the residents. I haven't shot no dope in three years because I knew that I had to be a role model for these guys we counsel." He paused for a moment, then added, "Under the circumstances, I may shoot some more dope. I don't know."

"That ain't the way to look at it, Big Red," Phil counseled.

"Well, what are we going to do?" Little John asked.

"We can't work without money," Tango interjected. "I know the white boys at prisoner's aid are going to pull out."

Tango was referring to the director and assistant director who controlled the money and met the expenses.

"Well," Phil said, "if we believe in what we are all about, why don't we hang in here and do the shit out of it for pure dedication?"

"Hey, man," Cocky said, "that is what we are all about. We got thirteen young men who depend on us to be strong, and if we close now, these guys are going back to prison, sure as hell."

Cocky looked at everyone for a moment and said, "Phil, since you decided that we'll hang in here, why don't we make you the director?"

"Good idea," Tango said approvingly.

At this approval, everyone else joined in, and Phil was made the official, unpaid director.

Phil's first task was to change the program's name and become incorporated, which he managed through a lawyer, Charles P. Howe, who donated his services. When he explained to him what his intentions were, he said, "Phil, this is a monumental task, but it will work." The encouraging thing he would always remember was that he gave the community residence center its first donation of cash.

His second task—visiting the Model Cities headquarters—was urgent because their eviction date had been announced and the movers had been sent to the program to pick up the furniture and clean out the building.

"Wait a minute," Phil said angrily to the rude movers who attempted to remove a typewriter from the secretary while it was in use. "Just hold off for one half hour. I am going to city hall to speak with officials to see if we can hold on to the furniture."

"Look," the mover in charge said, "we got orders to move.

Once they give us orders, they don't change their minds. But if you want to go down there and try, we'll wait a half hour."

He rushed to his car and was in the Model Cities Agency within eight minutes. The office complex was huge and located in the city hall building, a place that he had never visited. The very presence of the huge building frightened and awed him, but he didn't care. By now, Phil was quite angry and determined.

He thought, *Maybe I look a bit impressive with my briefcase and three-piece suit as I approach receptionist number one.*

"I'd like to speak to the Executive Director, Mr. Sky." His voice was firm and business-like.

"Do you have an appointment?"

"No, this is urgent. There is no time for an appointment."

She was tempted to refuse him, but something prompted her to say nothing. She indicated a direction with the wave of her arm to another receptionist twenty feet behind her.

Phil's approach was the same with the second receptionist. "My name is Phillip Avery. I'd like to speak to Mr. Sky."

"Sorry," she answered automatically, "Mr. Sky does not see people without an appointment."

"Look, Miss, I don't have an appointment. My situation is urgent, and I want to talk to someone right now."

His voice was intensified in sound, and he was not conscious of its loudness.

"Sir, I'm sorry, but you cannot see Mr. Sky. His assistant, Mrs. Elva, is here, but she, too, does not see people without appointments."

"Miss, I work at one of your programs that is closing today. I am concerned, and I want to talk to someone in charge."

"Sir, for the third time, you cannot—"

"I'll speak to the young man," a melodic, concerned voice interrupted. "Send him to my office."

"Yes, Mrs. Elva," the receptionist replied. "Mrs. Elva, the associate director, will see you, sir. Right this way."

She directed him to a large office just across from where she sat in the receptionist's area.

The lady sitting behind the long desk had large, soft, concerned eyes. She was very attractive, about forty, and was dressed in a stylish business suit which complemented her distinguished position.

"How may I help you, young man?"

Again her voice was warm and concerned, also authoritative.

"Mrs. Elva," he hesitated, calming himself, "my name is Phillip Avery. I work for the Model Cities' Community Residence Center at 310 East Lanvale Street. I believe in what I am doing; so does the staff. We want to keep working even though we know you have orders to withdraw the money. All I'm asking is that you give me permission to use the furniture and equipment in the building and let me know who owns the building."

She leaned back comfortably in her seat, as if to let what she had heard sink in. "Young man, do I understand you to say that you want to run that program without money or salary?"

"Yes, ma'am."

"You just want to use the furniture and you want the name of the owner of the building?"

"Yes, ma'am."

At this point, she looked at him as if she was trying to decide whether he was crazy or ignorant. "Do you know that it takes one hundred thousand dollars a year to run that program?"

"Yes, ma'am."

"And you are going to run it anyway?"

"I intend to, if we can keep the furniture."

"Young man, if you are that insane, I am insane enough to grant you that permission."

"Elated" wasn't the word to describe his feelings. What he felt had no adjective that could describe it. The program that he was to devote his life to had a chance.

"Mrs. Elva ... thank you! Thank you! Thank you!"

She reached into a file, retrieved a property list, and had him sign that he would be responsible for all property at 310 East Lanvale Street. Also, she gave him the property owner's name. She called the center, at his request, and had the movers return the furniture, which they had by now placed on the truck.

Noticing his elation, she smiled warmly as one would at a determined fool with a million problems that he would overcome.

"Good luck, young man," she said as he went out of the door.

When Phil returned to the center, he was the hero of the hour. The staff thought that he could do anything and were ready to follow.

The struggle was on. The next few months proved to be the test of true character. Many of the counselors became discouraged. Their spirits dwindled, and one by one they began to slip back into the hands of their old weaknesses—drugs, alcohol and crime. It was extremely disheartening for Phil to watch, even more so for the young residents who idolized them. Soon all of them left to return to a life of drugs, alcohol and crime. Cocky remained strong for as long as he could. He slipped a few times, pulled himself together and found employment.

Chapter 24

Having worked all day without anything to eat, Phil was very tired and hungry. He had thought about calling Vickie to see if she could meet him for a late dinner. Hoping she was still at work, he dialed her number. Just his luck; she was gone for the day. He decided to work a couple more hours at the center before leaving for the day. As he worked trying to complete all of that day's tasks, he was interrupted by a knock on the door. "Yeah?" he called out, thinking it was one of the parolees.

"Phil, are you in there?" It was Cynthia.

"Yeah."

"I've got to talk with you."

Phil was at the door as if lightning had struck him. "Hey, lady, what are you doing here this evening?" She stepped in where the light was shining on her face. "Cindy, who did that? Tango?"

"Who else? He beat me mercilessly last night, Phil. I called the police and had him locked up."

"What? You mean he's in jail?"

"Yeah, he is in jail, and I want you to go with me to get him out."

Phil didn't know what to do or say. He felt that he was being dragged into the middle of World War III. "Sure, Cindy. You want to go now?"

"Yeah, if you can leave now."

"Okay," he said, as he began straightening things. "Let's go."

They had to wait for two hours before all the papers were in order for Tango's release. Cindy was somewhat nervous. She felt that Tango was going to beat her for having him locked up, for he definitely didn't need any more data on his records. Phil looked at Cynthia's face and squeezed her hand.

"Phil, I'm scared." Her voice was trembling. "I—I'm scared that Tango will beat me again tonight."

"I don't think he will, Cindy."

"Phil, please talk to him for me, okay?"

"Okay, I'll talk to him, Cindy," said Phil, knowing that Tango would tell him to stay out of his business. He thought quickly. *Although I think Tango will tell me where to go fast, I'm not sure my talking will do any good.*

As they were talking, the sergeant at the desk called, "Ms. Davis."

Cynthia looked up with a jerk of her head. "Come on, Phil," she said as she pulled his arm for him to come along with her.

"Ma'am, you must sign these papers before the gentleman can be released." She signed the papers and looked as if she had signed her life away, because she knew that Tango would be facing her at any minute. She then looked at Phil with that same worried look.

Tango was brought out to where they were standing. He looked at her and kept walking. He didn't speak to either Phil or Cynthia. The sergeant looked at them and hunched his shoulders. He had noticed the reaction of Tango as he walked by them and out of the door.

Phil and Cynthia hurried to catch up with him. He was walking down the street as if he were going to put out a fire. They caught up with him and walked along beside him, not saying a word. Phil was hungry and tired. He certainly didn't want to walk a couple of miles playing catch-up with Tango. Phil thought he would make the first move to break the ice. "Say, Tango, let's take a cab, man. This walking ain't where it's at."

"Do what you wanna do. You ain't with me, 'cause I'm by myself."

Cynthia sped up her steps and walked along beside him. "Tango, baby, come on and let's go home. We can work things out. I know we can. We have always worked things out before."

Phil was hoping that Tango would reconcile with Cynthia and go home, so that he could get free of the intruding feeling that he had.

"Get away from me before I knock the hell out of you," said Tango.

Cynthia started crying. "Please come home," she said as she grabbed his arm.

Tango pulled away from her like she had leprosy. "Get your damned hands off me! I don't want you ever to touch me, bitch! You'll never have to call the police for me as long as you breathe, understand?"

"Tango, I didn't mean to call the police. I did it because you were hurting me. You were trying to kill me with your fists. That's why I called them, baby. Please forgive me; I didn't mean to do it." She was crying and in half-hysterics.

People were staring as they passed by.

Phil said, "Tango, let's all go home and talk about it."

"Man, stay out of this. This ain't your bag, dig?"

"Okay. Okay," said Phil, and threw up his hands as he walked beside Tango.

"You can take that bitch and go to west hell if you want to, because I ain't going no damned where with her."

Phil looked at Cynthia and felt sorry for her, she was crying so pitifully. "Cynthia, come on and let me take you home. We are fighting a losing battle for the time being."

Several days passed, and he had only talked with Cynthia once. He called her that afternoon. She sounded so depressed. "Cynthia, how are things going?"

"Phil, I don't know. Tango came knocking on the door at five o'clock this morning. He was all fired up, man. He had taken some heavy stuff. He crawled in bed, cursing me and calling me everything he could possibly think of. When I left for work this morning, he was still asleep. And I don't know where he is now. I see some of his clothes are gone."

"He'll come around, Cynthia. Just give him time to forget a little." They talked on for a few minutes, discussing Tango. Finally, Phil hung up the telephone and thought deeply. He wondered whether or not Tango was going back to Cynthia because he was one of those persons who felt that if someone had done him wrong, that was it. Besides, Tango had never bothered with the hard stuff before; this must have gotten next to him more than he let on.

Working in his office the following day, Phil was interrupted by the secretary. "There's a call for you from Ms. Cynthia Davis."

Phil immediately thought that Tango had beaten her again. "Hello, Cindy, what can I do for you?"

"Phil, come quickly. I can't wake Tango up. I think he has taken an overdose."

"I'll be right there."

When Phil arrived, Tango was spread-eagled on the floor, as naked as a newborn baby. Cynthia seemed a little embarrassed. "Phil, he came in last night and took his clothes off and slept here on the floor like this. I had some errands to run this morning, so I thought he would be up about the time I returned." Phil stooped down and looked at the pupils of Tango's eyes. Then he felt his pulse. "Phil, you think I should call an ambulance?"

"Let's see what we can do first. I'm going to try to revive him. Run a tub of cold water."

They put Tango in the cold water. He flinched a little. They slapped his face over and over as he sat there in the water. Finally, they got a little response. Phil took him out, and Cynthia dried him as Phil held him up. Cynthia got a robe, and she and Phil struggled to get him in it.

"Let's walk him," said Phil. They walked him backwards and forwards in the apartment, slapping his face. He finally opened his eyes a little and mumbled a word or two. Cynthia sighed with a gasp of relief. Tango was just beginning to respond to their conversation with him. He told them in broken sentences that he wanted to die.

Phil started to feed Tango his very own philosophy, which he had said to many young men who were in his shape. "Man, fight for the top. If you think you are a man, fight for the top. Don't stay at the bottom. It takes a lot of man to reach the top."

Tango looked at Phil and responded, "Don't want to hear that garbage." Phil felt a big relief; at least he was getting through to him. Tango was sitting at the table, looking as if he had been on a drunk for days.

Cynthia prepared a hot bowl of soup and said, "Eat this, Tango. You'll feel better."

He snapped at her, "How in the hell would you know?"

Phil had thought Tango was feeling differently about Cynthia, but he saw that he had that same hostile attitude. Phil told Cynthia that he had to go back to the center and take care of a few things before the end of the day. When he looked over at Tango to tell him that he would see him soon, Tango's eyes were filled with tears, and they began to run down his cheeks.

Cynthia looked at Tango and then at Phil. Then she spoke softly, "That's the depressed or down effect of the drug. He'll be that way for a day or so."

"I ain't gonna be here in a day or so. I'm tired of living this damned kind of no-good life," said Tango.

Phil stood up and put his hand on Tango's shoulder. "Man, you ain't tired of living yet because you and me are going to the senior citizens' home together. Just remember what you always told the man, and you'll come out of this smelling like a rose. I'll be back to see how you are doing, and I'll want a good report, okay?"

Tango nodded his head with tears running together under his chin and dripping on the table.

Cynthia walked to the door with Phil. "Phil, I'm a little worried. I've never heard Tango talk of death so invitingly. You don't suppose that he'll do something foolish, do you?"

"Naw, I think he just had a bad cut. He'll probably be all right after this wears off. Let me know how he's doing on a day-to-day basis, okay?"

Feeling like a cat on the prowl, Phil decided that he would go to see this young lady whom he had met while he was collecting money for the center. He had just stepped out of the shower when he heard a loud rap on his door. "Damn," he said as he tried to wipe the dripping water from his body. "Yeah, who is it?"

"The police."

"Who?"

"The police. Ms. Cynthia Davis sent us over here to get you."

Phil's head started to spin a mile a minute. "Just a minute." He grabbed his pants and scuffled into them. He opened the door.

The policeman said, "We'll wait for you in the car."

Phil grabbed a shirt and stuck his feet into his shoes. He knew that something terrible had gone wrong if Cynthia had summoned the police.

As Phil climbed into the back seat of the car, the police turned on the siren and the flashing light. "Could you tell me what is the matter?" Phil couldn't keep from asking, since the officers didn't volunteer any information.

"Your friend is attempting suicide." They didn't say any more, and Phil was afraid to ask any more questions. It seemed as if it took thirty minutes to get there instead of ten.

As the car came to a complete stop at the scene of the complex, a large crowd was standing outside, looking up. Several police cars were there and a fire engine. Phil could see a small figure on the edge of the roof, at the very top of the ten-story building. The firemen had a net and were holding it in a steady position directly under the point where Tango was standing. They moved alongside of the building, just in case Tango fell. Phil jumped out of the car and pushed through the crowd. He ran up to where several women were restraining Cynthia. "Cynthia! Cynthia!"

When she realized that it was Phil's voice, she broke loose from the women and ran to Phil. "Phil, oh, Phil," she said, sobbing, "please save him. He has had some LSD, and he said that he was going to fly away from here. He—He said that he was going to fly straight to hell."

Phil pushed Cynthia toward the women and said, "Stay here. I'll do my best."

While Phil climbed the fire escape ladder, balls of sweat

as large as mothballs were falling from his face. He just hoped that he could talk Tango out of it. As he got to the top, Tango was walking the edge of the roof like a trapeze acrobat. He had his arms stretched out while he walked slowly. Phil didn't want to frighten him. He thought that he had better walk closer and speak his name softly. "Tango, Tango." Tango didn't look around.

Phil then heard him saying, "Somebody is calling me, but I don't hear nobody."

Phil thought quickly and tried to use some psychology on him. "Tango, walk to the center of the roof. Phil wants to talk to you."

Tango kept walking. "Tell Phil I'm going flying. I don't want to talk now. Wait until I get through flying. Tell him I'm a bird now and birds don't talk. They just fly . . . z-o-o-m . . . z-o-o-m." Phil was just about in reach of Tango when he fell off the roof. You could hear the echoes of the women's screams a mile away. The firemen caught him in the net.

When Phil reached the ground, they had strapped him in the bed and were getting ready to put him into the ambulance. Cynthia was walking by his side as they wheeled him up to the door of the ambulance. To Phil's surprise, she was calm. Knowing that she wanted him to go with her, he got into the ambulance with her and Tango. It was awful for Phil to think that Tango might as well be dead because he was looking into space. Cynthia must have sensed what Phil was thinking, for she had worked as a nurse at Crownsville Hospital for several years.

She looked at Phil. "I believe his mind has snapped, Phil. I've seen too many patients at the hospital who have looked like this. That LSD has blown his mind." She bent down and kissed Tango. Tango didn't bat an eye. "What do you think they're going to do with him?"

"I reckon they'll keep him at the hospital in the psychiatric ward for some tests before they take him to Crownsville."

Phil thought to himself, *I wish I knew who sold you that bad cut, Tango. I would fix them good.* He felt very vengeful at that moment, for his friend would never be the same again. He thought back on the many things which might have caused this—no job, loss of his dignity, no money, and many other things. All Phil could say was—"Why? Why? Why?"

Little John and the secretary, Liz, stuck with Phil and the program.

"Well, boss," he said to Phil one day, "it's me, you and the secretary. Only the strong survive in the people's game."

"Right you are, John. We've got to see it to the end."

"You are going to get some money to run this program, Phil. I know you are."

"You will—you know," Liz was encouraged as her fingers worked the typewriter, just as efficiently as they did when she was receiving a salary.

They both spoke with such conviction that he felt that he had to come through.

"Little John," Phil said one day, "I tell you what. You guard the center and Liz and I will do some constructive hustling."

"I don't mind," Liz said eagerly. "We'll beg everyone in town for a dollar."

Chapter 25

For months, Liz and Phil walked the streets and begged donations from lawyers, businessmen and businesswomen all over the city. The initial response was overwhelming. Blacks and whites gave generously.

Eventually, Liz was forced to leave, out of necessity. This left Little John and himself. They both were now on the welfare roll as their unemployment checks had run out. A real shot in the arm came by way of a volunteer, Veda Wells. She heard about the plight of the program and joined forces. She had connections and knew people with influence. She lived in the Towson area and used her influence to solicit many donations from her wealthy neighbors. As a result, they were able to feed their residents, pay the house note, and meet expenses.

Occasionally, Phil spent time with Veda, but no one could substitute for Vickie. Vickie continued to be his inspiration, and he saw her twice a week and would do so until she left her husband.

Many times he thought of quitting and throwing in the towel, but Veda and Little John would always tell him he couldn't do it. "If it's meant to be, it's up to me." Phil kept focusing on this idea about the center. The center had provided a lot of good results, and Phil could not help but believe that someone would hear his plea and come to his rescue.

Phil organized a group to help collect money, food and clothing in order to keep the center open. He had eight of the men working with him. They were downtown in various neighborhoods, knocking on doors and soliciting help for the brothers lodging at the halfway house. People responded with nickels, dimes, quarters, half-dollars, and even some bills every now and then. Nevertheless, these coins were like manna from above. Every nickel was needed and used to its full monetary worth.

Phil was holding a sign which read, "Help us to remain in the mainstream of society—The Halfway House." They were standing on the corner of Howard and Fayette Streets in downtown Baltimore. One of the young men was collecting a donation from one of the motorists, while the other one was moving from car to car. Phil was walking backward and forward with the sign. He held the sign above his head so everyone could read it. As he was walking forward with the oncoming traffic at his back, he didn't know whether to jump or holler because this white Thunderbird was headed directly toward him as he glanced over his shoulders at the sound of the shrieking brakes. Then the car stopped, with the bumper pressing against his pants legs. Phil stood paralyzed, looking at the driver. All of a sudden the driver, wearing a big, wide-brimmed white hat, stuck his head out of the window and said, "I ought to kill you, sucker. You know you got it coming to you?"

Phil felt a big relief. As a matter of fact, he wondered if his pants were okay. He gave a big smile and said, "I'll be damned. How're you doing, man?"

Douglass reached his hand out and gave him a slap on the hand. "You're right. You ought to be damned." They slapped each other's hand again. Cars began to blow their horns in unison. Douglass reached into his pocket and gave Phil a fifty dollar bill. Phil was all smiles, for he knew Douglass didn't hold any grudges against him for not meeting him several months ago. The horns were not only blowing in unison, but heads were hanging out of the cars, calling them some very spicy names. Douglass waved his hand at the car behind him and gave the driver the "up" sign.

Phil said, "Man, get in touch with me at the center." He wanted him to move on before the police made them move from their spot for holding up traffic.

Douglass raced his motor and said, "Okay, man," as he burned rubber going down the street. Phil was smiling all over, because Douglass' donation was as much or more than all of them got. He thought as he walked backward and forward, *We'll make it*. He thought and wondered how Douglass could afford that new Thunderbird and give such a generous donation. No sooner had the thought left his mind when he heard a car's horn blowing. He looked above the three or four cars which had stopped at the traffic light.

Douglass was calling him, "Hey, Phil! Hey, Phil! Come take a break with me." He was half-leaning out of his car now.

Phil stretched, looked over the cars, and said, "What?"

"I said, come take a break with me."

Phil took his sign from above his head, gave it to one of the young men, and said, "Can you handle this for an hour?"

The young man responded, "Sure, man, go on." Phil hopped into Douglass' car, and they zoomed down the street.

They had driven four or five blocks before either had said

anything. "I like what you are doing," said Douglass. "It's a damned shame you have to be standing on the street corner, asking for charity pennies just to help the underdogs of society. I bet they ain't paying you hardly shit, huh? How much, Phil?"

"Uh—Uh, man, they've stopped paying me. The center is about to fold, but I ain't gonna let it."

Douglass interrupted, "Man, you mean they ain't paying you a M.F. thing? You crazy or something? Man, ain't nobody working for free these days. Who do you think you are, one of J.C.'s disciples?"

"Naw, naw, man," said Phil. "I just saw more good than bad come as a result of the center, until I just believe it will work if we show these suckers we can do it. You see, that's what they think. We are gonna go right back to that slave hole if they don't give us a little handout. As a matter of fact, they expect us to go back to the joint when they do give us little crummy jobs making two cents."

Douglass shook his head as he drove up in front of a bar. "All I can say, man, is that you are a good one. Let's have a drink." Phil and Douglass walked into the bar. Phil could tell this was Douglass' regular place for hanging out.

Douglass held up two fingers, and the barmaid was over with two Scotch and waters before they had gotten comfortable in their seats. Phil sipped his Scotch slowly and said, "Whew, good stuff."

"Yeah," replied Douglass. "Say, man, why didn't you meet me that night that we planned to stick up that spot?"

Phil had been waiting for that question ever since he had gotten in the car with Douglass. He took a big swallow of Scotch and said, "Well, man, it's a long story. My woman came by and changed my plans and made me feel as guilty as hell, so I couldn't let her down."

"Well, I kind of figured something like that happened,"

said Douglass, "because you are a man of your word."

"Thanks," said Phil. "I needed that, Douglass."

"Yeah, I mean it. I knew something must have happened."

Phil interrupted, "So did you go through with it?"

"Naw, man, but I pistol-whipped the hell out of one of those gray suckers as he walked to his car, and I got two hundred and twenty-four dollars."

"What?"

"Yeah, I sure did."

Phil was looking at him strangely. Douglass raised his fingers, and the barmaid brought them fresh drinks. "Uh, I didn't kill him, but he did end up in the hospital."

"You must be doing much better now. You look like you are living high on the hog," Phil said jokingly.

Douglass took a long sip and said, "Phil, that's the reason I came back after you. When I saw you standing out there, begging for charity, I said—"

Phil interrupted, "Man, it's not really begging for charity, it's soliciting for a worthy cause."

"Dress the shit up if you want to, but it's still begging for charity."

"It's the only way that I know of since Mr. Almighty Nixon cut off a lot of programs like these."

"No, man, it ain't the only way. You see this?" He pulled out a roll of bills from his pocket. "I'm pulling an eight-hour job from four to twelve, man, and cleaning some damned offices in order to keep me covered, but this scratch didn't come from an eight-hour job."

"I'm hip, man," said Phil.

"You damned straight," replied Douglass. "Eight hours a day won't get this kind of money. Then you won't have to be out there begging. By the way, how are you making it, anyway?"

"I'm doing odd jobs here and there."

"How do you survive doing shit like that?"

"I got a sweet sister who is helping. She's been damned good to me."

"Hell, man, I know what you mean. I've been in the same boat myself. Now back to what I was saying before we got sidetracked."

Phil was feeling just a bit pensive. He had a gut feeling of what Douglass was talking about. "You can have that halfway house in good shape before the month is out if you join the business." The barmaid interrupted with two more refills, and Douglass reached into his pocket and gave her a twenty-dollar bill. He patted her on the rear and said, "Keep the change, sweet stuff." She giggled as she walked away.

Phil took a big gulp of Scotch because he wanted to say yes, despite his inner feelings telling him that it was a one-way ticket back to the slammer.

"I can make connections for you today, man, and you can have at least five crispy one hundred dollar bills by this weekend."

Phil sighed a little and squirmed in his seat. "I don't know, man. This is very risky."

"Risky? Man, the big man is making millions while he's giving us a few crumbs from his table just to handle his shit. Man, it's easy. In no time, you can have a ride, money in your pockets, and plenty of women. Come on." He pulled at Phil's shoulder, and they got up and left.

There was a little voice inside of Phil saying, *You'd better stay clear. This is too risky to your freedom."*

They got in the car and drove away. Douglass said, "Now you just watch how easy this is going to be." All of a sudden, a weary feeling overtook Phil. He didn't want to get into trouble again when he was innocent. Douglass sensed Phil's mood and said, "Man, you'll be all right. Nothing is gonna happen to you. Trust me."

"I trust you, Douglass," Phil said reluctantly as they pulled up to a garage.

Douglass got out and went inside. The service attendant came out with a tool box and raised the hood of the car. He opened his tool box and took out a wrench and tightened a screw. At least he pretended he was tightening it, while with the other hand he placed a small package on a hook underneath the hood. Phil couldn't believe the transaction was being handled so smoothly. Things were happening a little too smoothly. It was as if he was looking at a television flick where they were caught right in the middle of the act. Phil looked around to see whether he saw anybody that looked like a plainclothes policeman.

Douglass put on another act as if he were actually paying the man. He took out his wallet and gave him a bill. The attendant reached into his pocket and gave Douglass five one hundred dollar bills. The transaction had taken place as quickly as one could count one-two-three. Douglass did a quick side bop and walked around the car while pretending to check his tires. After he got in the car, he sped off with a big grin on his face. "You see how easy that was, man? You can do the same thing. Come on and go with me to deliver the goods."

Phil felt a little apprehensive. He said, "Douglass, I've been gone too long. I'd better get back on my post."

"Man, you deserve one day or at least a half a day off. Come on and let me show you how easy it is. I want you to get off that street corner and join the business. How about it?"

"I don't know," said Phil.

"Nothing to it. You saw those five cool, green cabbage leaves I got, didn't ya? I'm what you call the pick up man. I simply pick the goods up and drop them off at another location. Man, I could get you on by tomorrow night. Come on and join me."

Phil needed money and he was really thinking seriously about this. "Let me think about it, man."

"Okay," said Douglass. "I'll be by tomorrow and see what you've come up with."

He drove up to Phil's spot. Phil got out, assuring him that he would think the thing through. The two guys were looking like they were getting ready to split the scene. "How did y'all do?"

"We did okay," one replied. "Only one thing wrong, not too much giving going on."

Phil said, "Let's call it a day."

That night, Phil had dinner with Tango and his lady. He told them about what had happened, and how the temptation was getting to him, especially since he was working for nothing. Tango said, "I thought it would get through to you, sooner or later. Now, can't you understand why I flaked out last week? I have had it, man. Fighting for the cause is one thing, and being broke is another."

Cynthia interrupted, "Somebody has got to hold up the banner. Phil, you are gonna make it. Some of these agencies are going to come to your rescue. Just don't get into any trouble."

"Shit," Tango interrupted as he got up and lit a cigarette. "Yeah, that's right, Phil. Don't get in any mess dealing with drugs."

She interrupted him with much force. "That's right, Phil. Don't get in any mess with drugs. That's what's killing off our people now, and if it doesn't kill them, they are screwed up for life."

Tango sat down and responded, "Look, let Phil do what he wants to do. Nobody needs no damned penniless advice."

"Oh, hell, Tango," she said as her voice rose, "I'm giving Phil sound advice, something that will keep him out of jail, and you are talking like a flat-headed fool."

Phil could see that a big argument was about to start. He

interrupted Cynthia, "May I have another piece of that apple pie? Boy, it's good."

She said, "Sure, you don't have to ask. Help yourself to as much as you want," as she pushed the pie towards him.

Tango got up and was mixing three drinks. Phil felt the tension dying down. He was glad because he didn't want them to get in a scrabble over him. Knowing that Tango had a hot temper, he certainly didn't want him to be angry at Cynthia. He would slap her and think nothing about it.

Phil finished the pie and said, "Well, folks, I hate to eat and run, but I've got a stop to make before I go home."

Tango said, "Okay, my good man, I can dig that. We have enjoyed having you tonight."

Cynthia patted his hand and said, "Be careful, Phil."

He kissed her on the cheek and said, "I will. Thanks."

Phil left with many mixed thoughts. He wondered whether or not he could go through with Douglass' plans this time. The run seemed so damned easy. He kept thinking in the back of his mind—what if he got caught? The image he had given to the parolees' minds would be torn to bits and pieces. They would never have confidence in any more counselors, especially an ex-offender counselor.

Phil was asleep in bed when he heard a loud rap on his door. He thought that he was dreaming.

"Phil! Phil! Phil!"

He sat straight up in bed. "Yeah, who is it?"

"It's Little John."

Phil sprang out of bed and opened the door. He said, "Man, what's wrong?"

"You'd better come quickly. Tango has taken a little too much this time, and we can't wake him up. We didn't want to take him to the hospital without your knowing about it first."

Phil said, "Where is he?"

"He's in the car. We thought we'd get you to go with us to the hospital because I think he's too far gone."

Phil scrambled into his pants, saying, "Bring him in. Let's walk him." They had brought Tango to the steps about the time Phil had gotten to the steps. Phil said, "That's okay. Let's walk him outside." Phil got on one side and Little John got on the other. They walked up and down the street, slapping Tango's face.

"Wake up, man. Wake up," Little John was saying. Finally, he began to mumble a few muffled sounds. Little John said, "You hear that, man? He's coming around!"

Phil said, "He's not out of the woods yet, man. We've gotta keep walking him." Phil's legs felt as if he'd already walked fifty miles.

A few hours later, Tango was stumbling a little by himself, saying broken phrases. "Man, I'm tired . . . bed . . . I—I wanna go . . . You bastards, turn loose . . ."

Little John smiled. "Phil, this S.O.B. is getting better. You heard what he called us after we have saved his stinkin' black hide?"

Phil said, "Let's take him back to the center. Keep walking him while I get my shirt."

That afternoon, Phil and Tango were in conference. Tango's eyes were still kind of glassy and wild-looking. He told Phil he just couldn't face another day with no work and hardly enough food to survive, so he had fired up.

After the conference, Phil knew that he would not go along with Douglass' plan. He would work together for the cause and leave the drug business to Douglass and others, for he had to be strong for the survival of his brothers.

Several days had passed, and Phil had not heard from Douglass as he had promised. Thinking of his decision, he was glad that Douglass hadn't come. He had planned some group counseling sessions for that day. He had hoped to try to give the group some encouragement to keep them thinking and moving forward. Because of many temptations leading toward indulgence, they were easy to elude one's mind. The men needed all the support in the world to keep them out of trouble. They felt the pains of being at the mercy of the people around them, especially when it involved food and clothes. This was enough pressure to turn any man back to the road of destruction.

Phil was getting his thoughts and plans organized when the new volunteer stepped inside the office and said, "Phil, there is a Mr. Douglass Wilson here to see you."

Phil looked startled, for he had been looking to see him for the past three days, although at that moment he wasn't thinking about him. "Okay," he said.

Phil got up and went to the door. As he reached it, Douglass walked in and gave him the hand slap. "How's it going, blood?"

"Okay, man, and yourself?" Phil pointed towards a chair. "Have a seat, man."

Douglass sat down and crossed his legs as if he were ready to do business with Dow Jones' stock market. "Everything is in order, man. You can start today and get paid today. I've talked with the head man by telephone and I told him all about you. He said that he wanted you to call him at this here number." He pulled out his wallet and was fumbling through it for a slip of paper. "I know I put it in here somewhere. Oh, yeah, here it is."

Phil sighed as he rubbed his chin. "Douglass, I had a man who almost died the other day from a bad cut. We couldn't even afford to take him to the hospital because of the bad publicity the center would have gotten. I know I need the money and I need it bad. It seems so easy and safe." Phil stood up and placed his hands in his pockets as he stood propped against the wall. "But I've got to renege on you again, and this time it is for good reasons. I can't do it. I've got to stay out here and continue to beg for charity."

"Phil," Douglass interrupted. "Man, it's easy. Come on and join me. We could bring in big money if we hooked up. You could run this here gig without any interruptions."

"Yeah, but what will these men think if they see me flashing money, or all at once I started buying things for the center? I couldn't afford to have money and let them suffer. Anyhow, they have done some of everything in the book. They would know what was going down. They could sense my game without any sweat and lose all confidence in me and this program. That's the way I see things. Man, I don't want to let you down—"

Douglass stood up and interrupted Phil, "Man, you are really strung out in this shit, ain't ya?"

"Yeah, I'm afraid that I'm in it all the way and I can't stop now."

"I wish you all the luck, my man, if that's any consolation to you, because I ain't working free for nobody. I don't care who it's going to help. Man, these dudes don't give a damn about you. You had better wake up and smell the coffee brewing, my man. You could be living on Easy Street instead of rolling with hard knocks. I don't understand you." Douglass looked at the floor, shaking his head in disbelief.

"I know I could, but I've got to stick to what I believe in."

"Okay, my man, I give up," Douglas said, throwing up his hands and walking toward the door.

Phil reached out for a handshake. They gripped each other's hands. "Douglass, don't think that I'm not appreciative for what you've done. I know you've gone out on a limb for me, and I hope you won't hold it against me."

"Naw, naw, man, I don't hold nothing against you. You've gotta do what you've gotta do." He patted Phil on the back as he walked out of the door.

Phil hated to let Douglass down, but it was better that way. He felt that he owed the men who had struggled with him more than a "pseudo" image. Anyway, that's what the center was all about, helping men to find a constructive way of living rather than a quick dollar and no hope for tomorrow.

Chapter 26

People, Phil had to admit, were really beautiful, especially his second mother, Mrs. Laura. She adopted the center as her own, and often sent food and other means of support to see them through. It was through her that he began to meet many political figures who became interested in what they were doing at the center.

"Phillip," Mrs. Laura always said, "if you want money for your program, you have to attend meetings." He did just that. He made contacts with everyone.

The newspapers became involved, and an editorial was written about the center, and how it was surviving without funds. The writer, Edgar Jones, wrote such a heartwarming story, describing their empty refrigerator and other needs, that people all over Maryland responded with donations of all sorts. This was a new surge of support, and it lasted about six months.

It was 1974 and Phil did not know where the two and a half years of struggle had gone. Little did he know how many people had heard about the center and had helped. It was hard to believe that many residents had passed through the program and had been helped.

The law of compensation was also beginning to pay off for the program. As it happened, he attended one of the town's meetings that Mrs. Laura encouraged him to attend. It was headed by the Urban Services Agency, an offspring of the old Model Cities Agency that went out of existence almost three years before. The lady who was speaking was vaguely familiar as she stood before the large audience, explaining that the Urban Services Agency had federal monies for existing programs to supplement their current funds.

When she finished explaining the Urban Services' funding and how much money they had to give, Phil asked, "Miss, do you have any funds for an existing program from the old Model Cities Agency that has no funds?"

"Sir," she answered from a distance, "there are no existing programs from the old Model Cities Agency that was abandoned three years ago."

"That is not quite true, Miss. My program was from the old Model Cities Agency program and I have been running it for three years without any federal, state or city funding."

"Would you see me after the meeting is over, sir?"

After the meeting was over, Phil walked over to the lady and they both recognized each other instantly.

"Why, you are that young man who came into my office three years ago and asked for the furniture. Lanvale Street, wasn't it?"

"Yes, ma'am."

"Anytime a young man can run a program that long without funds, you certainly should be able to work wonders with funds. You send me your proposal as soon as possible."

That year the Community Residence Center received thirty thousand dollars, which boosted their morale. Phil felt like a six-year-old on Christmas morning. He walked to the first telephone that he saw, dropped a dime in, and dialed Vickie's number. "May I speak to Dr. Dixson, please?"

Vickie didn't recognize Phil's voice with the traffic sounds muffling the receiver. "This is she speaking. May I help you?"

"Yes, ma'am, more than one way, too."

"Phil Avery! How dare you try to fool me like this."

"I believe I did, Doc."

"What's the nature of your call, love?"

Phil smiled as he teased Vickie. "Number one, I'm dying of loneliness and I need someone to talk to, and secondly, I need you right now." He laughed. "I'm serious, Vickie. I need to see you this afternoon and not tomorrow."

Vickie sighed, "Um-m-m, Phil, I don't—"

Phil interrupted, "I'm serious, Vickie. If you can spare but an hour or a half hour, please meet me at four-thirty at Sess' Restaurant."

"You sound serious, I'll be there."

"I'll see you at four-thirty. Don't be late," replied Phil. "I can't stand waiting for beautiful dames."

She laughed and said, "Okay, Mr. Fresh."

Phil was waiting for Vickie when she arrived. He could see her before she entered the restaurant. He stood up so that she could see where he was sitting. When she walked inside, she immediately flashed her eyes in his direction and put a broad smile on her face. He kissed her lightly. "Good timing, my love." He helped her to get seated comfortably. The waitress brought them a menu. She ordered a salad and iced tea. Phil said, "I'll have the same."

"Now, Mr. Avery, maybe you are ready to share with me what was so urgent in your voice this afternoon."

Phil said, "You'll never imagine what it is," as he unfolded the whole story about their getting thirty thousand dollars.

Vickie grabbed his hand and squeezed it very tightly. "I told you that you could do it, Phil. I always knew you could. I'm so proud of you."

Phil smiled and winked at her. "Does this call for a little celebration like tea for two?"

She smiled and said, "Yes, it does, but not this afternoon. I've got to go home early. I wish I could get out of this engagement, but I can't, Phil."

Phil smiled. "Well, I guess I'll just have to settle for looking and talking, which I always like to do."

The waitress returned with their orders. They talked and ate slowly, both wishing that those few minutes could last forever. Finally, they finished. Phil paid the waitress. They walked outside to her car. Vickie kissed Phil and they departed.

The next week, Phil spent hours budgeting the thirty thousand dollars. He wanted every penny to be accounted for and spent wisely. He felt good all over that his work had been recognized and rescued from the pits.

Within the next few months, Phil was in conference with various state and city officials. They were asking for suggestions that would help make the prison's situation better and how to work with parolees.

Phil made a speech at one conference:

"You cannot expect human beings to be ostracized and then brought back into society and function as if we were just lost for a few months, and now we have returned. We must have rehabilitation counselors for our mental and physical well-being."

He continued as he looked from one member to the other as his voice carried great emotional overtones.

"Yes, we have broken laws in our society. We understand that we did wrong regardless of the circumstances. Nevertheless, we have paid for them many times while being behind lock and key. However, when we do return to the mainstream of society, we have no alternative other than to return to those same locks and keys. Why? Because society does not accept us, does not work with us, and does not provide jobs for us. What else is there for us to do but return to the same path that we traveled before? And that path leads us back to cages with locks and keys.

"For example, we young men have no skills or knowledge for acquiring jobs, which will help us to maintain a livelihood. Yet society thinks that we should be able to enter the mainstream successfully because we have been paroled. No, this isn't the answer. We need to handle the program in a more positive and constructive manner.

"Here is another example—a young man who could not find employment was out of work and depressed to the point of desperation for a means of survival. What did he do? The first thing that came to his mind was to survive the best way he knew how. That way was mugging and robbing in order to have a few dollars in his pocket again. How much can a man take without a job to provide for himself?

"Then society judged him ten times as severely as it did the first time. Why? Because society thinks that it has given this person an opportunity to change his lifestyle, but society has been negligent in giving him assistance in a positive direction for employment by proper counseling and proper training in order to help him survive.

"Gentlemen, if you really want to help, let's see what we can do for these juveniles as far as counseling and rehabilitation is concerned instead of imprisonment. Secondly, let's visit the penitentiary and clean up the corruption and unjust practices which make the young men mentally and physically deranged in many ways.

"Finally, gentlemen, let's take a closer look at the ratio of black prisoners versus white prisoners incarcerated. Yes, we have a lot to have conferences over. I ask you to give what I said a few minutes of your time, and think these things over."

The councilmen gave Phil a big, hearty applause. Phil looked and listened to their comments. He found himself wondering if what he had said had an impact on the members or whether they were just wasted words.

Several weeks later, Phil was asked to give a speech to a certain segment of prisoners. He accepted with much enthusiasm. There were many faces which he hadn't seen before. Nevertheless, there were a lot he still remembered.

Phil made himself right at home with the men, and they had a rap session, not a speech ordeal. He tried to fill them with positive thoughts, which would help to release their minds of negativity.

Just as he was about to leave, a young man in despair ran up to him, with tears in his eyes. "Uh, Phil, please help me. I'm innocent. I didn't rob that store. They grabbed me and said I was the one. Please, I'm innocent. Please help me."

Phil immediately had a flashback of himself and Cowhand, who wrote his first letter of appeal for him. He put his arm around the young man's shoulder and said, "I'll need more information, then I'll see what I can do."

The young man said he would have it all ready for him when he returned on his next visit. Phil knew within his heart this was another project that he was going to undertake, and once he started it, he was going to work with it to the end.

That night, Phil kept hearing the different comments the inmates were making. It disturbed him greatly. Phil knew that he had made the best decision of keeping the program going, for the center was like heaven compared to prison.

Several months had gone by. Phil worked overtime in order to keep the center open and to keep it operating as smoothly as could be expected with understaffed personnel. The center needed more money than they had gotten from the city and federal governments in order for the program to be more effective.

Phil had prepared several proposals over and over, hoping that the city and state would extend them some funds. He was pleased with what they had received, but more money was needed in every way. He was racking his brains to the hilt in order to come up with a proposal that would persuade the councilmen to give more funds.

The second year, the program received one hundred and ten thousand dollars, and the third year, one hundred and seventy-five thousand dollars. The program began to expand from the one house on Lanvale Street to a total of ten houses around the city, helping thousands of inmates throughout the state of Maryland.

Phil was getting ready to write a new proposal to present to the officials the following day. As he began to write, he thought out loud, *If it's to be, it's up to me.*

His thoughts were interrupted by the secretary saying, "Phil, here is a letter you should read now!"

Mr. Avery:

> We have reviewed your proposal, and the councilmen have agreed that this program is to be granted $175,000 for the fiscal year of 1974-75 ...

Phil let out a yell that could be heard all over the building. He thought of all the new parolees that they would be able to house, and a million other things which they needed badly.

He sat there and thought of the long struggle of suffering they had undertaken in order to keep the center open.

Yes, I must write about all of this one day, for it has been and always will be a struggle for my brothers and me, who have been there, of course. We truly understand the plight. He thought more about the despairing faces that he remembered in the prison, looking toward him for a sign of hope and freedom. He could only think of how positive thoughts had helped him, and how he must continue to inject his brothers' minds with positive thoughts, for this was their only way to survive the system.

> *Think positively, my brothers!*
> *Think positively, and survive!*

THE NAKED SOUL OF ICEBERG SLIM

BY ROBERT BECK

NON-FICTION Don't cry for his soul because he's Black. Though Black is pain. Black is death. Black is despair. Black is the ghetto where he was born. And lived. As a pimp, dope addict, brutalizer of women—and other Blacks, but he cured himself of the ghetto rot. To write—as no other man ever has—about his people and his life. His name is Robert Beck. Better known by his ghetto name, Iceberg Slim. His first three books brought him fame. **PIMP: THE STORY OF MY LIFE, TRICK BABY,** and **MAMA BLACK WIDOW,** a tragic bitter family portrait. They were honest books—sensitive portraits of ghetto life and people. But this book, is his most disturbing. Because it has hope. Because it is now. Because he searches the artist's soul in a collection of personal essays that are full of passion and razor-sharp perception. And when his soul is naked, you see the hurt of a man who feels too much and cares too much.

HOLLOWAY HOUSE PUBLISHING CO.
8060 Melrose Ave., Los Angeles, CA 90046-7082

Gentlemen I enclose $ _____ ☐ check ☐ money order, payment in full for books ordered. I understand that if I am not completely satisfied, I may return my order within 10 days for a complete refund. (Add $1.00 per book to cover cost of shipping. California residents add 41¢ sales tax. Please allow six weeks for delivery.)

☐ BH758-6 THE NAKED SOUL OF ICEBERG SLIM $4.95

Name _____

Address _____

City _____ State _____ Zip _____

DEATH WISH

BY ROBERT BECK

Author Robert Beck, better known by his ghetto pseudonym, "Iceberg Slim," again displays his unique and compelling talent in this novel about the Mafia— an organization whose working details he knows intimately. It's an ideal setting for Beck's superb characterization as he portrays the greedy Don Jimmy Collucci, who wants nothing less than to rule the "Honored Society"...dedicated Black Warrior Jessie Taylor, who is driven to destroy it... and the dozens of people whose lives and fates are entwined with theirs. Vividly real, these powerful, implacable figures and their stubbornly loyal underlings stalk each other through pages teeming with life, love, lust and death.

HOLLOWAY HOUSE PUBLISHING CO.
8060 Melrose Ave., Los Angeles, CA 90046-7082

Gentlemen I enclose $ _____ ☐ check ☐ money order, payment in full for books ordered. I understand that if I am not completely satisfied, I may return my order within 10 days for a complete refund. (Add $1.00 per book to cover cost of shipping. California residents add 41¢ sales tax. Please allow six weeks for delivery.)

☐ BH755-1 DEATH WISH $4.95

Name _____

Address _____

City _____ State _____ Zip _____

LONG WHITE CON
BY ICEBERG SLIM

Robert Beck, better known by his ghetto pseudonym "Iceberg Slim," astounded and captivated readers with his first story of **TRICK BABY,** that blue-eyed, light-haired, white skinned black called "White Folks." Still the most incredible con man Beck has ever met, Folks rides again in this spellbinding new novel, playing for the biggest scores of his life! No chump change scores for him, he's out to prove that he's a "true blue nigger."

But the con game struggle between the greedy spider and the rich honkie fly is made all the more difficult by Folks' trauma visions of the past... the stigma of being a trick baby, a mother who was gang-raped, himself mercilessly violated by those who thought he was white.

Beck's unique talent for brilliant characterizations do justice to a superb cast of grifters including High Pockets Kate, the High Ass Marvel and the Vicksburg Kid. It's a modern masterpiece!

```
------------------------------------------------
        HOLLOWAY HOUSE PUBLISHING CO.
        8060 Melrose Ave., Los Angeles, CA 90046-7082

Gentlemen I enclose $ _____  ☐ check ☐ money order,
payment in full for books ordered. I understand that if I am not completely
satisfied, I may return my order within 10 days for a complete refund. (Add
$1.00 per book to cover cost of shipping. California residents add 41¢ sales
tax. Please allow six weeks for delivery.)

☐ BH756-X  LONG WHITE CON  $4.95

Name _____

Address _____

City _____ State _____ Zip _____
------------------------------------------------
```

TRICK BABY

BY ICEBERG SLIM

Author Robert Beck, better known by his ghetto pseudonym, "Iceberg Slim," tells the story of a blue-eyed, light-haired, white-skinned negro called "White Folks," the most incredible con man the ghetto ever spawned! Beck knew him well, knew where he was coming from. Folks was tormented by the hateful name, "Trick Baby," but he chose to stay in the black ghetto of southside Chicago because that's where he could turn the tables and exact his revenge! The petty triumphs of the white world weren't for him, but through the con game struggle between the spider and the fly he could overcome his deballing shame, lure his victims into traps and become a deadly predator in the inner city jungle! Beck tells his story in the gut level language of the con artist, with the bitterness and despair of the trick baby!

HOLLOWAY HOUSE PUBLISHING CO.
8060 Melrose Ave., Los Angeles, CA 90046-7082

Gentlemen I enclose $ _____ ☐ check ☐ money order, payment in full for books ordered. I understand that if I am not completely satisfied. I may return my order within 10 days for a complete refund. (Add $1.00 per book to cover cost of shipping. California residents add 41¢ sales tax. Please allow six weeks for delivery.)

☐ BH760-8 TRICK BABY $4.95

Name _____

Address _____

City _____ State _____ Zip _____

PIMP
THE STORY OF MY LIFE
BY ICEBERG SLIM

AUTOBIOGRAPHY—Iceberg Slim is the name he used in the black ghetto. His real name is Robert Beck and he was a pimp. This is his story, told without bitterness and with no pretense at moralizing...the smells, the sounds, the fears, the petty triumphs in the world of the pimp. No other book comes anywhere near this one in its description of the raw, brutal reality of the jungle that lurks beneath the surface of every city. Nobody but a pimp could tell his story and no one ever has...until Iceberg Slim. He was young, ambitious and blessed with a superior IQ. He spent twenty-five years of his life in Hell. Other pimps died in prison, or in insane asylums, or were shot down in the street. But Iceberg Slim escaped death and the drug habit to live in the square world with the woman he loves, and to write about his people and his life.

HOLLOWAY HOUSE PUBLISHING CO.
8060 Melrose Ave., Los Angeles, CA 90046-7082

Gentlemen I enclose $ _____ ☐ check ☐ money order, payment in full for books ordered. I understand that if I am not completely satisfied, I may return my order within 10 days for a complete refund. (Add $1.00 per book to cover cost of shipping. California residents add 41¢ sales tax. Please allow six weeks for delivery.)

☐ BH759-4 PIMP: THE STORY OF MY LIFE $4.95

Name _____

Address _____

City _____ State _____ Zip _____

MAMA BLACK WIDOW
BY ICEBERG SLIM

Author Robert Beck, better known by his ghetto pseudonym, "Iceberg Slim," tells the story of Otis Tilson, an incredibly comely and tragic homosexual queen. The dialogue is in the gut idiom of the queer—the black ghetto—the deep South—the underworld—the world of Iceberg Slim, Otis Tilson and his family. It is the story of the black men living in ghetto torture chambers. Men who have been and continue to be niggerized and deballed by the poisonous pus of double standard justice, racial bigotry and criminal economic freeze-out. And of the price paid by their children. In this case, Otis Tilson, his older brother and two beautiful sisters adrift in the dark world of pimpdom and crime and violence. This is Robert Beck's most vivid portrait of ghetto life. A masterpiece!

HOLLOWAY HOUSE PUBLISHING CO.
8060 Melrose Ave., Los Angeles, CA 90046-7082

Gentlemen I enclose $ _____ ☐ check ☐ money order, payment in full for books ordered. I understand that if I am not completely satisfied, I may return my order within 10 days for a complete refund. (Add $1.00 per book to cover cost of shipping. California residents add 41¢ sales tax. Please allow six weeks for delivery.)

☐ BH757-8 MAMA BLACK WIDOW $4.95

Name _____

Address _____

City _____ State _____ Zip _____

STREET PLAYERS

BY DONALD GOINES

This is Donald Goines' fourth novel, a gutsy account of an Inner City gold-hatted, high-bounding lover. And herein, Goines tests the tensile strength of a ghetto spawn who clawed his way to the top and fights like hell to stay there. He's known as Earl the Black Pearl, and he's up from the ghetto—way up. He views the streets from his fashionable penthouse with its wall-to-wall silk suits and women. He's everybody's mellow fellow, a big spender, the toast of the Inner City. He's as cool and sharp as an ice crystal. Even Joe Chink can't touch him. Then somebody put the heat on. Butcher knives flash and pistols bark, and Earl's friends begin dropping like flies, dragging Earl with them. But he's resilient and he bounces back—for a while...

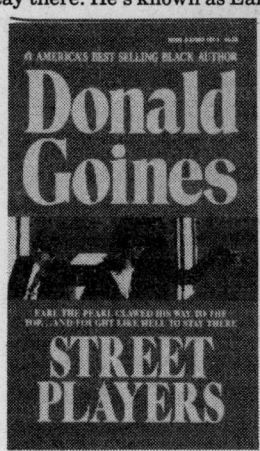

HOLLOWAY HOUSE PUBLISHING CO.
8060 Melrose Ave., Los Angeles, CA 90046-7082

Gentlemen I enclose $ _____ ☐ check ☐ money order, payment in full for books ordered. I understand that if I am not completely satisfied. I may return my order within 10 days for a complete refund. (Add $1.00 per book to cover cost of shipping. California residents add 29¢ sales tax. Please allow six weeks for delivery.)

☐ BH187-1 STREET PLAYERS $3.50

Name _____

Address _____

City _____ State _____ Zip _____

BLACK GIRL LOST

BY DONALD GOINES

Donald Goines has an established reputation as one of the foremost writers in the Black Experience genre. His previous novels have cast a glaring spotlight on the brutally harsh, sometimes nightmarish reality of the ghetto— the cool, clawing world of the pimp in **Street Players**, the cruel, violent conning of ghetto prostitution in **Whoreson**, the treacherous and sordid world of the man behind bars in **White Man's Justice: Black Man's Grief**, and the raw, secret world of the black junkie in **Dopefiend**. Now, in **Black Girl Lost**, Goines delves deep into yet another facet of the ghetto existence—the dark, despairing world of a black girl's soul! Sandra took to the streets when she was eight years old, and tried to fight off the hunger pangs by shoplifting. From shoplifting she moved into the profits of pushing drugs as she struggled to overcome her deprivation with quick money. And then she met Chink, and she discovered love and affection... and rape and murder!

HOLLOWAY HOUSE PUBLISHING CO.
8060 Melrose Ave., Los Angeles, CA 90046-7082

Gentlemen I enclose $ _____ ☐ check ☐ money order, payment in full for books ordered. I understand that if I am not completely satisfied, I may return my order within 10 days for a complete refund. (Add $1.00 per book to cover cost of shipping. California residents add 29¢ sales tax. Please allow six weeks for delivery.)

☐ BH186-3 BLACK GIRL LOST $3.50

Name _____

Address _____

City _____ State _____ Zip _____

DEATH LIST

BY DONALD GOINES

Donal Goines continues the gripping, gritty story of crime in the black ghetto begun in CRIME PARTNERS. They're all back for blood: Kenyatta, the ganglord with an army of brothers to deal deadly with crooked cops and dope dealers; Benson and Ryan, a black and white detective team, desperate in their fight to stop the black crime wave. It's doomsday when Kenyatta joins them in a war against a secret list of junk pushers.

DONALD GOINES, savagely gunned down at the age of 39, was the undisputed master of the Black Experience novel. He lived by the code of the streets and exposed in each of his 16 books the rage, frustration and torment spinning through the inner city maze. Each of his stories, classics in the Black Experience genre, were drawn from reality.

HOLLOWAY HOUSE PUBLISHING CO.
8060 Melrose Ave., Los Angeles, CA 90046-7082

Gentlemen I enclose $ _____ ☐ check ☐ money order, payment in full for books ordered. I understand that if I am not completely satisfied, I may return my order within 10 days for a complete refund. (Add $1.00 per book to cover cost of shipping. California residents add 29¢ sales tax. Please allow six weeks for delivery.)

☐ BH195-2 DEATH LIST $3.50

Name _____

Address _____

City _____ State _____ Zip _____

NEVER DIE ALONE

BY DONALD GOINES

FICTION—King David...he never let anything stand in his way in his clawing, grasping fight to rise up out of the streets. Sometimes it took busting open a woman's head with a Coke bottle to get her last dollars. Sometimes it meant mixing battery acid with cocaine in order to gain revenge. And once it meant copping out on a loan from some powerful Black underworld connections.

But then he makes it big, peddling heroin up from Mexico, and he returns to set things right with the gangsters...only to find that they're not about to forget his treachery.

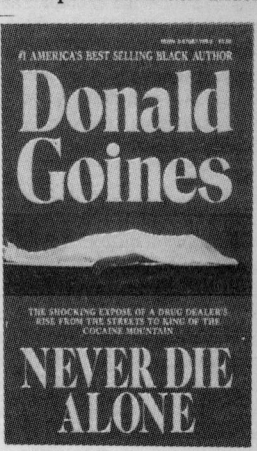

In his dying moments he leaves everything—his Cadillac, his ill-gained money and his diary—to down and out writer Paul Pawlowski.

Does Pawlowski inherit the curse of King David's vicious cruelty, or does he learn that even, in the ghetto success doesn't mean victimizing and hooking one's fellow man?

HOLLOWAY HOUSE PUBLISHING CO.
8060 Melrose Ave., Los Angeles, CA 90046-7082

Gentlemen I enclose $ _____ ☐ check ☐ money order, payment in full for books ordered. I understand that if I am not completely satisfied. I may return my order within 10 days for a complete refund. (Add $1.00 per book to cover cost of shipping. California residents add 29¢ sales tax. Please allow six weeks for delivery.)

☐ BH189-8 **NEVER DIE ALONE** **$3.50**

Name _____

Address _____

City _____ State _____ Zip _____

CRY REVENGE

BY DONALD GOINES

Crap games and smack pits the blacks and the Chicanos against each other in bloodbath of vengeance!

Young Curtis Carson doesn't mean to rip off the Chicanos in his back yard crap games. He just rolls the dice better. But the Chicanos don't see it that way, and when one of their brothers is brutally slaughtered in a shootout, because of Curtis's dealings with heroin pusher Fat George, the Mexicans cry revenge on Curtis, leaving his brother with a wrecked body that will forever prevent him from being the basketball star he'd always dreamed of being. Curtis swears vengeance of his own, as the ghetto streets run red with the blood of Black-Chicano warfare!

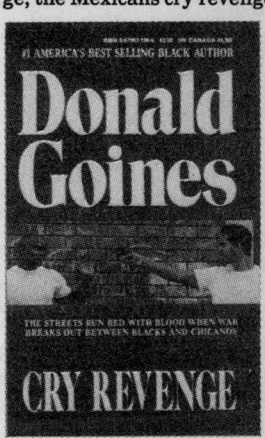

Author Donald Goines, whose established Black Experience best-sellers such as **Street Players, Dopefiend, White Man's Justice: Black Man's Grief** and **Black Gangster**, have ripped apart the curtain camouflaging Black life myth and fact, now reveals the bloody, gut-level truth of Black-Chicano hatred!

HOLLOWAY HOUSE PUBLISHING CO.
8060 Melrose Ave., Los Angeles, CA 90046-7082

Gentlemen I enclose $ _____ ☐ check ☐ money order, payment in full for books ordered. I understand that if I am not completely satisfied, I may return my order within 10 days for a complete refund. (Add $1.00 per book to cover cost of shipping. California residents add 29¢ sales tax. Please allow six weeks for delivery.)

☐ BH196-0 CRY REVENGE $3.50

Name _____

Address _____

City _____ State _____ Zip _____

SWAMP MAN

BY DONALD GOINES

Rape and murder sets off a savage manhunt through southern backwater country! George, a young black living in the samps of Mississippi, never had an easy life. As a child he, along with his sister Henrietta and his grandfather, stood by helplessly as the honkie hillbillies castrated and murdered his father. After his sister escaped the swamps with a scholarship to college, George learned to live with the evils of the southern swamps, whether it slithered like the water moccasins or walked on two legs like the vicious Ku Klux Klan.

But then Henrietta returns for a visit—a visit that becomes a bloody nightmare of rape and murder!

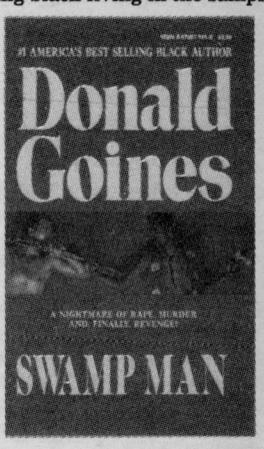

HOLLOWAY HOUSE PUBLISHING CO.
8060 Melrose Ave., Los Angeles, CA 90046-7082

Gentlemen I enclose $ _____ ☐ check ☐ money order, payment in full for books ordered. I understand that if I am not completely satisfied. I may return my order within 10 days for a complete refund. (Add $1.00 per book to cover cost of shipping. California residents add 29¢ sales tax. Please allow six weeks for delivery.)

☐ **BH191-X   SWAMP MAN $3.50**

Name _____

Address _____

City _____ State _____ Zip _____

WHITE MAN'S JUSTICE, BLACK MAN'S GRIEF

BY DONALD GOINES

Goines' classic novel of prison life, it has been called "one of the most revealing books ever written about prison life and bigotry built into our system." This is the story of Chester Himes, who thought he was the baddest man to come down the street. Behind prison walls he was nothing more than fresh meat.

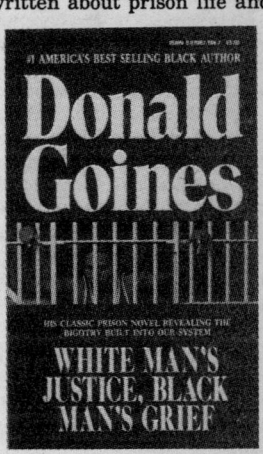

DONALD GOINES, savagely gunned down at the age of 39, was the undisputed master of the Black Experience novel. He lived by the code of the streets and exposed in each of his 16 books the rage, frustration and torment spinning through the inner city maze. Each of his stories, classics in the Black Experience genre, were drawn from reality.

HOLLOWAY HOUSE PUBLISHING CO.
8060 Melrose Ave., Los Angeles, CA 90046-7082

Gentlemen I enclose $ _____ ☐ check ☐ money order, payment in full for books ordered. I understand that if I am not completely satisfied. I may return my order within 10 days for a complete refund. (Add $1.00 per book to cover cost of shipping. California residents add 29¢ sales tax. Please allow six weeks for delivery.)

☐ BH184-7   WHITE MAN'S JUSTICE, BLACK MAN'S GRIEF $3.50

Name _____

Address _____

City _____ State _____ Zip _____

CRIME PARTNERS

BY DONALD GOINES

In this powerful novel Donald Goines lays bare the bloody, brutal world of crime in the black ghetto. *Crime Partners* is a gutsy, sometimes shocking story of Billy and Jackie, ex-prison buddies hot on the trigger to pull any job that pays the bread; of Benson, a black detective and his white partner Ryan, companions in the right against black organized crime; and of Kenyatta, a ghetto chieftain torn between two ambitions: cleaning the ghetto of all the drug traffic and gunning down all the white cops! This is a book that will grip you from first page to last!

```
┌─────────────────────────────────────────────────────────────────┐
            HOLLOWAY HOUSE PUBLISHING CO.
            8060 Melrose Ave., Los Angeles, CA 90046-7082

  Gentlemen I enclose $ _____  ☐ check ☐ money order,
  payment in full for books ordered. I understand that if I am not completely
  satisfied. I may return my order within 10 days for a complete refund. (Add
  $1.00 per book to cover cost of shipping. California residents add 29¢ sales
  tax. Please allow six weeks for delivery.)
  ☐ BH183-9   CRIME PARTNERS   $3.50

  Name _____

  Address _____

  City _____ State _____ Zip _____
└─────────────────────────────────────────────────────────────────┘
```